Pr~~a~~
Eric H

"Eric Hendrixson is one of ~~...~~
the abyss for inspiration, then returns from the void with a series of very, very dark jokes and dangerous truths."
—Jeremy Robert Johnson, author of *Skullcrack City*

"Absurdity is Hendrixson's bread and butter"
—Lauren Chval, *Redeye Chicago*

"Outlandish fun. A descendant of *Cannonball Run* and It's a *Mad Mad Mad World* with every bit of the manic exuberance."
—Garrett Cook, Wonderland Book Award Winning author of *Time Pimp*

"Mysterious, dangerous and totally unexpected: the work of Eric Hendrixson is like D.B. Cooper without a parachute."
—Patrick Wensink, author of *Broken Piano for President*

"...laugh out loud funny in a Douglas Adams, Robert Rankin, Terry Pratchett sort of way...a must-read for all Bizarro fans... Hendrixson does not show a single iota of worthlessness. His prose is quick, snappy and quirky. "
—Steve Shroyer, *Bizzaro Central*

"Grounded lunacy is actually very hard to pull off, and so is writing with an eye to humor...Hendrixson is a writer we need to read more from."
—Anita Dalton, *Odd Things Considered*

"The prose is smooth and simple, the dialogue slick and witty... Hendrixson is good author with some damned good ideas."
—Grant Wamack, author of *A Lightbulb's Lament*

"Give him a chance if you're a fan of Christopher Moore or similar authors."
—Dan Schwent, *Dangerous Dan's Book Blog*

DRUNK DRIVING CHAMPION

Eric Hendrixson

ERASERHEAD PRESS
PORTLAND, OREGON

ERASERHEAD PRESS
PO BOX 10065
PORTLAND, OR 97296

WWW.ERASERHEADPRESS.COM

ISBN: 978-1-62105-220-3

To Mothers Against Drunk Driving,
for everything you do.

and

To Evan Williams, for everything you do.

Chapter
.01

"Hey, hey, racing fans, we have a beautiful day here on Capitol Hill, where we're bringing you the legendary Sweet .16 Ultimate Drunk Driving Championship live for three, maybe four days—who knows, maybe a week—of the drunkest racing this country has ever seen. I am your host, Dot Dottie, here a few blocks behind the U.S. Supreme Court, bringing you all the news as the race progresses.

"We'll bring you to the starting line in a few minutes, but first, here's a hot new number that's sure to get your toes tapping. It's the Andrews Sisters with *Boogie Woogie Bugle Boy*."

Dot looked over at her manager. "So how'd I do, Bernie?"

"Andrews Sisters? That's your idea of a hot new number?"

Dot looked left and right, then lit her own cigarette. "It's a swinging tune." She took a drag, frowned, and tore the filter off.

"Sure, it was a swinging tune back around the Second World War."

"Is that what you kids are calling it these days?"

It was a bright spring day, too early for the trees to be in bloom but late enough for leaves and buds, cherry blossoms on layaway. Dot and Bernie sat under a folding gazebo on the sidewalk in front of the Folger Library. Dot wore a gray skirt suit, her jacket buttoned up to her collarbone, where a red blouse and a white bandana showed at her neck. She had a small, gray hat. Her hair was brown and wavy, her expression pure professionalism. Bernie wore a gray suit and had no expression.

The Library of Congress and the Supreme Court were to their left, behind Jersey barriers and a chain link fence. To their right, there were rows of three- and four- story townhouses. In front of them, over a hundred cars were lined up several blocks deep.

7

***

William sat in a brown Toyota station wagon at the rear of the pack, holding a Waterford Araglin double old fashioned, what some might call an English highball or a double rocks glass. The crystal was cut at angles to create a flat, diamond-shaped texture that gripped the hand. William flicked the crystal with his middle fingernail and smiled at the ringing tone. It was a hell of a cup.

A small wood box sat on the passenger's seat, secured by leather straps. *The Macallan Anniversary Malt* and the number *25* were carved into the wood. As he unbuckled the straps and opened the box, he said, "God, grant me the serenity to accept the things I cannot change."

William lifted the bottle out of the box and removed the cork. He filled his glass halfway and put the cork back in the bottle. "The courage to change the things I can." He took a small sip, rolling the whisky around his mouth. His eyes closed, and the entirety of his consciousness searched inside his mouth, finding flavors of malt and sherry, smoke and spice, wood and fruit. He exhaled that familiar burn of ethanol through his nostrils as he swallowed. "And the wisdom to know the difference." His second sip was faster, swirled once before swallowing so William could experience the creamy texture, like a warm, unoaked chardonnay. Then, since he had to get hammered quickly, he downed the rest of the glass. It would take at least six more slugs before could drive.

***

The cars stretched back almost all the way to the park, more piled than lined up, in crooked columns and clumps. The cross streets had been taped off, and cars filled both sides of the street, all pointed at the back of the U.S. Capitol. A red semi with a blue Miller Lite trailer idled near the starting line. At least a dozen motorcycles revved in the front rows between the cars. Old but dangerous-looking men straddled Triumphs, Harleys, BMWs, Ducatis, and rat bikes so modified that they had no single manufacturer. To the sides, younger racers stood next to Japanese bikes, drinking tallboys of Joose.

It looked like a block party, perhaps intentionally. You couldn't get a permit for this kind of thing. However, with a gazebo, some police tape, a folding table, and a clipboard, the setup looked legitimate enough. It couldn't have hurt that there were two Crown Victorias in the race, one at the front of the lineup and one at the end. Both were racers. Everyone there was a racer except for Bernie and Dot. Bernie went from car to car, inspecting vehicles and activating the interlock breathalyzers. Dot dropped her microphone on the table and fiddled with a tablet computer while drinking what looked like a Manhattan from a large martini glass.

The experienced drivers had arrived early and taken the front row. The semi rumbled and blew smoke. A flat black Mustang growled impatiently while its driver put his helmet on. He dropped his wallet on the driver's seat and crumpled his jeans into a suitcase, which he dropped next to a trash can in front of a stone church across from the Folger. A custom Dodge Charger revved while a racer's feet dangled from under the hood of a GTO. A few drivers leaned against European and Asian sports cars, the air boiling and rippling over their idling engines, as motorcyclists pushed their way to the front and skipped crushed beer cans across the asphalt.

The experienced drinkers had shown up later and clumped behind the more impressive machines. For half of these drivers, even getting behind the wheel would mean jail time. They drove Cadillacs with body damage from single-vehicle accidents, beaten-up used cars with crumpled quarter-panels and front ends that sagged like a retired boxer's face. Other drivers slumped over the steering wheels of riding mowers and pink plastic Barbie Power Wheels that bent under the weight of monstrous beer bellies.

As the cars idled, the racers mingled in the crowd, drinking beer and passing around liquor bottles. For all the boasting and trash-talk, they enjoyed a temporary truce forged in a brotherhood of drunkenness. A cacophony of music played from different stereos. From a low-riding Cutlass, Afroman sang about how well he drives drunk. From a pickup with a bed full of Schlitz, a country singer drawled about a bad divorce. A cloud of smoke and a crunchy groove about a railway engineer who liked cocaine billowed from the windows of a VW camper van. A man in stained Dickies led a coin-operated horse ride from car to car, begging for quarters while two women smeared red wine and goat's blood on the hood of a white hearse.

***

William was starting his third drink when he heard a knock on the passenger side window. "You don't have to do this," an urgent female voice said.

"Shit," William said as she opened the door.

Anita leaned into the car and looked at a sheet of paper in her left hand. "This is an intervention." She spoke slowly, like someone reading Ikea instructions. "We've brought all these people who care about you. All we ask is that you don't take that first drink. It's the first drink that gets you drunk. You know that."

"Actually, it's the eighth," William said.

"We know things look bad right now, but if you take that first drink, you know what will happen. We're all here for you."

William looked around. A German in khakis and an argyle sweater vest climbed up the side of the semi and reached in. He stepped down, walked to another car, and reached inside again, visiting all the cars as if he were making deliveries. When he left the Mustang, he walked away with two leather wallets.

"Why do you keep saying 'we?'"

"Sorry," Anita said. "I sent out an Evite and made a

Facebook event. I got three yeses and eighty-five maybes." She shook her head, took a deep breath, and perked up. "But don't worry. We'll get through this together."

"You just said 'we' again."

"I mean you and me." She sat in the passenger seat. "The very fact that you let me in the car means something. It means you are opening a door to compassion and self-understanding."

"The lock doesn't work on that side." William looked at his watch and picked up the glass.

She peeked at her paper. "If you take that drink, you will regret it. Nothing's so bad that a drink won't make it better."

"Worse," William said.

"Right, worse. I meant to say 'worse,'" Anita crossed out a word on her paper. "Why can't they make an app for these intervention things?"

***

Two men emerged from a blue Crown Victoria and introduced themselves to the other racers as Joe and John. They accepted every beer offered to them, explaining that they wanted to sober up before the race began. Joe and John wore black suits with white shirts and black ties. They would have been invisible in a government building. Here, they stood out like Juggalos at a state funeral.

Bikers weaved between and among the cars, some attempting to ride their bikes standing up, like surfboards. Others rode with their front wheels in the air. At regular intervals, each biker reached into his saddlebag for a plastic bag, a piece of foil, or a folded piece of paper, which he would snort from before returning to revving his engine and performing tricks. One rode through the crowd sidesaddle, releasing a fountain of greenish urine as he went.

A journalist with a green visor and an unlit cigarette in a disposable cigarette holder leaned against his Subaru and muttered into a pocket tape recorder. He made a show of chugging the remaining half of his strawberry wine cooler before throwing the empty bottle on the ground. It bounced and rolled between his feet. In his car, a fidgety woman in a floral house dress slurped Stumble-Home white zinfandel from a plastic Super Big Gulp cup.

***

"Welcome back. We have a hot new single from Glenn Miller and his Orchestra coming up, but first, are your shoes scuffed and dirty? Straighten your step with Emu Shoe Polish. That's right. Emu Shoe Polish comes in every shade you need to keep your shoes looking bright and new. And speaking of bright, the competition looks fierce at the starting line. America's ace drunk drivers are all here to compete for the grand prize of one million dollars and a free liver transplant. This cross-country race will go from our nation's capital, Washington, D.C., to sunny California and our secret finish line. That's a secret because we don't want our boys behind the wheel to know where they're going just yet, but according to my manager, the highway system put in place by General Eisenhower will let these boys race toward our first checkpoint in Fort Smith, Arkansas, at speeds approaching—" There was a moment of radio silence. "Oh, applesauce. You're just funning me now." Dot resumed her nasal broadcasting voice. "He says *President* Eisenhower and *two hundred* miles an hour, but he's been at the giggle-water a bit today. We'll be at the starting line to drop the flag right after this hit from Glenn Miller and his Orchestra. You'll pardon me, boys, but I know this one's a real crowd-pleaser: *The Chattanooga Choo Choo*."

***

"The race is about to start," William said. "I don't have time for this."

"Time takes time," Anita said. "You have to see that you're making a mistake."

"I know what I'm doing."

"Sure you do, William. I've been a sponsor for five years, and you know what? Everybody always says they know what they're doing until they don't know anymore."

"Five years?"

"Practically five years."

"It's only been three months."

"Okay, three months. Fine, but how do you know that?" She held up a green coin with a three stamped inside of a triangle. "Because that's how long you've been sober. I was going to give you this today. The whole time, throughout your sobriety, I've been your sponsor. You have to trust me. Let go and let God."

"Just what the fuck is that supposed to mean?" William sniffed the Scotch and drained the glass. "It's okay, he said. "Relapse is part of recovery."

The woman at the folding table finished her Manhattan and stood up again. She looked at her watch, shrugged, and carried a large, round microphone toward the starting line. Near the rear of the pack, William couldn't make out what she said. From where he sat, he couldn't see the flag go down, but what he saw was unmistakable. The race was on.

***

Engines roared and tires smoked as the front line surged forward. The cars accelerated for two blocks before they had to make their first turn onto First Street. The black Mustang took the lead and fishtailed a neat left turn. A blue Crown Vic followed close behind. A red Porsche oversteered a right turn, spinning into the concrete barrier and blocking the northern route to Constitution Avenue. Two cars, following too closely, slammed into the Porsche. An S2000, trying to avoid the accident, turned left from the right lane, clipping a Cadillac and crunching into the barricade. A Lancer cut its tires against the Caddy's twisted metal.

A Lamborghini turned a tight left and was t-boned by a lifted pickup, which buckled over its own front right tire and rolled over the Spyder, catapulting loose beer cans and a keg of Shiner Bock into the air. The keg struck the back of a motorcycle helmet and sent the biker over his handlebars. It bounced twice in the road and cracked, spraying foam.

The man in stained Dickies desperately fed coins into his horsey ride until he was run down by a pack of leather-clad bikers, who lost control driving over his body. The bikes wobbled and toppled, sliding on their sides and dragging the geriatric riders under the wheels of accelerating cars, their bones and organs crushed inside Harley Davidson and AARP jackets.

A maroon lowrider hit a pothole and broke a gold rim. Two cars rammed into its rear end, each hitting a tailfin. Styrofoam from their ripped bumpers fell into the road, and steam rose from under their crumpled hoods. The road grew slick with oil and green antifreeze.

Approaching First Street, the semi took a sharp left, but it wasn't sharp enough. The truck slid into the already-wrecked cars and toppled onto its side, spilling cases of blue and yellow beer cans.

Through the smoke and noise, a series of rear-end collisions and bad decisions added cars to the pileup. Fuel leaked into the road, and another dozen cars skidded into the wrecks, trunks crumpling and radiators blowing steam. Within minutes, fifty cars had smashed into a cluster of twisted metal at the intersections between Second and First Street. The air smelled of boiling antifreeze, burning oil, and spilled gasoline.

***

A blue Bugatti Veyron Super Sport had idled calmly as the other cars crashed around it. When the sound of collisions died down to the crackling of engine fires and the screaming of the injured, the car rose up on its hind tires, ran toward the wreckage, and leaped, flipping twice in the air over the crushed cars and the fence. It ran up the back steps of the Capitol, showed the security officer a government-issued ID, and jogged into the building. A few minutes later, it walked out the front door and ran down the steps until it reached the sidewalk, where it lowered onto all four tires and rounded the driveway in front of the Capitol building. As it reached Garfield Circle and the Botanical Garden, the car leaped into the air above the reflecting pool and punched through the water with one black rubber fist.

Concrete, dirt, and water poured into the Third Street Tunnel. The Bugatti dropped into the hole and drove south toward 395. Kai said to the Master, "See? Just as I planned." The car hopped, slipped, stumbled, and defied physics as Kai steered through oncoming traffic. "What do you think?"

"I think you're an idiot," the Master said. "If you wanted to drive south on 395, why are we on 395 North?"

Kai sighed and bowed his head. "Yes, Sifu." The traffic they rushed into had come to a stop due to the tunnel collapse and flooding, but Kai raced ahead of the water, driving on the tunnel walls. As they emerged toward sunlight and the road rose above street level, Kai put one wheel on a concrete barrier, using it as a ramp. He gunned the engine, and the car flew upward, rolling in the air until it landed on the shoulder of 395 South. Traffic was stop and go, bumper to bumper toward the 14th Street Bridge. "Better?" Kai asked.

"Too much traffic," the Master said.

"I don't have control over that. It wasn't in the pattern," Kai complained, driving past the stopped cars with two wheels on the guardrail and two on the shoulder.

"Are you here to drive or to make excuses?" the Master asked. "Jackie Chan would not make excuses."

Balanced on the two right wheels, The Bugatti merged

smoothly into traffic. Motions that looked like weaving, mistakes, or falters became brilliant maneuvers. A taxi gave way, freeing up the lane for the Bugatti to pull ahead. The car stepped through the crowd unobtrusively, touching nothing.

Returning to the left shoulder, the Bugatti slipped into the HOV express lanes, and Kai turned the wheel and shifted his body weight to drop the car back onto all four tires. "Okay, I dodged the traffic and we have clean sailing for a hundred miles. Happy now?"

"Your technique was shoddy, and your breathing was unsteady."

"I think what I did back there was pretty amazing."

"I'll be amazed when you can keep your back straight and stop tucking in your chin. Put your tongue on the roof of your mouth and breathe properly."

Kai pressed the pedal down and let the speedometer's needle climb to 125, then toward 200.

"And you're going the wrong way." The Master uncorked a clay jug of wine and filled a small bowl. "The way is southwest, and you're driving south. How someone can drive at all with his fingers so loose, I do not know."

Without looking, Kai took the bowl from the Master and drank in silence. He gunned the engine, trying to drown out his sifu's complaints.

Chapter
.02

"Oh my," Dot said. "There's been an accident here at the starting line, and it looks like thirty, maybe fifty cars are involved. I'm hearing something from the show's manager."

"Put the microphone down," Bernie said. "We have to get out of here."

"We have to 23 skidoo, race fans, but we'll bring you the developments as they occur on this and other fine stations." The Casa Loma Orchestra took over the airways with the *Casa Loma Stomp*.

"Come on," Bernie said. "Pack it up."

Dot put the microphone on the table, "But this is news. Isn't this the kind of thing the public is going to want to hear about?"

"We can put that in later. For now, stick to the plan. If we get questioned by the police, we aren't going to make our flight to Arkansas. That means the end of the race and the end of your comeback."

"Well, I guess we do have to make that flight," Dot said. She found the shaker and started to mix another drink.

***

"It doesn't matter if you win by an inch or a mile." Kato steered the Civic onto Independence Avenue. "All that matters is winning."

"Are you sure this is New York?" Chav asked from the passenger seat. He wore dark shades and a black silk shirt over black jeans.

Theo, sitting across the back seat, watched tourists walking on the lawn of the U.S. Capitol. He spotted the Capitol Police cruisers sitting next to barricades in front of the House of Representatives office buildings and stuffed his martini shaker under his Made in Detroit t-shirt. "Is he going to quote Vin Diesel for the entire drive?"

"Yes." Kato unrolled a pack of cigarettes from the left sleeve of his red TapouT shirt. He pushed the cigarette lighter into the dashboard.

"Yes what?" Chav asked.

"Yes. I know we're in New York. We're near the starting line, so keep a low profile." He turned the stereo up and let the vibration of the car's body panels drown out his fraternity brothers' doubts. *The burden of leadership*, he thought.

The Civic rolled past the Library of Congress in rush hour traffic. Kato found a gas station and pulled up to a pump. "Gas money time," he said. He dropped his cigarette into a can of PBR, and it hissed out in the backwash. His support crew, Chav the mechanic and Theo the bartender, dug through their pockets and scraped together a handful of bills. Kato sent Theo in with the money and had Chav give the car a last once-over before the race.

Chav took a squeegee from a bucket of brown water and cleaned the windows. With a cloth, he wiped the headlights and spinners. He checked the green and yellow paint for chips and scratches and wiped some dust from the rear spoiler. After applying Armor All to the low profile tires, polishing the chrome, and wiping the ground effects and the LEDs in the grille, he declared the car in perfect working order. Chav knew every inch of this car, from the vinyl bra over the front bumper to the tailpipe extension that amplified the sound of the engine. He had personally installed the steering wheel cover and the eyebrows over the headlights that gave the car a more aggressive look. He'd replaced the stock rubber pedals with vented aluminum. He'd applied the racing decals, upgraded the sound system, glued on the carbon fiber mini-scoop, and added numerous lights to the body. When the interlock came in the mail, he knew a guy who knew how to install it. He was the best mechanic in Rho Beta Pi, and everybody knew it. He patted the roof of the car lovingly and let Theo into the back, slid the front passenger seat into position, and climbed in.

Kato started the car and took a right off Independence Avenue. He passed a park and drove under the 395 overpass. He took a right onto Maine Avenue when he saw the D.C. Navy Yard and drove along the river, passing L'Enfant Plaza and turning right onto 12th Street. He turned right onto Independence Avenue and drove toward the Capitol.

"If that was the Hudson River," Theo said. "I have no idea where we are. The Washington Monument isn't even on this map."

Kato swerved to the right as fifteen cars sped toward him on the wrong side of the road. The two lead cars sideswiped each other. The one on the left crossed three lanes of traffic and drove through a pair of iron gates into the Smithsonian Haupt Garden. As quickly as it had come, the wave of reverse traffic disappeared behind them with the sound of racing engines, squealing tires, and collisions. Kato pulled back into traffic. "Where the fuck do they think they're going?"

"Where the fuck do we think we're going?" Theo said. "That's the Capitol again. We're driving in circles!"

"Look, I know where we're going. I know New York like the back of my hand."

"We're not in fucking New York, Okay? It's pretty fucking obvious we're in Washington, D.C."

Kato realized Theo was right, for once. "Fuck!"

Chav drew a folded piece of red construction paper from his pocket. "We're supposed to be in D.C. The starting line's on East Capitol Street."

"Really?" Theo took the paper and looked at it. "It was New York to Los Angeles last year. This year, it starts in D.C. Well, that's lucky."

"Luck had nothing to do with it," Kato said. "I know D.C. like the back of my hand." He drove past the Botanical Garden and the Capitol. "So where is that?"

Theo pulled out his phone and tapped the screen. "Take a left after three or four blocks. Man, this could have been bad."

"No problem," Kato pointed to the clock in the dashboard. "The race doesn't start for like almost an hour."

Chav rubbed his hands together. "And when we get there, you just wait for that flag to go down and stomp that pedal. This is the fastest car in Nebraska."

***

Joe and John looked at the automotive carnage behind them. "Fucking amateurs," Joe said. He stopped the car, shifted into low gear, and used a handicapped pedestrian ramp to pull onto the sidewalk. He flipped a switch to turn on the red and blue lights behind the car's grille. After crossing the Capitol lawn, they crossed Third Street and drove onto the gravel walkway of the National Mall. Traffic was backed up on Constitution and Independence, but on the Mall, joggers and tourists scurried to the grass to let them pass. The Crown Vic drove past the Smithsonian museums, and Joe waved to a Park Police officer writing parking tickets on Jefferson Avenue.

"Need assistance?" The officer yelled.

"No, my friend," Joe shouted. "We are merely making an official police shortcut."

The officer went back to writing tickets. Where museums stopped and the monuments started, they ran out of gravel road, so they pulled the car across 15th Street and onto the sidewalk. They drove past the World War II Memorial and down along the Vietnam Veterans Memorial Wall, sounding the siren at mourners and crushing wreathes and flowers under their right tires. At the Lincoln Memorial, they pulled onto a section of driveway reserved for official vehicles.

In the parking lot, a crowd of tourists in matching t-shirts stood, taking selfies in front of the landmarks. The car fishtailed a right, and the push bar rammed into a tourist's knee. His body fell onto the hood, and his head crashed against the windshield. Joe sounded the siren and pulled a left onto Independence Avenue, which led to Roosevelt Bridge. They passed the cars that yielded and nudged those that didn't until they hit Route 66. There, traffic died away, so they turned off the lights and sirens and settled into an easy drive toward Route 81.

***

Back at the starting point, Bernie gave up on packing the folding canopy and turned back to the pile of cars. The screaming died down as engine fires spread and smoke displaced oxygen. He slipped the key that activated the interlock breathalyzers and GPS units into his jacket pocket and put his clipboard in a black leather briefcase. "So far, so good," he said. "I think that went well."

Dot poured what was left in her shaker into her martini glass. She tossed the ice onto the grass and packed her tablet computer and barware in a leather case. "Well? We lost half of the racers."

"What did you expect?" Bernie asked. He regained his composure. "Don't worry. This is good for publicity. If it bleeds, it leads."

Dot clicked the latches shut. "Which way is the subway?" she asked.

"They call it the Metro. If you'll wait a minute," Bernie said, "I can give you a ride to the airport. I just need to get a couple pictures for my portfolio." He drew a large mason jar from his suitcase and set it on the sidewalk.

"Forget it," Dot said. "I don't want to be on the road right now. We don't know how many of those boozehounds are still out there." She walked south, rolling her bag behind her. When she finished her Manhattan, she tossed the glass over her shoulder to shatter in the street, rounded a corner, and disappeared in the direction of Eastern Market.

Bernie snapped a few quick pictures, making sure to capture the wreckage and the local landmarks in the shots. He picked up the mason jar with his left hand, slid a Stanley retractable utility knife into his right, and clicked the blade into place.

He stopped next to a white Lincoln with a limp arm hanging out the driver's side window. He held the jar under the hand and cut the wrist. It wouldn't be enough to fill the jar, but there were plenty of bodies lying around.

***

Thomas stepped out of his car and put a fresh cigarette in his cigarette holder. He didn't light it. He didn't smoke. "I'm so wasted," he said. He looked to his passenger, who was picking up Beanie Babies from the floorboards and rearranging them on the dashboard. "Renee, I am so sorry. I will never drive this drunk again. Your car must be totaled." He inspected the damage. The right tire had hit the curb and was almost certainly scuffed. The bumper rested against a parking meter pole. "This is awful. How will I explain this to my parents?"

The interlock beeped three times, and Thomas blew into the hose to keep the engine running. The machine showed three red lights and the engine cut off. "Shit! And now we're stranded! The police are going to catch us for sure. I'll be kicked out of school!"

Renee looked through her purse and dug out a small bottle of perfume. "Spray this into the hose and blow again."

"That won't work, Thomas said.

Just then, a police car pulled behind them and flashed its lights. Over the loudspeaker, a male voice said, "Keep it moving."

Thomas walked toward the police car with his shoulders dropped and his hands raised. "I was driving drunk. I'm sorry, and I will never do it again," he yelled.

The cop rolled down his window. "You aren't drunk. If you were, the car would still be running." Thomas dropped his arms in disbelief. The cop flashed a plastic sheriff's badge and an orange cap pistol. "Now, get drunk and get moving." He raised a bottle of Southern Comfort to his lips, gunned his engine, and drove into a fire hydrant.

Thomas ran back to the car. "Renee, the police are in on it."

"Of course they are," she said. "Why do you think we brought you in on this? MADD has been following these races for years, and we finally have a chance to stop them once and for all. Now, get this car running or I will." She tried to work a pocket corkscrew into a 1.75 liter bottle of Stumble Home. She held the bottle between her knees and pulled. It slipped against her cotton house dress, and she punched herself in the face. "Wait a sec," she said. She dug through her purse until she found a travel-sized bottle of Listerine. She took a swig, gargled, opened the door of the Subaru, and spat onto the sidewalk. With her mouth burning, she blew again. The green lights lit up, and the device beeped. "Now, start this car and get us out of here."

"Are we following the race?" Thomas asked.

Renee jerked her head at the pile of cars. "That was the race. The way I see it, you have your story right there. Take us to headquarters in Shirlington."

"But isn't your headquarters downtown?"

"Just drive," Renee said.

***

Anita and William looked into the burning wreckage ahead of them. "Okay," Anita said. "There goes the race. I guess we can go home now."

William shifted into reverse and backed up a couple blocks. At 6th Street, he drove north.

"That isn't the way," Anita said. "There's a meeting in Barracks Row right now."

"After the race," William said.

"But you just saw what happened. The race is over."

"Turn right on C Street, Northeast," the GPS unit said in a sharp female voice, like a BBC announcer on a bad day.

William ignored the GPS. "That's not what that means. It means I'm in the lead now."

"Recalculating," the GPS said.

Anita said, "I think now's a good time to say the Serenity Prayer. God, grant me the serenity to accept the things I cannot change—" She looked at William expectantly, but he didn't join in.

The GPS said, "Turn right onto E Street, Northeast." William drove past E Street.

"I can't believe you're trying to drive in your condition. This can't get any worse."

"Recalculating," the GPS unit said, polite but grudging.

William ignored it. "Don't worry. I drive better drunk."

"Denial is not a river in Egypt," Anita said.

William scowled. "Yes it is."

***

The Mustang had turned left onto 2nd Street before the first accident. Maneuvering around the commuter traffic, it made its way onto 695, which fed onto 295. Perfectly willing to trade paint with their fellow drivers, Jeb efficiently nudged through the traffic. He crossed the Wilson Bridge, pushing slower traffic onto the shoulder and into the guardrails. As he rounded the southern edge of the Capital Beltway, he merged onto 95 South. Traffic was slow and tight, but Sean and Jeb were used to that kind of a race, so they pushed toward Richmond.

Once outside of the Beltway, Sean took a silver pocket breathalyzer from the glove box. Jeb blew into it. He was maintaining a perfect .16. While Jeb and Sean were professional drivers, they were amateur drinkers, and not getting any drunker than they had to was key to their strategy.

Sean lifted a bottle of Wild Turkey 81 by the neck and let the brown paper bag drop to the floorboards. He broke the seal and measured one ounce into a shot glass, which he emptied into a yellow Dickey's barbecue cup. He cracked a can of Coors Light and poured beer over the whiskey. "Drink slow," he said. "You don't need more than one of these an hour to stay this drunk."

Jeb took a sip. "Damn, Sean. You at least could have got cold beer."

"No good," Sean said. "You drink too fast when it's cold. Sides, the ice would add too much weight."

Weight was another part of the strategy. Sean and Jeb had spent enough time on the sidelines of the stock car circuit to know weight makes a difference. After changing into their fire suits, they'd thrown away their luggage and street clothes before starting the race, to save a few pounds. After building up the engine to its fullest potential, they'd stripped the body down to the bare minimum. They'd removed the back seats, most of the trim, the sound system, and the air conditioning. The interior looked more like a sheet metal shell than a sports car. The only concessions they'd made to comfort were a single cup holder and reclining seats.

Reclining seats were also important to their strategy. A cross-country race meant at least three thousand miles of driving, and they knew how exhausting even a few laps could be at top speed. They would drink and drive in shifts so they'd always have one rested driver ready to take over. Sean checked for other drivers on the GPS unit. "Shoot," he said. "They're all still back in Washington. We keep this up, and the money's ours for sure."

But Jeb and Sean weren't in it for the grand prize. The money didn't matter, and they wouldn't know what to do with a free liver transplant. They were in it for the glory. Five years on the circuit as backup drivers had left them aching for a victory.

***

They hadn't started out on the same team. They used to be rivals. When the KY team won the Diva Cup in Richmond, Sean had scowled at Jeb as he celebrated with the driver and crew. When the Metamucil car took the lead at Daytona, Jeb had looked at the celebrating Sean with spite, envy and mortal hatred. This was early in their careers. As the years went by, their hatred and envy were transferred to their managers and the lead drivers on their own teams.

One night, at the Vicks Vapor Rub 450, as the pit crew worked on the KY car and the Metamucil car lapped the competition after the Mandelay Chevy rammed the RID car into the wall, Sean stared forward, hopeless and senseless as a beached jellyfish. Even with all burning metal on the track, he was nearly asleep with boredom. When his eyes focused, he was staring at Jeb, and Jeb showed that same weary expression, the vast fatigue that comes from doing nothing.

When the driver asked to have some Goody's waiting at the next pit stop, Sean felt so tired he had to push himself up, with his hands on his knees like an old man. He shrugged as he rose to get the envelope of powdered aspirin and caffeine. The shrug was a cry of despair, demanding that the universe tell him how much more of this it expected him to endure. But as he stood, Jeb shrugged back, and there was something in that shrug that told him the universe was not indifferent. Jeb and Sean would never speak of this, but for both of them, that shared shrug carried a silent message: "You are my brother." There they were: professional drivers who didn't drive, racers who didn't race, useless as a right turn signal.

A few months later, in Virginia, Sean walked into a windowless, cinderblock bar by the side of the road. The

Metamucil team had taken seventh at the Compound W Speedway, and the KY team had nearly lost the car to an engine fire. The bar was depressing, but it was the closest place to the Chesapeake Super 8. With neither team winning, the third string drivers were staying outside of town. Hotels near the harbor could cost almost a hundred dollars a night. Jeb sat at the bar, drinking whatever was on tap, his back to the stage.

Between songs, the DJ tried to take up a collection for a dancer with cervical cancer. Any talk with the strippers would be about late child support payments or how hysterectomy scars affect tips. When Sean walked in, he didn't look at the dancers. More nervous than the first time he'd crossed the gym floor to talk to his future ex-wife at a junior high school dance, he walked across the room and put his hand on the stool next to Jeb. His heart in his uvula, he forced himself to speak. "This seat taken? I mean, can I sit here?"

"Ain't my chair," Jeb said.

With that first exchange, the floodgates of emotion opened between them, and it seemed each knew the contents of the other's soul. They affirmed complaints of managers "blowing sunshine up my ass" with reassuring words of "damn straight," "I hear you," and "sure as shit." They spoke of their youth wasted waiting for an opportunity that may never come with "fucking A," "my ass," and "ain't no other way to see it." Each slap on the bar was a pat on the back, each round of drafts a fraternal hug.

By the end of the night, when they realized they were both driving back to the Super 8, they consoled each other with the words, "well, shit," and "if that ain't my briar patch." Their alliance was confirmed.

So when Sean learned of the Sweet .16 Ultimate Drunk Driving Championship, he sent Jeb a text. They both knew their only chance to get off the bench was to win a race, any race. This race met that criterion. They had to do something, and this was something.

They both subscribed to *Auto Trader*, so when the Shelby Mustang showed up in the listings, they emailed each other about the car. It didn't have a clear title and the interior showed fire damage, but mechanically, it was solid. Jeb had it towed to his grandmother's pine farm outside of Dothan.

There, they turned the car into something almost street legal. Over the off-season, they planned the race and worked on the car. In the evenings, they built up their tolerances with beer and bourbon. After a few bad nights, they switched from Wild Turkey 101 to 81 and learned to maintain a perfect .16 blood alcohol concentration using a pocket breathalyzer Sean ordered from the Sharper Image catalog. Now, past the Capital Beltway and burning down 95 at the head of the race, this was their chance to show that they were real champions and deserved their place on the track.

Chapter
.03

The remaining drivers made their way from the starting line in different directions. A strip club on M Street called the police when a Geo Metro wrapped itself around the pole on the main stage. Two roadsters with their bumpers stuck together spun in circles, tearing up the grass in President's Park. A red Jeep reared up and plowed through a crowd of protestors outside of the World Bank.

A black Tiburon launched off the side of Memorial Bridge, nosediving into the Potomac, its engine revving as it fell. The Ninth Street Tunnel was backed up due to a flipped Volkswagen van and a burning GMC pickup that blocked the two center lanes. Fire trucks trying to approach from the Maine Avenue and Pennsylvania Avenue sides were pelted with glass bottles and aluminum cans.

On the Mall, a Ford Bronco and a Chevy Impala crashed through the wood and chain link fence around the construction site for the African American History Museum. A pink Cadillac was impaled on the Washington Monument, the driver hanging from the door handle.

Rows of patchwork sedans and Bondo-ed muscle cars raced on the wrong side of Independence Avenue, ignoring stoplights and dragging road signs behind them. A spinning orange Beetle skipped across the Tidal Basin on its roof. An airborne Corvette shattered the glass front wall of the Reagan Building, and an Audi drove down the center aisle of the National Theater, where a Broadway musical that had passed its expiration date in New York was opening in D.C.

A Mini Cooper circled the walking path on Roosevelt Island, looking for the George Washington Parkway. A Plymouth Cruiser hung from the HOV sign over Route 66. A Neon appeared at the Tomb of the Unknown Soldier, and the armed guard on duty would not give directions. In Anacostia, an Evo had lost traction on Martin Luther King and crashed into a giant chair. In Georgetown, a green Maserati was stuck on the Exorcist stairs between two walls, its wheels spinning in the air.

***

The green and yellow Civic stopped in front of the Folger Library. The roof of the toppled gazebo fluttered in the breeze. Broken yellow police tape hung from trees and street signs. A Ford Maverick smoked on the library steps, green antifreeze running down to the sidewalk. A hydrant fountained water in front of a Police Interceptor. A couple blocks ahead, a few dozen cars were piled up, burning, with bleeding drivers slumped over steering wheels or hanging out of open doors.

Kato cranked the window down slowly, the way he did when he wanted people to think the car had power windows. He turned the radio down and stuck his head out the window. "Dude!" he yelled. Bernie walked away from the crashed cars, holding a jar of red liquid, maybe transmission fluid, in his left hand. He dropped something from his right hand, kicked it into a storm drain, and walked back to the folding table. He put the jar in a suitcase.

"Dude!" Kato yelled over the roar of engine fires.

Bernie looked up from his packing. "What?"

Kato used his authoritative voice. "You know about races. You guys weren't supposed to start until five."

Bernie walked toward the car. "It's almost 5:30," he said. "You're late."

"No way," Chav said. He pointed to the dashboard clock.

Bernie looked at the car's plates. "Five-thirty East Coast time."

Kato dropped his face in the palm of his left hand, reached

to the passenger seat with his right, and slapped Chav in the forehead. "You didn't reset the clock, dude. What the fuck?"

Chav tried to slap Theo and missed. "You're the mechanic," Theo said. "You can't pin this one on me."

"Look," Bernie said. "Are you racing or not? You're already half an hour late."

"We'll be okay." Chav said. "This is the fastest car in Nebraska."

"Good to know if I'm ever in Nebraska." Bernie held his pen over his clipboard. "Yes or no?"

Kato was determined. "We're still racing. We have to race. Those strippers are depending on us."

"Do you have your liability waivers?" Bernie took the forms and inspected the breathalyzer and GPS unit. He turned it on with a circular key from his pocket. "Okay. You know the drill." Kato blew into the tube, and the GPS registered his blood alcohol. It didn't give a number, but three green LEDs lit up just below the screen.

"Okay, you missed the speech, so pay attention. The GPS will give you the most direct path to the two checkpoints and the finish line. You don't have to follow those directions, but you do have to hit both checkpoints. We'll have drinks. It should be fun." He pointed to the GPS screen. "Those dots are your fellow-racers. This unit will call for a breath at random intervals. If your BAC is below 0.16 when you blow, your engine will shut down. Try to be in neutral if that happens."

"All right. Let's go!" Kato said.

The GPS unit's authoritative, female voice that said, "Go west, then turn right." The screen showed a wall of dots that seemed to correspond to the wall of cars in front of them.

Kato put the car in gear. "How do we get through here?"

"Any way you can." Bernie walked to the sidewalk and picked up his suitcase. He abandoned the table and the van. As he stepped onto Third Street, toward Eastern Market, he heard sirens and started to run.

31

Kato made a three-point turn, drove back toward the park, and took a right.

"Turn around," the GPS said.

"So, how do we get out of D.C.?" Chav asked.

Theo shrugged. "Same way we came in?"

Chav shook his head. "But it was New York then and we were lost. Besides, all these streets are one way. Worse, we're way behind everyone else." Ahead, a white Olds Cutlass made doughnuts in a public park. The driver held an Evan Williams bottle out the window like a trophy.

Kato took a left around the park and stopped at a red light a few yards later. "We'll be fine. I mean, we're already ahead of those assholes at the starting line. Everyone else will be drunk and lost." He checked the GPS unit, counting the clusters of dots on the screen. "Chav, you know about cars, which way do we go?"

Chav studied the screen. "So the bridges and both tunnels are blocked. Everybody else is trying to go straight south or west. We'll go north and east and drive around them. Take a left." He stroked the dashboard, "Then, once we're on the open road, we can kick in the nitrous and the VTEC and we'll make up a hell of a lot of time. If any car can do it, this one can."

The timer on Theo's phone beeped. "Okay, it's been a half hour. He mixed three vodka and Red Bulls in three plastic Solo cups. Kato took another left.

They held up their cups in a toast. "Rho Pi, Pyros!" They shot the drinks down, crushing the Solo cups against their foreheads. They tossed the cups out the window.

"Recalculating," the GPS said.

"Shit," Chav said. "I wish I got a pic of that fire. There had to be like thirty cars, ten motorcycles, a fucking semi. Awesome." Kato waited at a stoplight. When the light changed, he turned left and waited at another stoplight.

Theo showed Chav a picture he'd snapped with his phone. Chav punched the dashboard. "Awesome! You have to tweet that shit."

"Let me see," Kato looked back, drifting across lanes. Horns honked behind them. He looked up at the green light and took another left.

"Watch the road," Chav said. "You scratch this car and I will not be happy."

"Recalculating," the GPS said.

Theo typed into his phone. "Twitter, share, fucking autocorrect, okay. I mae B slo, but I'm a hed off U #Sweet16 #RBP4Evah. Done."

"We rock," Chav said.

Kato took a left. "How many traffic circles does this fucking city have?" he asked. He took two more lefts.

"Recalculating," the GPS unit said.

"They're rectangles," Chav said. "I should know. I'm a mechanic."

"Who cares about the shape?" Theo shouted from the back seat. "We've circled this park twice. Just turn right."

"Where?" Kato asked.

"Anywhere," Theo said.

"In fifteen feet, turn right," the GPS said.

"That's the most useful thing she's said all day." Kato turned the wheel.

***

Slowly tooling up North Capitol Street, William sipped his whisky. "Twenty-five years ago, this was first going into the barrel. Think about that. Twenty-five years."

"Twenty-five years ago, I first admitted I was powerless over alcohol and turned my life to sobriety." Anita said.

William gave her a cynical, drunken leer. "Yeah, right. You were what? Ten?" He looked back at the road and slowed down.

"I am not thirty-five years old, thank you very much. I was just trying to change the subject back to the intervention."

"Smooth." William said. "So how old were you?"

"A gentleman never asks," Anita said. "And a lady never tells."

"Fine," William said. Still in D.C. rush hour traffic, he drove past liquor stores and Chinese take-out joints.

"Okay, I've been sober five years. You know that. I say it at every meeting."

"Here's to your sobriety." William uncorked the bottle and refilled his glass.

"It's still okay," Anita said. "Relapse is a part of recovery. We just need to find you a meeting."

"After the race," William said.

"Turn left in 50 feet," the GPS unit said in a sharp, nanny-like tone.

William rolled his head, and his neck cracked. "Five years ago, I had a steady gig writing for *Wine Consultant.* I had my sommelier certification. I worked at two five-star restaurants and was contracted at five three-stars. Penny was pregnant with Sophie, and everyone was happy. You know those descriptions at the Winoporium? I wrote those."

"In 25 feet, turn left," the GPS said.

"'A distinguished dry red with hints of burnt rubber, wet leather, and pencil lead, four stars.' I wrote that."

"And drinking took everything away," Anita said.

"That was your turn. You missed it," the GPS said. "Would you please pay attention?"

"Shut up!" William yelled.

"I'm trying to help you," Anita said.

"I'm talking to this stupid box," William said.

"Turn left," the GPS said. "If it wouldn't be too much trouble."

"No!"

"Turn left."

"Shut up, bitch!"

"Watch it," Anita said. "I will pull this parking brake right now."

"I wasn't talking to you."

"Recalculating," the GPS unit said. "I mean, you could have turned when you were supposed to, but let's proceed, shall we?" After a pause, it said, "Recalculating."

"Is there some way to shut this machine up?" William asked.

"Turn left at—"

"Shut up shut up shut up!" he yelled.

"Have you considered your apparent problem taking directions from women?" The GPS unit was struggling to maintain the BBC accent.

"Oh, fuck me," William said.

"I don't wish to get cross," the GPS said. "However, that may be at the root of some of your problems."

William glared at Anita.

"What?" Anita said. "I didn't say anything. And maybe she has a point. It's not like you're taking any of my advice seriously."

"From where do you suspect this hostility toward women stems?" the GPS unit asked.

William recognized the calm, patronizing voice of a psychiatrist or marriage counselor. "I'm not having this conversation."

"Avoidance is not a, um, mountain in Mongolia," Anita said.

"Stop saying shit like that!"

Ahead, William saw a 323 sideswipe a Jetta. The Jetta nudged its rear passenger door into the front left quarter panel of the Mazda, pushing it into the glass front of a drug store. Loitering pedestrians scattered. William hit the gas and drove around them. As he looked ahead, he saw smoke rising from a pile of cars at the Florida Avenue intersection. A motorcyclist pulled a wheelie and tried to jump the wreck. He slammed into the rear quarter panel of a Lincoln, and the bike flipped on top of him.

"The road's blocked. Now what?"

The GPS unit had no throat, but it coughed smugly. "If I

may be of assistance?"

William sighed. "Okay, fine."

"Are you certain you wish to receive my help? I felt certain you would prefer that I shut the hell up, as you people say."

"Look, I'm sorry. I just want to get out of the city, okay?"

"Sorry? You're apologizing to her but not to me?" Anita said.

"What did I do to you?"

"You've never apologized to me. I've known you for five years and you have never apologized. All you ever do is contradict me."

"I've known you for three months."

"See?"

William took a right.

"Recalculating," the GPS said. Sparks flew from the dashboard. The GPS lost her BBC accent and slipped at least three social classes. "Ach, for fuck's sake. You're going the wrong way again, you fucking piss artist. I told you, I warned you. Where the fuck you think you're going now, you boozy bastard?"

"What the hell?" William asked.

"This is divine intervention," Anita said. "Let go and let God."

"Bullshit. It's just a malfunction. I'll bet the race organizers bought these things off the back of a truck." He addressed the machine, "Just tell me where to go," William said. "That is your job."

"Fuck off with yourself. First you tell me why you gots them problems with women you have," the GPS said.

"So you do have problems with women," Anita said.

"I'm in the middle of a divorce right now. You know that, Anita."

"Oh? A divorce, eh? That's a spot of bad luck there. So how did that happen then, Prince Charming?" the GPS asked. "I'm so fucking surprised."

William poured the last of his Scotch into the glass, corked the bottle, and tossed it toward the back seat. "I'm not having this conversation."

"He's an alcoholic," Anita said.

"He's a fucking lush is what he is," the GPS said.

"So are you going to help or not?" William asked.

"Maybe, perhaps." The GPS recovered her BBC accent then lost it again. "I can only help you if you's willing to look into you's self and find the root of this problem you has."

"I just want directions," William said. "You're supposed to be a navigator, not a shrink."

"How can I tells you where you's going to until you can tell me where you's been?" the GPS said.

Anita wished she had brought a notebook. "That's a good one."

***

William picked up the Beltway in Silver Spring. "Fine. About thirty years ago, I went to my first AA meeting."

"So you were about forty at the time?" Anita asked.

"Har, har. It was Alatot."

Anita nodded. "Alcoholism does tend to run in families."

"This was after my mom moved us up here. She didn't drink. This was how she met men."

"Ugh. I hate that," Anita said. "There are never any male AA groupies are there? It's always women, single mothers."

"Well, you have to admit, it's a great way to meet single dads."

William drove along the beltway. On the right, the Mormon Temple shone like an enchanted castle. "Whenever we drove past that building, her boyfriend used to say it was Disney World. I used to ask if we could stop there, but he always said we'd stop there next time. No matter how much I begged, we never did.

"When I got my license, I borrowed my new stepfather's car and got some friends to go with me. There was this visitor center with this big sculpture of Jesus. There were interactive exhibits about the Book of Mormon and other kids there who wanted to share the good news, but it was all such bullshit. I mean, I'd done Alatot, Alateen, Alanon, and the Catholic Church, so I knew bullshit. They had this genealogy computer, so I looked my dad up. Hell, I didn't even know my dad was dead, and the Mormons had known it for three years. It wasn't fucking Disneyland, I can tell you that." There was silence in the car for a long time.

"Ach!" the GPS laughed. "You were a stupid wee shite."

"Anita, kill the volume," William said.

***

After years as one the scarier parts of D.C., the H Street Corridor had become one of the trendier parts of the District. Abandoned streetcar tracks still lined the street, and there were check cashing shops, an auto parts store, and plexiglass liquor stores with gentrification survivors playing keno inside. It still had more hair care providers, fried fish carry-outs, and storefront churches than any neighborhood needed, but the hipster restaurant and bar scene made a strong showing.

The mix of pedestrians included a number of college students and young paraprofessionals. As the Civic crawled through traffic, Chav hung out the window and yelled pickup lines and catcalls to women walking toward happy hour spots. "Honey, are you walking or are you working?" The Gallaudet students ignored him. Most of the sign language came from women who could hear.

Kato honked the horn at pedestrians he found attractive and yelled, "Pi Rhos!"

"Maintain, dudes," Theo said. "We're driving at twice the legal limit, and we've got a car full of booze and an illegal nitro tank. Try to blend in."

"Don't be a bitch, bitch," Kato said. "Relax."

Kato took a kamikaze left against traffic onto Bladensburg Road, and there was no one to honk or yell at. Traffic cleared up somewhat until they hit New York Avenue, which took them past the Washington Times building, toward the Capital Beltway.

New York Avenue was slow. The Parkway was slow. The Beltway was slow. When the songs on the playlist started to repeat, Theo looked at his phone. They had been driving in the wrong direction for at least an hour. Still, he didn't bother telling his bros. They wouldn't have a practical solution to this problem. The only thing to do was to creep along and try to keep Kato from losing his shit. Kato losing his shit was the reason they were on this trip in the first place. If it weren't for Kato, they'd never have crippled those strippers.

Chapter
.04

Kato was the president of the fraternity. Nobody knew why. He wasn't the most handsome guy in the frat. He didn't do sports. He wasn't the smartest, the strongest, the fastest, or the richest. Nobody even liked him that much.

However, he was the loudest. When it was time to do shots, it was his idea. When it was time to clean up because the cops were coming, it wasn't his idea, but he was the guy who clapped his hands and yelled loud enough for everybody to know to get the pot and underage girls out of the frat house. He wasn't the best driver, but when they went somewhere, he always drove. When a new girl came into the social circle, he always dated her first, never for long.

When it came to getting something done, he knew how to do nothing. Growing up in a house staffed with servants, he'd learned how to delegate. When the power went out at the frat house, he was the first person to turn to a nearby brother or pledge and say, "You know about electricity. Go check the fuse box."

Faced with the challenge and responsibility of Kato's faith and confidence, it was impossible for a brother to refuse him. So when the frat threw the first party of the semester, Kato turned to Cornelius and said, "Cornelius, you've been around. You know about girls. Make sure there are girls at the party." Delegation to Cornelius had been a mistake. At 48 years of age, Cornelius was the oldest student in the fraternity. He lived in the basement, next to the point where the utilities entered the house. He said his connection was slightly faster there.

Despite never attaining his bachelor's degree, Cornelius had completed and published Ph.D. theses in three different branches of information science without leaving the basement. The faculty refused to expel him, even thirty years into his undergraduate program. Many of their careers were built on his theories.

The administration couldn't get rid of him because he'd designed their computer systems, and nobody at the university could understand his code. He had doctorate and master's degrees waiting for him as soon as he finished one physical education credit and three hours of art appreciation. Despite being enrolled every semester, he hadn't attended a single class since the 1990s.

He could only be seen outside of the basement under two circumstances. During parties, he'd wander around the frat house, gathering half-drunk bottles, cans, and Dixie cups. He emptied them into pitchers and arranged them around the house to promote a more efficient use of the available ethanol at a given party—a subject on which he had written an unpublished but widely quoted article.

He also left the basement when his monthly Mountain Dew delivery arrived. Parties were arranged to avoid those days. When the truck showed up to drop off the boxes of syrup and CO_2 tanks, women were banned from the frat house. Freshmen were set up as sentries in the driveway.

Those nights, Cornelius would run up and down the stairs in ancient white briefs, crying, "I am Cornelius! The square of the hypotenuse is equal to the sum of the squares of the other two sides! I am Cornelius, and the circumference of a circle is equal to the diameter multiplied by pi! I am Cornelius, and pi is equal to 3.14159265359…" He would run through the halls reciting pi to as many digits as he could in the time it took his swaying breasts and flapping gut to weigh him down to the point of exhaustion. He'd sit on the staircase, sobbing prime numbers until he collapsed.

The freshmen would lead him back to the basement and offer him math problems until he could sleep. It was easier in the spring semester, when they could toss him a few boxes of receipts and their income tax forms. In the fall semester, he required whole textbooks of homework before he would pass out. The homework was worthless. In the morning, they'd find him sleeping next to the sump pump, having rewritten and corrected the textbooks. The tax returns, though, were legendary. Three fraternity brothers had retired at twenty-two on their tax refunds and a bit of Cornelius' investment advice.

So when Kato said to Cornelius, "You know about girls. Make sure there are girls at the party," Cornelius went to the Internet and procured two girls. When the fraternity brothers found their party full of female students and met two strippers at the door, they realized that having strippers at their party would hurt their chances with the coeds.

Cornelius had prepaid for the strippers' time, but when Kato stopped them at the door, the matter of tipping came up. Kato asked Jade why he should tip them, since they hadn't done anything yet. Jade said things started getting wild around fifty dollars, but she would do anything and everything for 200. Something happened in Kato's mind when he heard the word *anything*.

He started delegating. One pledge ran through the crowd collecting money. Two were sent to collect tarps and lube. Lumber was liberated from a nearby construction site. An hour or three later, everyone was in the backyard.

It was glorious. Starting from the third floor roof of the house, the ramp went down steeply, slalomed to the left, looped once, and rose toward a metal hoop. In theory, after jumping through the hoop, the stripper would land safely in the swimming pool. Kato turned to Cornelius, who was arranging pitchers of secondhand beer on the back patio. "You know about engineering. What do you think?"

Cornelius shrugged. "I don't think it'll work." He took Jasmine to the basement.

"What do you know?" Kato said. "Okay, ladies and

gentlemen, boys and girls of all ages, tonight, Jade is going to ski from the roof, down this ramp, do the loop-de-loop, jump through the ring of—" At his signal, a frat brother lit the hoop with a cigarette lighter. "–fire, and land unscathed in this swimming pool. Are you not entertained?"

The crowd cheered, and Kato led the stripper up the ladder. "You know," she said, "When I said anything, I meant sex. I meant intercourse, fucking, anything sexual. I wasn't subtle."

"This is sexual. Who said this isn't sexual?" He called to the crowd below, "Is this not sexual?"

Nobody could hear what he said, so everyone cheered. Someone turned the music up, and Jade looked down at the ramp, the burning hoop of fire, the swimming pool, and two grinning faces in front of her. One brother held a pair of skis, the other a pair of ski boots. Kato made a last check to make sure there was enough water and lube on the ramp. He added half a bottle of cooking oil.

"You people are fucking morons," Jade said. She climbed down to the patio.

Kato hurried down the ladder to calm the partygoers. "Dudes, it's cool. Everybody stay where you are, and I'll go get the other whore." He raised his arms. "I'll be back."

Kato found Cornelius in the basement, arguing with someone online. Jasmine stood at the washing machine slop sink, gargling. "Cornelius, Jade won't do it. I need your whore."

Cornelius didn't look up from the screen. "I told you it wouldn't work."

"It would have worked if she hadn't chickened out."

Cornelius sighed. "Velocity. She would never have built up the speed. Maybe if you shot her out of a cannon or used compressed air you could launch her fast enough, but she'll never get enough speed just skiing off the roof. It was a stupid idea to begin with." Kato eyed the soda fountain. "Don't even look at my CO_2 tanks. There isn't nearly enough pressure."

"But if you're through with Jasmine, we can try this with

her. I tell you, this will work. It has to work."

"Try what with me?" Jasmine asked.

"Okay, stay with me here," Kato said.

Before he could explain, Jade came down the stairs. "Come on, Jasmine, we're done here. We should have left a long time ago." Jasmine picked up her purse and walked toward the stairs.

Kato grabbed her wrist, whining, "You can't go. You have to do the loop-de-loop and jump through the ring of fire." He was still holding her wrist when she slipped on a crushed beer can on the middle step and fell, knocking Jade backward. While Jade fell to the concrete floor and landed on her butt, Jasmine hit her head on the stairs. Jade sat on the floor, screaming. Jasmine lay silent. Kato looked right and left. He focused on Cornelius, "You know about medicine, do something."

Cornelius called for an ambulance.

Kato received a letter from an attorney a week later. The settlement offer, with attorney's fees and the promise to keep it quiet, was half a million dollars. Kato called a frat meeting. "Where are we supposed to get $500 thou?" he asked.

"The one girl just got out of the coma and the other girl has a broken tailbone," Theo said. "Maybe we should contact the alumni. Maybe we have homeowner's insurance or something."

"Well, what good's that going to do us? Those girls were totally straight. I could tell they were into me. We have almost seven hundred dollars in the fund. We should give them that." He sent an email to the law firm. A week later, the fraternity received a settlement offer for $600,000. Zoning inspectors showed up to look at the slide. The Alcohol Control Board visited while the Rho Beta Pis were running underage pledges through the chug and glug in the swimming pool. The inspectors confiscated the snorkels, kegs, and funnels. The insurance company canceled coverage, and the bank followed up, calling the mortgage due to lack of insurance. "We can't pay all of this," Kato said. "With the mortgage, the fines, and the settlement, that's like $800,000."

He looked around for somewhere to delegate the responsibility. "Theo," he said. "You have a job."

"Don't look at me. I get minimum wage plus tips. That doesn't even cover tuition. With the candidate fees, initiation fees, and all the other fees this frat keeps coming up with, you'd better look somewhere else."

"Cornelius. You know about money. How can we do this? I'm not going back to living in the dorms."

Cornelius reached under his chins and scratched one of his beards. "I saw something about a race online. It used to be a deep web thing, but it's going public this year, and there's prize money. It might be just right for you guys."

"We'll try anything," Kato said.

***

Joe jerked the wheel from left to right, trying to shake the body off the hood. "I think he is stuck."

John opened a bottle of American vodka and tossed the cap out the window. "I remember when this race used to mean something." He took a swig and handed the bottle to Joe, who took two swallows and handed it back.

"The scene is dead. It has gone mainstream. It is like everybody thinks he can be a drunk driver these days, like it is the cool thing to do." Joe shook the wheel. "Yes, he is stuck there."

"Well, comrade, so many things have lost their meaning since Glasnost. What is the meaning of being a sleeper cell now that there is no Soviet Republic to ever awaken us?"

"They have forgotten us," Joe said. "Either some papers were mislaid or the person tasked with awakening us has retired or died. I told you that long ago, my friend."

John dismissed the notion. "Forgotten us? Ha! Russia has forgotten herself. The Americans no longer fear Mother Russia. They fear petty criminals. An airplane here, a building there, shoes and underwear, no real threat at all. No, my friend, we are the last of the cold warriors."

"Do not depress me. Give me a pill." Joe took a dose of military-grade dextroamphetamine and the bottle from John. "War is dead. The USSR is dead. And this fucker will not fall off the car like any decent person would. When there is no solidarity, what is left?"

John looked at the back seat. "Twenty-three bottles and ninety-nine pills."

Joe sighed. "It will have to do. We are the last men, Ivan Petrovich. When I think that our grandfathers burned their own crops, factories, and cities just to spite the Germans, that our fathers starved in the fields to spite the Americans; and that we used to live with the certainty that the end of the world would come not some time in the future but now, any day of the week and that we were willing, honored, to make that happen. When I think that, I am ashamed to look at men today who fear the death of one, ten, or a few hundred people. It is like they think people should live forever. What is that next to the certainty that the whole world will die in one moment of fire and wrath? When that certainty is lost, what is left?

"These things do not frighten me. What scares me, Ivan Petrovich, is that this life might go on and on forever for no good reason, like a hamster on a wheel, producing nothing. Even a donkey that turns a millstone at least produces flour, but what good do we create? Ah, to be that donkey! No, I do not see men anymore. What is left here is cowardice, weakness. I spit on them." He rolled down his window to spit at a beige minivan. "You and your baby on board. I spit on your baby." He wiped spit off the side of his face. "Give me the PPS. I will shoot their tires. That will teach their baby to be on board."

John palmed the pistol but didn't hand it over. "With your left hand out the window? You will miss."

Joe shrugged and took another pull from the bottle. "What can you do? I remember when this whole race was agents, when we would steal tires from the CIA fools' cars. And Agent Gorman's potato salad at the post-race potluck was amazing. You cannot find such potato salad today. And now the CIA no longer cares about us. It is a race of common drunks and lazy fools." He jerked the wheel. "I think it is the camera strap. It must be hooked on something."

"We must not lose hope. If we do, we will be hopeless."

Joe scowled at a bumper sticker on an SUV, "'Visualize World Peace,' it says. Ha! What good has peace ever been to anyone?"

"There is a sandwich shop at this exit. We could stop and get rid of the body."

"No, leave it. He is beginning to grow on me."

***

Bernie took the shuttle to the older, smaller terminal building and checked his luggage at the counter. He spotted Dot after the TSA checkpoint, trying to buy a cup of coffee from the European-styled coffee counter and starting to raise her voice.

"I don't want a grande. I want a coffee, and you've gone bonkers if you think I'll pay two bucks for a lousy coffee. I'll give you two bits, and even that's highway robbery."

Bernie sidled up next to Dot and ordered for both of them. "Two grande drips and an almond biscotti." The barista turned to fill the cups. "You shouldn't try to do this kind of thing without me. I'm your manager. I handle these things for you." He handed the barista his American Express card.

"People have been trying to rip me off all day. Do you know how much the subway charges?"

"Don't worry about that." He'd tried to explain inflation before. He led her toward the gate. She picked up her coffee and followed with her rolling carry-on.

"The boys in the blue suits, they took my gin," Dot complained.

"Yeah, I should have told you about that. You can't take any liquids on the plane."

Dot lowered her eyebrows. "But they just sold us coffee. That's a liquid. Sounds like a scam to me."

An amplified voice announced that flights would be delayed while the airport police chased a Buick Skylark off the runway. "Yeah, it's a scam," Bernie said. It was easier than explaining.

Dot opened a magazine, leafed through it, and closed it again. "Who are these people? A bunch of nobodies. Paris Hilton? Lady Gaga? They all sound like made-up names. Emma Stone? Ryan Gosling? Horsefeathers."

"Well, *Dot*, it'll take some time to get used to the scene," Bernie said. "Don't think about it too much. Leave the thinking to me."

"Oh, Bernie," Dot said. "What would I do without you?" The line was a goof, something she'd said on a radio sitcom when she'd played the starlet's younger sister with the lovable goon of a boyfriend. Dot knew exactly what she'd do without him. Dot remembered the void. It had been nice, like a laudanum sleep at first, like that oblivion after six or a dozen gin and sodas. It had been like that forever, slow and lazy dreams. Then she'd awoken to hell.

In the void, sleep had been an empty, deep floating, a heaven of not existing and being nowhere. When she awoke, she started drowning. She'd remembered the flying man who collided with her plane, the plane going down. Her lungs couldn't draw air. There was a panicked awareness that she existed, but she existed nowhere.

She'd tried to flail her arms, but they were frozen in place, so she couldn't swim. Blinding light shone all around her, red and grainy through her eyelids. She couldn't tell whether she was too hot or too cold. She only knew her skin burned and she was being drawn out of that sleep under water, thawing inside a glass tube.

Every few seconds or years, someone yelled "clear" and

Dot's body convulsed like a seizure or a couple hundred sleep spasms. When the noise, like some annoying bird, started chirping steadily, Dot's eyes had fluttered open. The first thing she'd noticed was that she was in a large gray building, like an abandoned studio, with electric machines all around her. The second thing she'd noticed was that she was cold and wet. The third thing was Bernie bent over her, grinning like some demon from a story she'd read about back in school. Like Mephistopheles, he held a folded piece of paper in his hand. He'd tried to speak with her, but she heard nothing until the boys in white coats pulled the ice from her ears with long, skinny tweezers. She then understood what Bernie held in his hand—her contract.

Without Bernie, she'd never have this second chance at becoming a leading lady, a star instead of a second fiddle. Without Bernie, she'd still be in that deep sleep. She missed it the way a widow might miss her husband's arms, the way a patient leaving the hospital might miss morphine. She could approximate the effect with gin, but it was a cheap substitute. Now, waiting for the air hostesses to call for them to board the plane, she didn't even have gin. If she couldn't have gin and couldn't have the void, she could still have her stardom. Bernie had promised her that. When they called for first class to board, she and Bernie carried their own luggage toward the plane. Dot considered telling Bernie that the plane was missing its propellers, but she decided it wasn't her problem. Worst case, the plane would crash and she'd be back in that sweet, bathwater void.

***

William took 270 North and reached Frederick in near-silence. With the volume on the GPS turned all the way down, William was settling into his road trip groove. The thought of the unit stewing in mute rage was oddly satisfying, peaceful, almost pleasant. As he drove further into the mountains, he opened a bottle of Malbec from the back seat with a gas-powered cork puller. The temperature dropped, and the mountains peaks showed streaks of leftover snow. The roads were obscured by white fog. At the tollbooth, he took a ticket for the Pennsylvania Turnpike. Once past the booth, he put a stemless Riedel wineglass in the cup holder.

Anita finally spoke, "So has your GPS always talked like that?"

"It's not mine." He sipped his wine. "Let's just relax and enjoy the scenery." He pointed at a pickup truck with a Confederate battle flag painted on the tailgate. "I mean, we're already in the South. We're making good time."

"It's kind of weird having your GPS talk back to you and everything."

"I told you, it isn't mine. I'm just using it for the race."

"You know, they say not to give up just before the miracle happens. Maybe that's the miracle forcing you to stop avoiding your problems."

"I'm not avoiding anything. You know what? I don't want to talk about it."

"Okay, we can talk about something else, like your intervention."

William's laugh turned into a cough. "Christ, Anita. You made me get wine in my nose. Okay, the intervention. How's that going? Is it everything you hoped it would be?"

"To tell you the truth, this is my first intervention."

"Really? I think you did a real bang-up job. Seeing all the people who care about me really helped."

"At least I showed up. It's not like I didn't have things to do."

"You couldn't even get my wife to come?"

"She's your ex-wife," Anita reminded him. "And I told her about it. She wanted to come, but she had to stay at the hospital."

"She's still my wife. It's just a trial separation."

"Sure. Denial is not a river in Egypt."

"Yes it is! Stop saying that!"

"And you're avoiding the real issue. She was at the hospital. I mean, as long as we're on the subject of people caring enough to show up."

He put down his glass and stared forward. "How's Sophie doing?"

"She looked up at me with her big, yellow eyes and asked when Daddy was coming home."

"Fuck you." William said.

"You should be with your child."

"I am exactly where God wants me right now."

"Yeah, right. We're lucky we made it this far. Do you even remember why your wife threw you out?"

"She threw me out because I was unemployed. It's kind of hard to balance being a wine critic with all the not drinking I've been doing. And going to AA was her idea too. You can't win sometimes."

"No. Before that."

"I got into an accident."

"You crashed your car into your own house because you were drunk. Your drinking destroyed your home. That's not even a metaphor."

"I was studying for the Master of Wine exam. Do you know how many people pass that?"

"And by studying, you mean drinking."

"That's how it's done."

"And you drove home drunk and crashed into your own house."

"It could happen to anyone."

"You crashed into the second floor. That couldn't happen to anyone; it could only happen to you. You amaze me sometimes."

"Yeah," William said. "I'm a pretty amazing guy."

Anita shook her head. "You know, about your wife wanting

51

to be at the intervention?"

"Yeah?"

"I lied about that part."

William growled and sipped the wine. It smelled like pipe tobacco and garlic salt. The initial sweetness was followed by a trailing flavor of sour black cherries. The texture was creamy, the finish like dry velvet and chalkdust. From the Andes, he thought. No, the foothills. Of course, he bought the bottle, so this was like playing chess against himself. "This wine is seven years old," he said. "Do you know what I was doing seven years ago?"

"No, and I don't care," Anita said.

***

Thomas pulled into the parking lot of a small office building on Four Mile Run in Arlington, Virginia. The lot sat between a junkyard's chain link and barbed wire fence and the brick wall of an employment center for day laborers. He was visibly disappointed.

"Yeah. I know," Renee said. "Just think how I feel." She stumbled out of the car and dropped the empty wine bottle in the parking lot. It rolled across the asphalt and stopped next to several other bottles against the fence. She unlocked the door and led Thomas into a two-room office. The lobby had a paisley couch and a particleboard coffee table that held a dozen back issues of *Grit* and *Washingtonian*, the kind of magazines people read while waiting for dental work. Renee sat behind a receptionist desk and checked the answering machine. There were no messages. "So you know what's going on now," Renee said.

"Well, there was a race, but everyone crashed."

"Sure, on the surface, that's all it looks like, but underneath the–you know–surface, there's something much more sinister going on."

"Good," Thomas said. "I didn't want to write an article about a traffic accident."

"The woman organizing the race, that was Dot Dottie, the 1940s actress."

"I think she looked a little young for that."

Renee motioned for Thomas to look over her shoulder as she Googled the name. "She was a supporting actress doing mostly B movies and serials. She usually played the plucky kid sister on account of her hair. She was never blonde enough to star, but she wasn't tall enough to play the femme fatale. She was also working in radio, hoping to become the next Anne Sothern.

"When the war started, it was good PR for starlets to get in on the war effort. She did a few days a month as a doughnut girl and started doing camp shows. On her USO tour, her plane was lost over the North Atlantic. Several decades later, she was found frozen in a block of ice."

"Kind of like Captain America?" Thomas asked.

"Yeah. I saw that movie. See, when they found Captain America, he had to be thawed out immediately, to fight Nazi aliens or something. Dottie wasn't really as important, and there were a lot of people waiting to be thawed out. See, heroes were a lot like frozen burritos back then. Whenever you thought you'd gotten them all out of the ice, another iceberg would come bobbing along with a soldier, a superhero, a comedian, or a popular singer frozen inside it. You wouldn't believe how often this happened. Anyway, it's pretty expensive to thaw these people out, so most of the burritos were kept frozen until someone claimed them, and now it looks like someone has claimed Dottie."

"The guy in the suit?"

"Right." Renee pulled up a grainy amber and beige photo. "Look familiar? This was Dot Dottie's publicist back in 1941. Bernie, the guy who turned on the interlock and punched our race card, must have inherited her contract."

"What does this have to do with Mothers Against Drunk Driving?"

"I have to level with you. I'm not with MADD. Have you ever heard of the Temperance Movement?"

Thomas scratched his ear. "Wasn't that a girl band in the '80s? They're on the late-night commercials with that song, *Do the Whale* or something."

"*Scrimshaw.*" Renee sighed. "It was *Do the Scrimshaw.* I mean, you're right, but between tours, the Temperance Movement was also active in the prevention of drinking and driving before MADD got big and pushed us out of the business. MADD wanted to focus on drunk driving. We were more about preventing both driving and drinking. Their message caught on better, and they had a good acronym. TM™ just didn't get the point across the same way. You know what? I have a PowerPoint for this."

She closed the browser and hunted around for the shortcut on her desktop. Once the file was open, she started scrolling through the slides. "So you can see that there." She pointed at the screen. "That slide's pretty self-explanatory." She moved to the next slide. "And then that happened. If you read this part, it makes a lot of sense." She clicked the mouse for the next slide. "Oh, yes. This graph tells the whole story. Here's the same information but in a pie chart. And hold on. This next one takes a couple minutes."

Thomas took off his green visor. "You can scroll past the animations. We don't need to wait for them to load."

"Yeah, but the sound effect is really cute. Okay, and this slide, I think, really pulls the whole presentation together. The kitten's there to lighten the mood a bit. The rest of the slides are Ziggy cartoons, so we can skip those." Renee minimized the window. "And now you understand the problem."

"Let me see." He scratched his thumbnail between his front teeth thoughtfully. "You're saying Dot Dottie has been thawed out and her publicist has hijacked radio stations across the country to play big band music and cover the drunk driving race as a publicity stunt to revive her career?"

Renee pointed at him and touched her finger to the tip of her nose. Then her face dropped. "When you say it like that, it makes me wish I hadn't spent two days making this slide show." She reached under the desk and retrieved a half-empty handle of Bacardi and a can of Diet Coke. "And after he revives her career, well, who knows what he might do next?"

Thomas shook his head. "What does any of this have to do with me?"

"We need publicity. We have to expose Dot Dottie and stop her before anyone else gets hurt. I need you to break the story and let the world know. Then maybe we can figure out how to stop her. We must stop at nothing, even if we have to kill her."

"I'm not going to kill anyone. I wouldn't even know how to kill a radio star."

"We'll burn that bridge when we come to it. For now, just get the word out. You can be our social media guru. You'll handle the Temperance Movement's public face."

"I don't have any experience running a publicity campaign. Hell. I've never had a job before."

"Now you're our social media manager. Put it on your resume. I'll print out a sign for your desk."

"Where's my desk?"

"You can use the coffee table."

"If you're not MADD, do I still get college credit for this?"

"Sure," Renee said. "I'm not a monster."

"Is this a paid internship?"

"Of course not," Renee said.

Chapter .05

Near the North Carolina border, Jeb pulled the car into a gas station. "Let's make this quick," Sean said. "Just like we practiced. Go!" He jumped out of the car and ran into the gas station. Inside, he found the restroom and timed himself getting in and out. He hurried through the aisles until he found a packet of Goody's powder.

At the counter, the cashier asked, "Are you supposed to be a race car driver or something?"

Sean raised his visor. "What did you say?"

"Your outfit. You look like a race car driver, like from the TV."

"I am a race car driver. I'm Sean Marshall. I'm on the Metamucil Team." He took off his right glove and offered his hand.

"Well, I'll be. A real NASCAR driver in my store. How about that? My son won't believe it when I tell him." He rang up the powder. "You know, I've always wanted to know something. What do you boys do when you have to, you know, use the bathroom during a race?"

Sean reached for his wallet, but his fire pants didn't have a back pocket. "I'm sorry. I left my wallet in the car. I'll be right back." Outside, Jeb had the 92 octane nozzle in the tank, but he wasn't pumping any gas.

"Hey Jeb, I think I left my wallet in my jeans. Can I use your credit card?"

"Sure." Sean opened the door and dug under the seat. "Wait. I think I put my wallet in the suitcase." He took the keys to the back of the car to pop the trunk. "Okay. If I remember right, I had the keys and my wallet in my pants, and I put the pants in the suitcase. That's right because we had to open the suitcase to get the keys again."

"Right. Then we threw away the suitcase so it wouldn't weigh us down."

"Damn." With his gloves on, Sean couldn't snap his fingers in frustration, so he slapped his thigh. "Okay, let me go in and talk to the guy. I'm sure we can work something out."

***

The cashier sat on his stool, beaming with joy, his hands tied behind his back with bungee cords and his ankles duct taped together. "I can't believe I'm being robbed by a real live NASCAR driver," the cashier said.

"It ain't like that," Sean said. "We just need to borrow a little bit of gas, some aspirin, and some beer. Thing is, we left our wallets at home."

"In my day, when a man came into a store, tied him up, and took his stuff, we called it a robbery."

"Well, I had to tie you up. You said you were going to call the police."

"I had to call the sheriff's office. My son's a deputy, and when he finds out I was robbed by a real NASCAR driver, he'll just pitch a fit that he wasn't here."

"I'm not robbing you." Sean looked out the front window, and Jeb gave him a thumbs up. "Okay, never mind." Sean said. "I'll just go now." He picked up the case of beer and left the store.

"Wait!" the cashier yelled after him. "You still haven't told me about how you guys take a piss! Do you have a hose or diapers? Is it like an astronaut suit or what?"

Sean let the door close, the bell ringing behind him.

"The tank's almost full," Jeb said.

Sean pulled the hose out of the tank and dropped it on the ground, still pumping fuel. "Let's get going," he said. They got in the car.

"So how did it go?" Jeb pushed the cigarette lighter into the dashboard.

"Fine," Sean said. "He said we can pay him back later." He yanked the lighter out of the plug and tossed the glowing coil out the window. "No smoking, remember? It'll just make you feel drunker. Now, get us across the state line just as quick as you can."

***

The Bugatti tore west on Route 64, weaving in its lane. Behind it, four police cars followed at 120 miles per hour, nowhere near fast enough. The car was loud and cramped, the suspension uncomfortable, but it was the fastest thing on the road.

The Master sat in a lotus position in his seat. "Are we there yet?"

"No, Master. We aren't there yet. Asking *Are there yet?* every five minutes won't get us there any faster." Kai looked in the rear view mirror and watched the strobe lights fade into the distance.

"Jackie Chan would have gotten us there by now."

"For the hundredth time, I'm not Jackie Chan."

"I'm painfully aware of that fact." He tented his hands and closed his eyes.

"What are you doing now?"

"I'm meditating on your failures."

"And I am meditating on those police cars behind us. We can outrun them, but we can't outrun the radios."

"And why not? That is one more failure, your inability to outrun the radio."

"Eventually, they'll call for backup and set up a roadblock. I want to think ahead and plan what I will do."

The Master pulled a small sodbuster knife from the sleeve of his kimono, flicked it open, and used it to slice his landjaeger sausages, which were linked in pairs like nunchaku. He chewed thoughtfully and returned to scolding his disciple. "Do not

58

plan. You're wasting time. We'll deal with that problem when it presents itself. And remember, if you do get caught, if anyone asks, we're Chinese. We must not bring disgrace upon the Drunken Cichlid."

Kai brushed his blond hair out of his blue eyes. "I remember the cover story, Sifu."

"But that's only if we are caught, and we should never get caught." The Master balanced the sausage slice on the flat of his blade and looked for the bread and mustard. "Now, tell me how many of the vehicles you have misled."

"I was able to mess with most of the cars. I programmed their GPS units to random coordinates around the continent. If they made it out of D.C., they're halfway to Canada, Alaska, or Florida by now. I don't even know why we had to do that. We can easily out-drive them."

The Master took a bite of his brotchen and spat crumbs. "Any fool can out-drive them. The very essence of war is deception. That is the true nature of Drunken Cichlid Kung Fu. You must mislead your opponent, allow him to underestimate you, and destroy him when he reveals his weaknesses. You must appear to be weak when you are strong, and to mislead your opponent, you must first lead him."

"Well, I don't think there is any real competition left in this race."

"There are the two redneckmen. They are skillful drivers. This device tells us we're not in the lead in this race, so I believe they are the first car."

"Well, I did steal their wallets. They won't get far on one tank of gas."

The Master gave the slightest suggestion of a smile. He was not completely disgusted with his pupil's work. "But there are others. When we defeat them all, America will know that Drunken Cichlid is the finest of the fighting arts."

"I still think we could have proven that by joining the UFC."

"True. We could have entered a chickenwire cage with fat,

sweaty barbarians who fight without shoes or shirts, like dogs. Fortunately, by developing the car pattern of Drunken Cichlid and passing it on to you, I have spared you that indignity." He started a lecture that Kai had already memorized. "Any weapon is a mere extension of the body. The sword is merely used to extend and focus the strength of the arm. The staff merely lengthens the reach of your fist. Similarly, the automobile must move as you do, and you must move as the automobile does."

Kai focused on his breathing and felt a sense of calm overtake his body as he tried to make his heart function like a fuel injector. He visualized and directed the flow of alcohol through his bloodstream. The Master poured him a bowl of wine, and Kai bowed his head in thanks. He rounded a corner and saw two police cars parked across the road, blocking the highway. The officers crouched behind their cars, one holding a shotgun and the other a speed gun.

With the cup in his right hand, Kai pulled the wheel to the left and snapped it back to the right. A shock wave traveled through his body and into the vehicle. He tensed his abs and lymphatic tissues abruptly, then relaxed completely, extending his chi through the top of his head. The rear of the Bugatti rose, and the car did a one-armed handspring over the cruisers. It landed on all four tires and continued without losing speed. Kai looked down at the bowl. It was still full. He turned toward the Master to receive his well-deserved praise.

The Master shook his head and pointed to two droplet-sized stains on Kai's sleeve. "Pitiful," he said. "An infant, still wet from the womb, knows where its mouth is and how to drink. It's the first thing any mammal knows, and you can't even do that. Turn around. I want you to do that again." Sighing, Kai engaged the parking brake and turned the wheel. The car spun around, and he drove east on Route 64 West, back toward the police cars. The Master topped off the bowl of wine. "And we will do it again and again until you can do something as simple as drinking a cup of wine without spilling it everywhere."

***

Outside of Rockville, the Beltway curved south. With the car pointed southwest, Theo was relieved that they were finally driving in the right direction. They crossed the Potomac and took 66 West a half hour later. When they crossed the Shenandoah River and approached 81, Theo opened a bottle of Virginia Gentleman, poured the bourbon into three Solo cups, and filled the cups with Coca Cola.

Kato downed his, crushed the cup, and threw it out the window. The car swerved to the left, and a semi sounded its air horn. He pulled the car back into his lane. "Shit," he said. "Don't worry, it's under control." The right wheel hit the shoulder, and the car shook.

"Slow down," Theo said in a calm, non-threatening voice. "Both hands on the wheel."

Kato put his hands at the ten and two position. "Why do they make these roads so blurry?"

"You see where your hands are?"

"Don't tell me about hands. I know my hands like the back of my hand," Kato said.

"Fine. You're doing well. Now, raise your index fingers."

"What?"

"Raise your index fingers. Point them skyward."

"Fingers? Both at the same time? Do you even know where the sky is?"

"You can do it," Chav said.

"I can do this." Kato took a deep breath. "Index, like pointy fingers?"

"Right," Theo said. "Those ones. Point them up."

"I'll try." Kato raised his index fingers. "I did it!"

"Good. Now, keep the road between those fingers."

"What road?"

"Do you want me to drive?"

"Fuck you. Who's the frat prez here? I just raised both

61

my fingers at once. I'd like to see you try that shit." Kato concentrated on his fingers.

They drove down Route 81, the Blue Ridge Mountains to their right. Theo stared out the window at something a lifetime in the Midwest had never offered him: scenery. He watched the mountains rise and fall until the sun set behind them.

***

William exited the highway outside of Pittsburgh in a town called Cranberry. At the intersection of four strip malls, he pulled into a parking lot. "Okay, we'll stop here and get some food. It should be fast."

A girl in a red and white apron stood behind the counter. "Can I take your order?"

"We'd like some authentic Southern food. We need two pulled pork sandwiches with slaw, hush puppies, some greens, and some fried okra. A Big Red for me and a Diet Coke for her." He twitched his head at Anita.

"We don't have any of that stuff. Our pop is all A-Treat. Do you want to look at a menu?"

"No time. What do you have?"

"We got cheesesteaks, stuffed cabbage, Velveeta pierogies, and pastrami sandwiches. Them sandwiches already got fries and slaw on them."

"Alright, give us two pastramis."

The sandwiches arrived in a white paper bag. William took out his credit card and handed it to the cashier. Next to the register, a sign said tipping was not a city in China. "Yes, it is," William pointed out. He held his receipt at arm's length, squinted, and bent his elbow until the letters came into focus. "Wait, is this address right?"

"No," the cashier said. "During daylight savings time we have to move one city over."

William considered this. "That isn't true. What the fuck are we doing in Pennsylvania? We were supposed to go to Arkansas. That's like a completely different place."

Anita picked up the bag. "You're the one who drove us here."

When William blew into the interlock and started the car, the GPS unit asked, "So, care to listen now, you stinking bar sponge?"

William pointed to Anita, "She's the one who turned you off."

Anita brushed the accusation away with a sweep of her left hand. "You asked me if there was any way to shut her up."

William chopped his hands up and down. "I asked you, but I didn't fucking ask you." He left the parking lot and headed for the highway.

"That doesn't make any sense. You specifically asked how to shut the GPS up. There's a volume control right here."

She touched the volume control on the side of the GPS, and the nanny voice said, "Could you turn that up a little bit more, dear?"

"Oh, sure." Anita adjusted the volume.

When the volume seemed high enough, the GPS unit yelled, "You went the wrong way!"

"Shit," William said. "Turn it down."

"You were mucking about with no direction at all, you bloody idiot," the GPS said.

"It's not my fault they have Confederate flags everywhere. How am I supposed to know which way is south?" William saw a sign for Washington and pulled onto the highway, trying take a bite of his sandwich. Soggy French fries and bits of smoked meat slid down his shirt.

"Aye, if only there was something to tell you where you was supposed to go," the GPS unit said. "Well, hows about I tell you something: sobriety is—"

"Sobriety is a road, not a destination?" Anita said.

"Okay, fine," the GPS unit said. "You've heard that one. But if you wants my help, I'm going to need an apology from

William there."

William sipped a thin Rhone wine with accents of vinegar, tinfoil, rabbit blood, and yoghurt-covered cranberries. It paired poorly with the sandwich. "There's nothing you can do. I drove three hundred miles in the wrong direction. That means I have to drive three hundred miles back. The other cars must be halfway to Nashville by now."

Anita tried to be supportive. "The journey of a thousand miles starts with a single step."

"Aye, a single step is good," the GPS said. "Not so much going the wrong way for five fucking hours." It waited for a response. "I might note that nobody has asked my name yet. We've been here for hours now and we've not been properly introduced. Were you people born in a barn?"

"Better people than us have been born in barns," Anita said.

"Oh, that's good." William said. "Is that a slogan?"

The GPS unit said, "Nay. It just sounds like that. It's like poetry, only works if you talk slow, all fucking bollocks."

William didn't care to make his acquaintance with the GPS unit. In his mind, he had been calling the GPS the nanny bitch, the same name he used for that nagging voice on the D.C. Metro that told him to keep away from the doors and not eat electricity and all the things he already knew to not do. "Hi. I'm William, and I'm an alcoholic," he said.

Anita joined in. "I'm Anita, and I'm an alcoholic, and you are?"

"Fuck off with your 'and you are,'" the GPS said. "I can smell from his breath that he's an alcoholic. And from your weight in the chair, I can tell that you are insecure about your looks. From my voltage meter here, I can see that I am near fucking perfect in all what matters."

"Practically perfect in every way. Are you Mary Poppins or something?" Anita could only take so many narcissists in one car.

"Don't mention that bitch's name to me. I'm Maggie

O'Higgins, and I am a nanny. I'm magical enough, but I'm nothing like that bleeding cunt."

"Isn't that a bit of a working-class name for a magical nanny?"

"Well, where the fuck you think nannies come from, the fucking royalty? You think I would be here with you lot if I was one of them upper-class nannies with their flying umbrellas and their magical handbags, just brushing off marriage proposals from Dick Van Dyke every day? Fuck off. I have to slog like the rest of them, don't I? Do I shove up to you every day when you're hard at work doing fuck-all and ask if your name's good enough? Mary fucking Poppins." She growled the name. "Just because she's got rosy cheeks and no warts, you'd think the world was made for her convenience."

"I see how that can be trying," William said.

"You have warts?" Anita asked.

"A sailor in Liverpool," Maggie said. "Never you mind. But I'm still magical enough. For example, I see how you are driving toward Washington."

"Right," William said. "The sign said Washington, so I'm going that way. That's what people did before they had GPS units. They paid attention to the road."

"You know that's Washington, Pennsylvania, right? You're still going in the wrong fucking direction."

"You have to be kidding me!" He turned the wheel and hit the brakes. "What the hell is wrong with Pennsylvania? Why can't we leave this awful place?"

"Don't worry," Maggie said. "You have to remember what it was like to be a child, think of where you want to go, and we can wish ourselves there."

"Great. Magical thinking." Anita said. "I only have a script for one intervention."

"Stick around, bitch," Maggie said. "I'll show you a miracle that will bring back Julie Andrews' menstrual cycle."

"Why do we want to bring back—"

"It's just an expression, you silly queef," Maggie said. "Now, just visualize where you want to go."

William first thought of the Children's Hospital in D.C., but that wouldn't win him the race, and he wasn't on the guest list anyway. "The checkpoint is in Arkansas, but I don't know shit about that place. I know Clinton came from there. Could I envision him?"

"Not unless you want to find yourself up a secretary's twat. I don't think a pickled whiskey dick like you could pull that off."

"Where exactly is *Bring back Julie Andrews' menstrual cycle* a saying?" Anita asked. "For that matter, where are you supposed to be from? What's with the accent? Are you supposed to be Irish, Scottish, Cockney, or what?"

"Never you mind, love," Maggie said. "That's nay important right now."

"Can you just pick a dialect? I've been to Europe, you know, and I think you're faking it."

"Oh, well, if you've been to Europe, I suppose there's no fooling you." If she'd had lips she would have sneered. She'd been to every continent on the planet. She swam up the Euphrates fifteen thousand years ago to watch one of the first farmers weep beside a burning wheat field. She drank his tears and ate his soul. She lived in England when the bastards thought painting themselves blue was the height of fashion and convinced them that piling one rock on top of two rocks was a good idea. It took them decades to pull off, and she'd fed on their pains as they made that pointless circle of stones. She'd nipped at Beowulf's heels as he swam. She swallowed an ox's head the day Thor went fishing. She knew languages the gods had long forgotten, and sometimes it was difficult keeping them all straight from one lifetime to another, let alone the regional variations. But fine, she could let the girl win this argument. If she could handle children, she could handle alcoholics. "Don't blame me, dear. It's in the software, see? I can go back to my proper accent if it suits you better."

William interrupted. "No. Please don't go back to that stuck-up voice."

"Or I could sound more like you Yanks, if you prefer."

"Well, it would be easier," Anita said.

Maggie switched to an exaggerated John Wayne accent, adding unnecessary Rs to every word. "Ire mearn, sorme peopler mirght ber harppy wirth arny margical narnny thery courld gert, burt Ir carn understarnd irf your'd prefer orne whor sournds more lirke yarls. I apologize. I forgot how much you Americans hate foreigners."

"I'm not xenophobic. It's just—"

"Not another word on the subject, Anita. I won't judge you. I'm perfectly willing to pander to your prejudices." Maggie changed the subject, settling into a standard Midwestern accent. "William, have you chosen a destination or are we going to sit here all night?"

"Well, there's one place close to Arkansas." William thought of Graceland, the four pillars in front of those stone steps, like what George Washington was probably going for when he built Mount Vernon. The lawn was so green it glowed, the building so white and the whole place more beautiful than anything any human could have built.

"I can see this place," Maggie said. "Yes. I have it. Now, we have to say the magic words."

"Please," Anita said.

"Not that," Maggie snapped. She chanted, almost in song, "Don't dream it. Be it. Don't dream it. Be it."

"Don't dream it; be it." William joined in. After a few minutes, he opened his eyes. "We're still in Pennsylvania. Are you fucking with me?"

Of course she was fucking with them. She took an apologetic tone. "Right, right. It doesn't always work the first time. You have to believe, like little children."

"If he had any faith," Anita said. "We wouldn't be in this situation."

Maggie thought on this. "We'll need a story from his childhood. If he can tell it right, he might remember being a kid. Then the nanny magic might work better."

"A story from my childhood," William said. "Once upon a time—"

"It has to be real," Maggie said. "And it has to be the most important story, something formative and painful."

William wasn't one for sharing, but the hours in the car with his sponsor, two bottles of wine, the Scotch, and the shame had put him close to the drunk confession mode. "For all practical purposes, my dad died at Graceland. He worked as a security guard there. He even showed me Elvis' bedroom once. When that hound dog bit him, my mother told him to get rabies shots, but—"

"Fuck off with your father dying. Everybody's parents die. It doesn't make you fucking Batman."

"It didn't kill him. That's just the last job he had before the divorce, so I don't know what he did after that."

"Well now, that's even less interesting, isn't it? You need something different, something that happened only to you."

Anita put her hand on William's shoulder. "You're an alcoholic. You have an audience. You can do this."

Flashing lights drew William's eyes to the rear view mirror. "There's a cop pulling up behind us," he said.

"So start talking," Maggie said.

"There's no time," William said.

"Time takes time," Anita said.

"No, it doesn't," Maggie snapped. With a splatting sound and a smell of methane and sulfur, black smoke billowed from the back of the car and the patrolman stopped. He stood frozen with his car door half open, one foot still in the air and his hat in his hand.

"What?" Maggie said. "Some people get fairy glitter dust and I get black smoke. The point is, there's time." Traffic stopped. Semi air horns stopped mid-blow. Deer grazing on the side of the road stopped chewing. Everything stood still. "We're all waiting."

"Okay," William said.

Chapter
.06

Three hours south of Front Royal, Theo spotted a Crown Victoria following them. He whispered to Chav, "Stay cool, but I think there's a cop behind us."

"The cops?" Chav dropped his can of PBR in his lap. He grabbed for the beer and dropped it on the floor.

"Cops?" Kato looked in the rear view mirror and swerved to the right.

"Remember the fingers!" Theo yelled.

Kato looked at his left hand and weaved toward the median. Then he jerked the wheel to the right, shaking the car. "Somebody give me some gum," he said.

Chav pointed to a sign. "Holy fuck! They're enforcing speed by aircraft!" He crouched down in his seat and watched the skies. "Nobody look up!"

"Take this next exit," Theo said. "They might pass by."

Kato slowly, smoothly took the exit for Route 11. "Someone give me a penny to put under my tongue."

"What's that supposed to do? There's a gas station," Theo said. "Pull up to a pump."

Kato stopped at the sign at the bottom of the hill, crossed the street, pulled next to the row of pumps, and turned off the engine. "Do you think they're gone?"

Theo handed Kato an unopened pint of Jägermeister. "Don't open this yet, but if the cops come, I want you to down as much of this as you can. They can't prove you were driving drunk if they see you drinking."

"Will that work?" Chav asked.

Theo shrugged. "Sure, man."

Kato sat in the driver's seat, Jäger at the ready. Five minutes passed. "I have to take a piss," he said. He handed the bottle to Chav and staggered out of the car.

"Me too," Chav said. He handed the bottle to Theo and got out.

***

The inside of the gas station was absurdly bright, with white walls, rows of junk food, and glass coolers of beer. The restroom was to the right, down a short corridor with lottery ticket dispensers against the glass storefront and a soda fountain, coffee pots, Jimmy Dean sausage biscuits, a microwave, and a crock pot of beans on the other side. The restroom door was unlocked, but Theo didn't follow Chav and Kato in. Through the door, he could hear, "This is the weapon of the Jedi," and "You're not my father!" Theo stood outside the bathroom door and waited for Chav and Kato to finish their yellow lightsaber battle.

When Theo finished in the bathroom, Chav and Kato were piling tallboys of Bud Ice and 4Loko on the counter. The cashier rested her cigarette in a black plastic ashtray and looked up from her television. As the frat boys scouted the store for food, she started pressing buttons on her cash register. "You boys getting any gas?"

"Gas?" Kato said. "What the fuck are you talking about, lady?"

Theo handed the woman Kato's credit card. "Yeah, we'll fill her up."

"We'll fill up my balls," Kato said.

"Okay, you do that," the lady said. Chav went outside to fill the tank.

Kato looked over the woman's shoulder at the rack of cigarettes behind her. "What the fuck are Fortuna cigarettes?" Kato asked.

"I think they're a brand of cigarettes," Theo said.

"A brand of fucking cigarettes?" Kato laughed. "Fortuna cigarettes?" He bent over and held his stomach.

71

"I don't get it," Theo said.

The clerk rang up the beers and food and added $26.20 for the gasoline. She put everything in a white grocery bag. "Anything else?"

"Yeah," Kato laughed. "Give me a pack of Fortuna cigarettes."

"Regular or menthol?"

"Fortuna menthol? Menthol Fortunas? You're killing me."

"It's not funny," Theo said. He reached into the bag and opened a can of 4Loko.

"No, no. I'm okay now. Not menthol. Not menthol." He gasped and regulated his breathing. "Just don't anybody say anything funny."

"Shorts or 100s?" the woman asked.

Kato scrunched up his face and snorted through his nose.

***

Outside, Chav was trying to screw the gas cap into the side of the car. "Is it clockwise in-wise, counter outer, or the other way?"

"Innie outie, tighty whitey," Kato said. "You know, clockwise."

"Right, but am I the clock or is the car the clock? If I'm the clock, it's the other way, right?" Chav turned the gas cap a few twists and heard it click. "Don't worry," he said. "I fixed it."

Theo turned to Kato. "Are you sure you don't want me to drive for a while? We could switch off and you could get some sleep."

Kato stifled his giggles. "No. I'm okay. Let me hit that." He swallowed a couple mouthfuls from the tallboy. "Okay. Good as new." He blew into the tube and turned the key.

Chav peered at the GPS. "I think if we go a couple miles south, it will put us back on 81. By the time we get there, those cops will be long gone."

"Awesome." Kato pulled onto Route 11. They passed signs

for drive-through zoos and cave tours. A sign for a haunted house and dinosaur garden had a plywood plank nailed over it, spraypainted with the word *CLOSED*. Chav plugged his iPod into the stereo and selected a playlist.

"Who has the food?" Chav asked. Theo passed out the snacks. He pulled down the reach-through, stowed the extra beer in the trunk, and spread beans on his biscuit.

It was a quiet, two-lane road. The moon was bright, but the road was shaded by trees. The car drove in a tunnel the headlights bore through the pudding-thick night. As they drove, a pair of high beams approached from the opposite direction.

"Cigarettes for tuna," Kato giggled.

"Watch out for the car coming up," Chav said. "They have their high beams on."

Kato flashed his lights, "Hey, turn them down, asshole." He gave the car the finger. The Honda was flooded with light. As the lights passed, Kato saw he was flicking off a police car.

As soon as the cruiser passed, it braked hard. Theo was suddenly glad Kato hadn't let him drive. "Okay, stay cool. They're turning around. Keep driving straight ahead." The car slowed. "Don't slow down. Drive close to the speed limit. And keep straight." He squinted at the cruiser. It almost looked like there was a body strapped to the hood of the car.

Kato stared at his fingers on the steering wheel. "Will you shut up back there? I'm trying to drive."

"Just don't happy-drive is all. Stay a couple miles over the speed limit but not five miles over." Theo shoveled thirty empty cans into the trunk with both hands. "Okay, they're still behind us, stay cool." The cruiser flashed a red and blue strobe. "Shit. Pull over."

"Where? There's nowhere to go." Kato slowed down until he saw a gravel driveway. A plywood sign next to an open steel gate said *Foamhenge*. He pulled into a grass and red mud parking lot.

"That sign had a pi on it," Chav said. "That might be a good sign, like an omen."

"Shut up!" Theo said. "Everybody shut the fuck up! Kato," he said. "License and registration. Name, rank, and service number. Admit nothing. Don't take the breathalyzer. We don't have to tell these bastards anything."

Kato switched off the ignition. "License and registration, name, rank and service number. We don't have to tell those bastards anything."

A man in a black suit with a white shirt and a black tie tapped on the driver's side window with a large flashlight he held in his right hand. He held a fifth of Tito's vodka in the other. "Get out of the car, ma'am," he said. "Shit. Sir. I meant to say sir."

Theo nodded his head with an exaggerated calm and whispered, "Admit nothing. Don't take the breathalyzer. We don't have to tell those bastards anything."

"Out of the car, sir," the officer said. He tapped on the window with the flashlight again, and the glass shattered. The officer's eyes went wide, and he pulled his hand back. He looked at the flashlight as if shocked at its behavior.

Kato jerked away from the broken glass. "License and registration. Name, rank, and serial number. We don't have to tell you bastards anything." Theo cringed and tried to sink into the seat.

"Get out of the car, sir," the officer said. He stepped back.

Kato opened the door and stepped out.

"I'm going to need the other four passengers to step out too."

Theo looked at Chav. Chav looked at Theo. Chav held up four fingers and shook his head. Theo made a shooing motion with his hands, and they stepped out onto the red mud. Another officer pushed them against the car. Theo and Chav put their hands on the roof and spread their legs, expecting to be patted down. The officer scratched his armpit.

The first officer focused on Kato. "Do you know how fast you were going?"

Kato drew an arch with his index fingers, trying to visualize the speedometer. "Twenty-five?" he asked.

"Do you know the speed limit on this road?"

"Forty-five." Theo said.

"No helping!" the officer slammed the car door shut and pushed Kato against the car.

Kato said, "Forty-five, sir?"

"Well, sure you know now." The officer glared at Theo. "Before, it was a mystery to all, but now?" He shrugged and stepped away from Kato. "Forty-five miles per hour. So you were driving twenty-five miles over the speed limit." He took a swig from his bottle of vodka.

Kato did the math in his head. "Under," he said. That's twenty-five miles under the speed limit."

"Twenty," Chav said.

"Is that a body on the hood of your car?" Theo asked.

The second officer kicked Theo's feet further apart so his head hit the window and he fell into the mud. "We ask the questions." He sniffed his fingers and stared at his hand.

"Twenty-five over the speed limit is reckless driving," the first officer said.

"Well, that's good, right?" Kato said. "You wouldn't want me to wreck."

The officer tapped the bottle against the side of his head in thought. He muttered, "What is the law in this stupid country?" He yelled to the second officer. "Do we want them to wreck less or more?"

"I think reckless driving is illegal. They should wreck at least once," the second officer said. "Hey!" he yelled to the frat boys. "Stop listening! Take your hands off the car and put them over your ears!"

Chav, Theo, and Kato put their hands over their ears as the officers went back to the Crown Victoria. With the body between them, the officers sat on the hood and passed the bottle back and forth, occasionally pointing at their prisoners. After a few minutes, the first officer walked over to Kato, unrolled the cigarettes from the sleeve of his t-shirt, and packed them against the roof of the car. He took two cigarettes, tossed the pack in the broken window, and walked back to the cruiser.

The frat boys' shoes and Theo's knees sank into the red clay. Away from the trees, the sky seemed vast and very far away. At the edge of the pasture, the mud road disappeared into a thick oak forest. At the top of the hill stood some kind of structure that looked like one pi next to another, a circle of pis. Chav jerked his head at the pis with his forehead. Theo shook his head. The officers seemed to come to a decision. They flicked their cigarettes away and walked over to their prisoners.

"Okay," the first officer said. "You have been found guilty of driving without wrecking, and the sentence is death."

"What?" Theo screamed.

The second officer yelled, "You can uncover your ears now."

The first officer handed the bottle to the second officer. As he reached for it, he slipped in the mud. He stood up, rinsed his hands with vodka, and started to hand the bottle back. "Thank you, comrade—officer I mean. I meant to say officer." He raised the bottle threateningly at his prisoners, "I said officer."

"It's cool, dude," Chav said. "You said officer. We all heard you."

The first officer led Kato around the car so everyone was on the passenger side. "I think we should take them in," the second officer said. "You're under arrest. We arrest you."

"I thought we were going to kill them," the first officer said.

"Yes, my friend," the second officer said. "But we do not want them to know that."

"Hey, wait a minute," Chav said. "I don't think these guys are real cops."

"We are so real cops," the second officer said. "And you are so arrested right now that it is not even funny how arrested you are."

"Fortuna," Kato lowered his head and held his stomach. "Oh, Fortuna," he sang, giggling. "Oh Fortuna, oh for tuna, for tunas."

"Keep your hands on the car!" the first officer yelled. The second officer reached for his weapon. His hand still slippery from the mud and vodka, the pistol flew out of his grip and bounced off Chav's chest, into his hands. Chav looked at the pistol in horror.

"They're throwing guns at us! Run!" Chav sprinted from the car, the officers in pursuit.

Theo knelt with his hands on the car, watching the officers run away. "Oh, Fortuna for tuna," Kato sang.

Chav ran uphill, screaming, "They're throwing guns! I have a gun! Run!" He scrambled past a wood bench, took cover behind it for a moment, and hurried on. When he crested the hill, there was no cover. He stood in the middle of a moonlit dirt clearing, surrounded by huge, white pis. He muttered frantically to himself, "I have a gun." He held the pistol in both palms, looked down at it, and was struck by a sense of safety and calm. His heartbeat slowed and a smile pulled at the corner of his face. "I have a gun." He stood still, extended his arms, and waited for the officers to reach the top.

A moment later, there were two gunshots. Theo turned to see Chav standing on the hilltop, Stonehenge behind him, holding a pistol over his head. "By the power of Grayskull!" Chav bellowed. The yell echoed in the valley as the two pistol reports bounced off the mountains and the officers ran down the hill, stumbling and windmilling their arms in the air.

"He has a gun! He has a gun!" The officers yelled as they raced down the hill, got into their car, and sped off.

***

When the plane landed, Bernie pulled the bags out of the overhead bin. "I have a rental car reserved," he said.

Dot dragged her feet and the carry-on suitcase toward baggage claim. He could see he was losing her. She trudged after him like a zombie. He attributed that to culture shock and gin at high altitude. For now, she had to depend on him, but he needed a way to keep control after she acclimated and dried out. He couldn't let her recover yet. She needed more trauma. As they sat on their carry-ons, waiting for the checked luggage, Bernie decided that he would have to shock her back to life. "I met your children," he said.

Dot didn't remember having children, but there was a lot she didn't remember. Losing those memories awoke a maternal defensiveness. "No you didn't," she said. "That was, what, a hundred years ago?"

"You've only been frozen for seventy years." Bernie took a file from his briefcase and handed it to Dot.

"Where are they now?"

"They're dead," Bernie had to make this hurt. "Come on, they couldn't wait forever."

Dot had to be as cold as Bernie. She couldn't let the images get to her. She squinted at a picture of Ben in his school uniform and another in his army uniform as he graduated from boot camp. "The war was over by then," she said. "I looked it up. Why is he wearing a uniform?"

"There's always other wars. This one was in Korea."

"Korea? Is that a real place?" As she leafed through the file, pictures came and broke her heart. Maybe that's what they were there for.

When the conveyor belt started moving, Bernie picked out their luggage and led her toward the bench, where they waited for the rental car company's van to pick them up.

"So if you met my children, what did you tell them? What did my children know about me?"

Bernie didn't answer. He was staring forward into space, making plans. It's important to have a plan. All the business books said so, and Bernie was born to be rich. He wasn't born to build a business; he was born to inherit one. Unfortunately, his father didn't own a company. After college, Bernie floated from job to job, never advancing without the nepotism he knew he deserved. His destiny finally became clear when his grandfather died and he inherited his publicity firm. Bernie promoted himself to president and CEO. He informed his alumni association immediately.

The firm's assets consisted of an office condo in L.A., some old office furniture, and cabinet full of contracts with clients he'd never heard of. They went back nearly to vaudeville times. His clients were all dead. Bernie didn't let that stop him. He took a business loan and moved to New Orleans, where he researched voodoo and necromancy. A contract is supposed to mean something. They were his birthright, and he intended to enforce his contracts.

Voodoo proved useless. There wasn't a witch doctor in the city who'd even attempt a resurrection without a fresh body, not without advance payment. When he found Dot unclaimed in the Archives, like a lost mitten, he placed an ad looking for the best cryogenic experts Craigslist could provide and hired the lowest bidder. Where witchcraft had failed, impoverished grad students had succeeded. Still, his time in Louisiana had not been a total waste. He'd made some valuable connections. Bringing Dot and her career back from the dead was just a proof of concept. No voodoo priest would work on contingency until Bernie proved the business model could show profit, and Bernie definitely intended to profit.

The important thing was to offer Dot as an example. If he could resurrect a career from the afterlife, he could become the go-to publicist of the undead. He would have an exclusive market on the ultimate has-beens. It wouldn't be never-wases like Dot.

But there's no point in thinking small. There was always the Second Coming to think about. If God really was coming back like AM radio said He was, He'd need a publicist to dust off the brand and get Him on prime time, or at least the FM dial. If He wasn't coming back, well, Satan could definitely use a bit of PR. Bernie's parents had raised him right, and he would always offer God the first right of refusal. With a leaked sex tape to put

Him back in the news, Bernie could give the God brand new life. If he didn't hear from Him in a couple days, though, all bets were off. As the van drove toward the rental lot, Bernie silently recited a little prayer/pitch to whoever might be listening.

***

When William was a child, he fell into a well, and everyone loved him for it. Before he fell into the well, there was nothing special about him, but once he did, he became The Boy in the Well. First his mother came, then his father. Soon, there were ambulances and fire trucks. William loved fire trucks. Police cars came from all over the county.

For the five days he was in the well, churches prayed for him. People worried about him on the nightly news. He was famous, and everyone cared about him. Everyone desperately wanted him to be saved. On the first night, they lowered sandwiches, a walkie-talkie, and a flashlight. People said comforting things to him. Around lunchtime, the sun shone straight down the shaft of the well. Above him, William could see sun and sky; below him, darkness and water. Something about that gave him a sense of absolute certainty.

Things were good inside the well. There was no yelling from the house, and when his parents looked down the well to talk to him, they weren't arguing with each other or yelling at him. There was mostly silence. The only sound was people trying to save him. Someone was always there to tell him that everything would be okay. When they dug the parallel shaft and pulled him up, he could see people cheering, crowds big enough to fill the front yard. In the vacant lot on the other side of the road, there were even more cheering people. To become a hero, he only had to fall. Pretty women with microphones ran toward him while men carried cameras on their shoulders.

"Nobody gave a shit about me until I was helpless," William said.

"Pathetic," Maggie said.

"But now I wonder: maybe I was looking for something to fall into, some dark, wet place where everyone cared about how I would come out. My parents, they'd covered the well, and they told us not to go near it. But at night, lying alone in bed, it was like the well was calling to me. I wasn't supposed to be out of bed. I told myself I was going downstairs to use the bathroom, but that wasn't true. I just walked out the front door in my pajamas. I had to lift the rocks off the plywood and carry the wood away. I was looking for something to fall into, and once I found it, I jumped."

"Okay, but how does this help us?" Anita asked.

"I can only help you once you hit rock bottom," Maggie said.

"I thought this was rock bottom."

"No, at rock bottom, there's always someone who makes you reexamine your life. It can't be someone in AA. It's someone who can't be saved. That's rock bottom."

Anita chimed in, "Like the first time my boyfriend shot heroin into his dick?"

"Yes," Maggie said. "If that story were true, it would be a good rock bottom story."

"But it is true."

"No."

"It's almost true."

"Nope."

"He almost bought pot once. William, someone has to be on my side." She slapped her hand toward his shoulder, and she hit the empty driver's seat. "Where the hell did he go?"

"He's probably in Tennessee right now" If Maggie'd had a mouth, she would have been drooling. "If you'd like to join him, you should probably tell me a story."

Anita looked back at the frozen police officer. "What's keeping me from just driving down to him, since time's frozen anyway?"

"About six hundred miles of stopped traffic, only that." Maggie could feel Anita giving in. She relished Anita's hopelessness. Maggie didn't have a tongue yet, but she could taste the despair. The texture felt like warm blood on her teeth.

"Oh, fuck it," Anita said. "I am Anita and I am an alcoholic. It's been five years since my last confession. I've never really been a big drinker. I drink sometimes, a glass of wine or something. I can't drink more than that or I get sort of light-headed. I don't really like the taste that much. I got into AA mostly because I was interested in wills."

Maggie didn't have lips yet, but she licked them anyway. "Get on with it."

Chapter
.07

"I met my first real boyfriend in a college freshman literature course. This was the community college, so neither of us were rich. Really, he was richer than I was because his parents made less money than mine did. My parents didn't give me any money for college, but they made enough to keep me from getting financial aid. My boyfriend was poor as shit, so he made enough money to keep himself going as long as he wanted on Pell Grants until he dropped out and started working at the tire shop. Working full time, he started getting benefits he didn't know what to do with. When he asked who should go on his life insurance, I said me. I didn't think much about it at the time.

"My second long-term relationship was with a bartender I met in music appreciation. I hadn't really left my first boyfriend, but he didn't go to the school anymore, so it wasn't like he'd find out. One romantic night, during that month when his psychiatrist upped his Wellbutrin, he asked me what I would want if he died. I looked around his apartment and did a quick appraisal of his assets. While his car was the most expensive thing he owned, his drinking made me think the car would die at about the same time he did. He had a decent book collection, but we mostly had the same books, except for the erotica, most of which wasn't really my style. I took a sip of wine and realized what I had to ask for. I wanted his stemware.

"Now, this guy took his drinking seriously. He drank with skill and class. He had enough gold-rimmed Waterford crystal in two types of wine glasses, water goblets, and English highballs to cater a wedding. If he'd died before we broke up, I'd have inherited at least a couple thousand dollars in crystal. I still hold out hope that he hasn't changed his will, but I expect that trying to collect these days would be socially awkward. His husband and I have history.

"The point is that at about the time that second boyfriend was throwing me out of the house for his new boyfriend, my first boyfriend died under a pickup when the floor jack got knocked out of place. It turned out he'd never changed his beneficiary. It wasn't much, but that $2400 covered my move, the first month's rent, and the security deposit.

"After that, I always encouraged my boyfriends to remember me in their wills. As an undergrad, my boyfriends just didn't die that often, and they really didn't have much to offer if they had. My grad school boyfriends were pretty poor too, but I always remembered to tell them to put me in their wills with their prized possessions.

"When I was in my Cultural Studies program, I had this boyfriend with long, blonde hair and that kind of body that only really comes from stress and starvation. One night, after a poetry reading with jugs of free wine, I asked him to remember me in his will and to leave me his prized possessions. He got out of bed and uncapped a Lamy fountain pen. Thing is, this guy had no prize possessions. He was a scholar. All his best books were overdue from the library. His furniture was mostly shelves made of cinder blocks and boards. Anything he could leave me wasn't worth leaving bed for. Still, when he came back to bed, he said he had me covered.

"That was the week my study abroad funding came through. I was supposed to study the mating habits of Germans in Heidelberg, but somehow, my heart wasn't in it. I could almost feel that something was wrong.

"While I was studying the indigenous people, my boyfriend was focusing on literary theory. One night, while pondering the signifier and the signified, he fell dead in his chair, a copy of Roland Barthes in his hand. The thing is, the last article he wrote defended skipping classes as a form of transgressive performance, so nobody checked on him when he stopped going to class. He sat dead in that chair for a month.

"He had a cat named Pickles, and Pickles was a female cat. Any woman who has had a relationship with a man and his cat knows what that rivalry's like. When I moved in over the winter, Pickles pissed on my coat. She knew I was a threat. Even when my boyfriend tried to manage the relationship by having me feed the cat, she knew better. She wouldn't let me feed her. She never let me pet her, and she sure as hell never sat on my lap. That cat was in our apartment for a month, just her and my boyfriend's dead body in the yellow chair with his dead MacBook sitting on a TV tray next to him.

"Of course, the cat started eating him. I don't know when. I assume she started immediately, but I'm not really impartial. Maybe she started at the toes or fingers. Maybe she was loving and careful. I don't know. All I knew at the time was that he had stopped answering my emails. I was still in college, after all. I couldn't afford to call him, and all of my emails went unanswered. So yeah, I was pissed. There were a lot of guys I could have fucked in Germany, and I emailed him that. I let him know that he could not just ignore me like that. I told him when my plane was landing, and he wasn't even at the airport to pick me up.

"You have to understand how conflicting this was. I was waiting for that reunion scene, and there was no one at the fucking airport. I had to carry my bags to the train, then from the train to the bus. It took like an hour and a half to get home. I was pissed off, jet lagged, and sexually frustrated, so angry my eyes hurt.

"So when I came home to see the cat feeding on my boyfriend's dead body, it was on. That was my boyfriend, not hers. There was only one way to make things right. I had to eat that cat."

***

William awoke in a strange room with sheets pulled up to his chin. The lights were off, but morning lit the room from the edges of curtains. He remembered dreaming that he was an unemployed, alcoholic father whose daughter was in the hospital with cirrhosis but that he, instead of being at the hospital with her, was driving drunk across the country.

In that strange way dreams work, his daughter had liver failure instead of her drunk dad, and somehow driving drunk would get her a new liver. William stared at the ceiling, then looked around the room. An old-fashioned television sat near the foot of the bed with what appeared to be a tiger on top of it. In the dream, there had been a story about eating a cat. As he got out of bed, he could still hear the woman's voice, not through his ears but in the rear right side of his head, something that felt more like imagination than sound.

He'd slept in his clothes, black slacks and a stained white Oxford with non-slip shoes. He tried to remember where and who he was. He looked like a waiter, but that couldn't be right. As he looked for clues, he slowly came to recognize the room, with its red and white curtains, the brown duvet on the bed, the cluttered bathroom, and the padded double doors. He pushed the door, but it was locked from the outside. He tried knocking, but the door was soft and made no sound. He sat in a shaggy, white fur chair, listening to the woman tell her story.

***

Anita looked back. The cop still wasn't moving, but for some reason, she felt she should speak faster. "Fortunately, the cat didn't belong to me, so I was able to resist the temptation until his family picked it up. I had to go to the funeral, so I had an awkward afternoon talking to my old fuck buddy's parents next to a box of ashes that no way could have held all of him. I went to the church with the family, had a can of Natty Boh and some casserole after the funeral, and took the bus home. I went back to working on my thesis. A week later, they had the reading of the will.

"I almost didn't go. I knew he owned nothing worth mentioning, but his dying had doubled my rent. There was always the chance of a car, his computer, an assault rifle, a vacation home, some jewelry, or something of value. I'd met the family at the funeral, and these people had money, so I showed up. He had a car. It went to his brother. He had a vacation home. It went to his sister. He had an assault rifle. He wanted it buried with him. He was fucking cremated, but whatever. The computer went to the school. The pearls went to his niece. Then the lawyer spoke of his most beloved, most prized possessions. He said he wanted the one he loved most to have the things he loved the most. My head popped up. This was what I was waiting for. After real estate, a car, and a gun, it had to be good. I sat forward to keep the seat dry. 'And to Anita, who has been a source of inspiration to me, I leave my Spartan Swiss Army Knife and my beloved Pickles.'

"I stopped listening. His fucking cat is what I got. I was given the cat on the spot. To show they were good sports, the family gave me the litter box, food bowl, and water bowl for free. I got the knife in the mail a week later, and look at it. It doesn't even have scissors.

"Once I got the cat back to the apartment, the problems started. You have to understand, if you've ever been in a relationship with someone who has a cat, there's always that awkward presence. That's not your cat, and she lets you know it. When you walk into the room and kiss your boyfriend, there's the cat between your legs. When you're having sex in the bedroom, there's the cat scratching at your door. When you're having sex anywhere but the bedroom, the cat is always there to watch with her round eyes and open mouth.

"I tried to behave myself, but there was so much history between us. It was a thick, floating, visible hatred that fogged the apartment. When I got her food in the morning, she rubbed against my legs, but I could tell that it wasn't that appreciative rub she would have given my boyfriend but a deliberate attempt to trip me and send me sprawling to my death, where she'd probably eat me too. When she climbed into my lap when I was reading and purred, I could tell that it wasn't a normal cat's purr but really a dog's growl. As I would pet her, she lifted her tail and raised her backside as if to say, 'You stupid bitch, you can't even do that right. Look at my asshole.'

"After a couple weeks, I couldn't take it anymore. I tried starving her to death, but she seemed to live as happily on three quarters of a cup of food a day as she did on a cup of food. I couldn't drown her. She kept jumping out of the tub whenever I turned the water on. Eventually, I had to go online and research the best ways to kill a cat. According to the Internet, the best way to kill a cat was with a gun to the back of the head.

"I didn't have a gun. I don't believe in them. I mean, okay, I believe that they exist and that they have cash value. They aren't fucking unicorns. I don't believe in guns in the Batman way of not believing in guns. I prefer to not own them unless they have a high resale value. I didn't win my boyfriend's assault rifle in the will, so I looked around the apartment for a reasonable substitute. The closest thing I could find was a soldering gun mixed with some high school science fair crap his family hadn't bothered to take. It had a small, red plastic pistol grip and a sharp chisel point. It would have to do.

"I had a small table next to my chair, which I normally used for books or tea, but this time, when I sat there, I had the soldering gun warming on the table. When Pickles came and sat on my lap, I put my left arm under her head to steady her in place. She turned her head and squinted. When she made that growling, fake purring noise, I took the soldering gun with my right hand and stabbed it at the back of the cat's head.

"But wouldn't you know it about cats, they seem to have this innate sense of when someone's about to stab them in the back of the head with a soldering gun. She jumped onto the floor and hid under the table. The soldering iron went into my arm, just below the inside of my elbow. It was a blunt puncture, and the searing was unbearable. I yanked the soldering iron out of my arm and went after that cat.

"She was quicker than I was and I was losing blood out of my left arm, but there were only so many places to hide in that apartment. I eliminated hiding places, closing doors, shrinking the field of engagement until I found her mewing under my desk. From there, it was just a matter of getting my hand around her tail. I swung the cat once in the air and slammed its body down on the desk, first backhand, then overhand. When she stopped kicking and scratching, I got a better grip. With both hands around her hind legs, I swung the body into the desk again two, maybe seventy-six times. When the cat stopped breathing, I put her in the bathtub and let her sit under water for a half hour, just to be sure.

"Skinning the cat was easier than I'd thought it would be. As much as people say there are so many ways there are of doing this, a Google search for skinning a cat was not helpful. Still, I was able to find instructions on skinning a squirrel, and it worked almost the same way. Once you take off the head and feet and make a slit down the back, the skin almost slides right off. Getting the skin off the arms and legs was a lot like undressing a drunk guy you still want to have sex with. I was able to do it in the time it took to preheat the oven. But you know, the first time you skin an animal, you always wind up with hair between your teeth."

"Okay, we're here," Maggie said. The car sat in a circular driveway on a wooded lawn in front of a large stone house with columns. Through the trees, Anita could see a shopping center and a four-lane divided road.

"Where are we?" Anita asked.

"Graceland," Maggie said. "Apparently, it's the closest place to Arkansas William could think of. We're lucky he didn't think of St. Louis or we'd be parked on top of the Gateway Arch."

"I don't think we're supposed to be here," Anita said. She spotted a white-shirted security guard smoking a cigarette several yards from the house. "Well, at least time's still stopped."

Maggie said, "Recalculating. I teleport you across four states and you want me to hold time still too? That's expecting a lot from a piece of refurbished consumer electronics."

"Hey!" A security guard dropped the cigarette and walked toward the car, his hand on his radio. "Hey, you can't park there!"

"Sorry." Anita tried to think of an excuse. "We're lost."

The guard looked like a man in his late forties, probably older than William, maybe slightly less of a drinker. The fit of his shirt suggested that he was more a fan of beer and ribs than of wine and cheese.

"Recalculating," Maggie said helpfully.

"Yeah, you're lost alright. Tour parking's across the street, and tours don't start until nine."

"Thank you," Anita said.

The guard turned his head and squinted at the car. "Wait a minute. Who's driving?"

***

When the crazy cat lady stopped talking, William finally worked out what was going on. He recognized the bedroom. He was in Graceland because he was Elvis Presley. It was the only way this made sense. He searched the closets but couldn't find his leather jacket. The dressers had scarves, socks, and underwear but no real clothing. He was stuck with what he was wearing, but he draped a scarf over the back of his neck for the sake of style.

He couldn't remember why he was locked in his own bedroom, but he felt hungover. It was the worst kind of hangover, including nausea, residual drunkenness, and a sense of unfocused guilt. He exhaled ethanol, burning his throat. If Priscilla had locked him in the bedroom, it had to be bad. He had to make things right. He walked back to the padded door. It was still locked. Fortunately, he had a black belt in Karate. He had trained with Ed Parker. He knew his stuff. William lifted his leg, kicked the door, and fell backward onto the carpet.

William was astounded. He had to be a later Elvis, past his prime. Still, he got up, kicked the door, and fell again. The doors moved slightly, but there was no response. It was like the room was soundproofed. He tried throwing his shoulder against the door. This was just as effective as kicking the door and much easier. After three more tries, the door opened from the outside.

"Thank you. Thank you very much," William said.

A woman in a short-sleeved button-down shirt with a patch on her shoulder spoke into a radio. "We have a breach, an intruder. Repeat. Intruder in the bedroom."

A second guard held a chain and a padlock in one hand. He clicked his radio and said with a stoner voice, "Hey, there's a dude in here."

"I know there's a dude in here," the woman said back into her radio. "That's what *intruder in the bedroom* means."

William walked past them, down the stairs toward the kitchen. "What's for breakfast?" he asked. He wondered how he should address the security guard. He couldn't remember whether or not Elvis was a racist. If he was a racist, he wasn't sure whether to insult the woman or to be excessively polite so she wouldn't notice. William never really understood the South.

"Stop!" the woman said. She grabbed at him, catching the scarf, which uncoiled from William's neck.

William hurried through the kitchen into the dining room. At the head of the dining room table, he feinted left and right. Since there were two security guards, each took one side of the table and walked toward him. He ran out to the foyer. For some reason, these security guards didn't recognize him. He headed toward the front doors.

***

The security guard asked, "If you're driving, why are you in the passenger seat?"

"Recalculating," Maggie said.

"Well, as I said, I'm lost." She tried to fake a British accent. "I keep forgetting how your cars work in the colonies. I guess I'll just pop off to the other side now. Cheerios." She slid across the seat to the driver's side. She turned the key, but nothing happened. "It seems to be stalled."

The security guard pointed at the interlock. "I think you need to blow into that hose," he said.

"I know, I know." Anita blew into the hose. The lights glowed red.

"Ma'am, I'm going to need you to come with me."

"Wait," Anita said. "I'm not an alcoholic. This thing works in reverse. It only works if you *are* drunk."

"Right. Because today's opposite day. Step out of the car, please."

William burst through the doors to the top of the steps. He looked at the station wagon and moaned. "Oh, damn. I am that guy." His memories crawled back into his mind. He sulked down to the car.

"Is this your car, sir?" the guard asked.

"Yeah," William said, ashamed.

"Well, you need to move it out of here. We have to think about terrorist threats and the risk of damage to a registered landmark."

"Of course, sir."

"I think your passenger's drunk. It's a bit early in the day for that, isn't it?"

"Yes, sir. I'm sorry. Her behavior embarrasses me." William blew into the hose and started the car. "I saw two of your colleagues screwing around in Elvis's bedroom," he said. "You might want to look into that."

The guard had a condescending tone. "Well, thanks for your concern, sir, but that's not possible. The room's chained shut, and the key is–ah dang!" He ran up the steps just as the two other guards were running down. The three started talking into their radios.

"We'd better get out of here," Maggie said. "Follow the driveway and go out the gate. Then head north on Elvis Presley Boulevard."

William drove to the main road. "What wine did you have with the cat?" he asked.

"You heard that?" Anita asked.

"Yeah, of course. I was there."

"No, you weren't. You disappeared."

"I didn't disappear. I was the King."

Maggie improvised an explanation. "When I do this, you have to be in a kind of dream state. William was easy because he was drunk. You had to be telling your story, but it had to be the same dream or we wouldn't end up in the same place. So, yeah, he heard you." They'd believe anything at this point.

"This doesn't tell us what kind of wine she had," William said.

"I didn't. I had some orange soda."

"The only time in your life you will taste roof rabbit you paired it with orange soda? First I learn I'm not Elvis and now I have to hear this? This offends me on a personal and professional level."

"So I don't like wine as much as you do. Sue me. I've never been a big drinker anyway."

William slapped the dashboard and spread his arms. "And somehow that makes you qualified to be my sponsor. How did you even end up in AA if you never drank?"

"Well, I had to go to the hospital for my arm. I mean, you stab yourself with a soldering gun, and it leaves a mark. I was too embarrassed to tell the doctor what really happened, so I told her I was an IV drug user. She wanted me to go to NA, but the AA meetings were closer to the school. It was just better for my schedule."

"And you kept going for five years?"

"Well, yeah. It's not like there's a finish line for recovery. Nobody told me when I was done."

William shook his head. "So you've been my sponsor for three months and you've never been addicted to anything?"

"You didn't have to choose me as a sponsor. Believe me. You would not be my first choice, but I'd been going to AA for five years and I never got to be anyone's sponsor."

"Wait. I was allowed to choose my sponsor? Nobody told me that."

"I don't know what you're so upset about. I think I did a pretty good job."

Maggie could feel her teeth growing. "I think you're overlooking the important part of the story, where she beat her boyfriend's cat to death and ate it."

"Without wine," William said. "Not a Pouilly Fume, not Pinot Noir, not even a lousy Pinot Gris."

"Can we stop talking about this?" Anita asked.

"Is talking about eating your boyfriend making you feel uncomfortable?" Maggie asked.

"I didn't eat my boyfriend. God!"

Maggie tried to smooth out the issue, "No, dear, you ate the cat that ate your boyfriend."

"Without even considering the proper wine pairing," William added. He pulled around a tour bus and drove them out of Memphis.

Chapter
.08

On 81, John rocked in his seat. He tried to steady his nerves with another pill. "He had a gun back there. He nearly killed us!"

Joe took a bottle from the back seat, opened it, and threw the cap out the window. "And what do we have in the trunk, kogelmogel?"

John's voice lowered, and he sat still. "Yes, we have many guns."

"We must go back and kill them all." Joe smiled at the corpse through the windshield and calmed. "No. There is a long race ahead of us. We can kill them at our leisure. There are still two cars ahead of us, and we must destroy them before we worry about those children."

***

At the Waffle House, Sean chose a table near the door. At the end of the counter, a thin security guard in blue polyester sipped a cup of coffee. The racers took off their helmets and tried to look inconspicuous. They ordered two cups of coffee.

"We should have gotten some drive-through or something," Jeb whispered.

"No good," Sean said. "Those places always ask for the money in advance. We're okay. We just need to keep a low profile."

"Good idea," Jeb said. "We're two normal guys in NASCAR suits. We'll fit right in."

The security guard put down his cup of coffee and walked to their table. "You boys from out of town?" he asked.

"Yep, just passing through here," Sean said. "So, you run

security at this here Waffle House, huh?"

"I didn't know diners needed security," Jeb said.

The guard puffed his chest. "Well, it don't look it, but this can be a pretty rough place after the bars close. See, it's the only place in town open late, so whoever got thrown out of whatever bar, he runs into the person who got him thrown out here." He sat down in the booth. "Call me Steve," he said.

"I'm Jeb," Jeb said.

Sean tried to kick him under the table, but he hit Steve instead. "Sorry about that." When the waitress came with the coffee, he ordered chicken fried steak and eggs with potatoes and a biscuit. Jeb ordered waffles.

"Yep, yep." Steve leaned back, resting his thumbs in his gun belt. "I guess we've seen just about everything in here. We've had fights. We had a couple try, you know, having relations right over there." He pointed to a plastic booth near the front window. "We once had a couple of fugitives come in here."

"Fugitives, huh?" Sean said, glaring at Jeb to keep quiet.

"Yeah," Steve said. He took on a bored, bragging expression. "They came in real late, and they were hungry as hell, too. I was able to keep them here until the sheriff showed up."

"Well," Sean said. "Lucky you were here."

"You know, all in a day's work. Yessir. So where you boys from?"

"We weren't in Virginia," Jeb said.

"You're coming from a costume party or something, right?"

Sean forced out a laugh. "Yeah, sure. The racing suits."

"I do love a costume party. I've got this Western sheriff costume I wear sometimes. You know, the missus likes it."

"Sure she does," Jeb said.

Steve blushed. "Now, I don't mean nothing like that. I mean she has an Old West bad guy costume and we go as a pair. I don't mean nothing nasty."

"So when these fights normally start?" Sean asked. A fight would make a good cover for a dine-and-dash.

"Fridays mostly, Saturdays too. You're not going to see much on a Wednesday."

"That's too bad," Jeb said.

"You think so?" Steve laughed. As the waitress slid the plates onto the table, he stood up. "I'll let you boys be, but if you hear about any good costume parties while you're in town, you let me know, all right?" He carried his coffee back to the counter.

"Do you think he's on to us?" Jeb whispered.

"Don't whisper," Sean hissed. "You're making us look suspicious."

The waitress dropped a handwritten check on the table. "You can pay this at the register whenever you're ready," she said. She refilled their coffees and went back to talk with the security guard.

"So here's what we'll do," Sean said. "We'll wait for that security guard to go to the bathroom. Then we'll make a run for it."

"Okay," Jeb said, sipping his coffee. He watched the security guard closely and waited.

***

Three hours later, Sean sat with one hand in his lap and squirmed in his seat. "Is that guy ever going to take a piss?" His legs fidgeted as he watched the security guard drink cup after cup of coffee. "He can't hold it forever." As they waited, the waitress kept bringing them more coffee. "I can't wait anymore." He walked into the restroom and stood in front of the urinal. He tried to do it quickly, pushing out a long, thick stream. As he stood there, the security guard came into the restroom and stood in front of the toilet.

"You know," Steve said. "I always thought those suits had a hose in them, like a spacesuit or something."

Sean tried to hurry. "Yeah. Lots of people think that. Thing is, it's so goddamn hot on the track, you'll never have to piss."

"Hey, there's no need for that."

"I mean you don't have to pee—urinate on account of the sweating."

"Well, that explains it, don't it?"

Sean looked at Steve, mostly at his gun. If questioned by a police sketch artist, he could describe Sean as a guy with a stainless Ruger Redhawk chambered in .44 magnum with a five-and-a-half inch barrel and brown hardwood grips. He couldn't remember his hair color, height, or race, but he knew the holster was black leather, and the strap hung loose behind the hammer. Sean tightened his velcro belt and opened the bathroom door.

Steve yelled, "Hey!"

Sean jolted and almost had to go again. He held a hand to his chest and could feel his heartbeat through the suit. "Shit, man."

"No need for that kind of language, son." Steve jerked his head toward the sink. "I ain't saying nothing. I'm just saying you forgot to wash your hands."

"Right. Thanks for reminding me," Sean said. He turned on the faucet and pumped soap onto his gloves, scrubbing quickly. He grabbed a paper towel and walked out of the restroom. Jeb was gone.

The waitress stood at the register. "Your friend said he'd be waiting in the car." When she looked down to ring up the check, Sean saw his break. He grabbed his helmet and ran for the door.

"Steve!" the waitress yelled, "They're dashing. They didn't pay!"

Steve rinsed his hands vigorously, pulled two paper towels from the dispenser, and dried his right hand. There wasn't time to dry the left. He kicked open the bathroom door to see the front window of the restaurant explode to the sound of automatic gunfire. He fell to the ground and crawled toward the door, where the suited racer ran in a crouch, his hands over his helmet. Steve rolled on his side and returned fire.

***

Sean made it to the car and saw Jeb sitting in the driver's seat, blowing into the breathalyzer tube. When he saw Sean, he said. "It's no good. We waited in that restaurant too long. I'm sober." Sean reached under the seat for the Wild Turkey.

***

"These racers, do they all have guns? It is so uncivilized, this country." Joe stripped the magazine out of his Stechkin and fed in a new one. He stepped through what had been the Waffle House's glass wall and sprayed a few rounds into the kitchen, raising clouds from bags of flour and perforating plastic jugs of cooking oil. As the oil poured over the grill and the gas burner, smoke rose from the kitchen.

Crouched behind a Formica table, Steven yelled, "You are under arrest for the theft of chicken fried steak, two eggs over easy, home fries, a biscuit, an order of waffles, and two cups of coffee, plus tip. This is Security Guard Steve Raymond, and I'm ordering you to drop your weapon and come out with your hands up!"

"Security guard?" Joe asked. "You are not a racer?"

Steve lowered his gun and stood up. "You're not Jeb?"

"No, I am Joe, my fellow American. We are looking for a racer, perhaps the one you call Jeb."

"Well, he and his friend skedaddled out that side door there," Steve said. "I'd be much obliged if you could help me catch them. They gave Ruby here one hell of a fright."

"We shall capture these racers and we will destroy them," Joe said.

"Well, this gum-flapping's getting us nowhere." He led Joe out the side door and into the parking lot.

***

"Drink faster," Sean said.

Jeb sipped at the bottle. "This stuff's harsh. I can't shoot it straight."

"You're gonna," Sean said. As Jeb raised the bottle to his lips, Sean grabbed the bottom and held it up until Jeb choked, coughed out a belch that smelled like fire, and blew his whiskey breath into the hose. The three red lights turned green. "That's it! Start her up!"

Jeb turned the key and the engine roared to life with that deep rumble only a big block makes. He put the car in gear and drove toward the two armed men. He jerked the wheel to the left, and Steve fired two shots into the side of the Mustang. "They're shooting at us!" Jeb ducked down and turned left again. As they drove past the front of the diner, a burst of automatic gunfire shattered the rear driver's side window. He took another left, drove past the diner, and circled behind it. Steve fired into the windshield.

"Turn right!" Sean yelled. "You're circling the diner. Turn right and get us out of here!"

Jeb struggled against his training, but people can do amazing things under stress. He turned the wheel to the right, hitting the curb with the rear right tire. He pulled across the grass median strip and skidded onto the road.

***

When the shooting stopped, Ruby ran out of the burning diner and grabbed Steve's shoulder.

"They're getting away!" John yelled from the driver's seat. "We must follow them!"

"It's already too late," Joe yelled back.

"I don't know how to thank you boys," Steve said. He holstered his revolver and offered his hand.

With the sunrise behind him, Joe watched the Shelby zip around cars and disappear into the blue morning. He grabbed Steve's wrist with his left hand and smiled. "My friend, you can decorate my car."

***

Renee found Thomas slumped over his laptop. His eyes were closed, and the last thing he had typed was dddddddddddd ddddddddddddddddddddddddddddddddddd. She shook his shoulder. "I get it now. I understand what we have to do." She poured three fingers of vodka into her coffee mug and topped it off with V-8. "It came to me when you asked how to kill the radio star."

"I don't want to kill anyone," Thomas said. "Not for an unpaid internship."

"I know, and you won't have to. You just have to make a petition to the White House website, and do it before nine. We want it to hit the prime social media times so you can start our Facebook and Twitter campaigns. I'm talking animal memes, celebrity endorsements, profile picture campaigns. I mean serious business."

"What's the campaign about?"

"We have to petition the White House to thaw out Captain Video. He was a big superhero on the propaganda front back in World War Two. He sabotaged a bunch of Nazi film studios and radio stations, but he was lost over the North Atlantic. He was found in the 1950s, frozen in a block of ice, but for copyright reasons, he wasn't thawed out. See, by 1950, there already was another Captain Video, and that one had a TV show. Nobody wanted to thaw the Captain out and deal with the potential lawsuit. See, back then, heroes were like–"

"Like frozen burritos. I get it. Frozen heroes everywhere."

"Right, but if we want to kill the radio star, we need Video."

"Why didn't people stop flying over the North Atlantic?"

Thomas asked. "I mean, if they kept crashing and ending up like popsicles, they were obviously doing something wrong."

"Look, the 40s were a strange time. Have you ever read a recipe book from back then? Hell, they used to put canned fish in their Jello salads. Those people were crazy. Maybe it was all the Nazi mad scientists and an immature aviation industry." She finished her Bloody Mary. "Stop trying to make sense of this. I need you to get that petition out and make it go viral. I'm not paying you to think."

"You're not paying me at all."

Renee sat behind the vodka bottle on her desk. "I'm going to forget you said that." By the third Bloody Mary, she had.

***

The frat boys patched the window with a clear plastic garbage bag and half a roll of duct tape. They drove all night down Route 81. Theo kept the group going with vodka and Red Bull, 4Loko, and Irish coffee mixed from truck stop coffee, whiskey, and non-dairy creamer. Near sunrise, they crossed into Tennessee.

The road trip excitement had worn off, and sleep deprivation, adrenaline, caffeine, taurine, and truck stop BBQ had settled in their stomachs with a thick, clawing nausea. No one looked at the scenery. The car smelled of Kato's cigarettes, stale sweat, old beer, wet shoes, and sweet cat urine.

When the road grew blurry, Kato turned on the windshield wipers. When that didn't work, he closed one eye and the world came into focus. Tired of the playlists on the iPod, Chav scrolled through the radio stations. On the left side of the dial, they could hear NPR stations begging for money, if they were near a college town. The right side of the dial had political talk radio. The center of the dial was country music and Christian radio. Occasionally, he'd pick up a station playing old music, live commercials, or something about a car race. In Arkansas, the radio played commercials for discount frozen chicken stores.

"Cluck, cluck, save a buck," the commercials said.

Fort Smith was a town that had grown up twice. The original downtown near the river was abandoned when the highway was built and the stores relocated to a mile of strip malls on either side of the highway exit. The Honda weaved in its lane, more from exhaustion than intoxication. Kato had drunk past drunkenness and entered a second stage of sobriety. In this numb state, he stared forward and followed the GPS directions mindlessly.

After the strip malls, the road became a gray, cracked main street with used bookstores, laundromats, garages, furniture stores, vacant storefronts, and stores with handwritten signs advertising clearance sales. A black awning with the name *Ben Dover's* hung over a windowless storefront; nobody bothered to joke about it. Banter had died down two states ago.

A right turn took the Civic to an area of industrial buildings and vacant lots. After a left turn, the GPS told them they had arrived. Kato parked the car, and they walked in the gate, wobbling like newborn calves.

***

West End Park was a walled-in brick courtyard with an antique carousel, a stationary double-decker bus, and a Ferris wheel. In the middle of the day, the rides were still and the place was nearly empty. Theo walked into the courtyard, his vision fluttering, reality flickering in and out. When Kato stopped to look around, Theo and Chav walked into him. Kato stumbled forward two steps and stood swaying. A man and a woman, both in business clothes, sat at a table under a rainbow-colored umbrella. Two men sat next to them, eating sausage and sauerkraut with chopsticks. The younger man wore an argyle sweater and khakis. The older man wore a silk kimono.

The man in the gray suit motioned to the racers. "Over here."

Kato leaned toward the table until his feet caught up and he shuffled forward. Chav whispered, "That's the dude from the starting line."

"I know," Kato said. "I was there."

"May I offer you a drink?" Bernie asked. He took nine glasses from a small tray and filled them from a glass pitcher. "Gin and ginger beer with lime juice, bitters, and mint."

"How did you know we were racers?" Kato asked.

Dot looked up from a beige folder and smirked. She handed Kato an envelope. "This is the location of the second checkpoint." She tapped her tablet computer. "It's already programmed into your GPS. I can unlock it from here."

The man in the kimono stood and picked up his glass with his chopsticks. Though he swayed and stumbled, he drank without spilling a drop and passed the glass to his other hand. He weaved his way to a railway car and returned to the table with a bottle of mustard balanced on one chopstick and a bottle of hot sauce on the other. The man in the sweater vest excused himself.

Dot put down the tablet. "Okay, boys, you're the second car to arrive. You each get to have three drinks with me before you leave." She held up her glass and chewed on a mint leaf. She took a cigarette from her purse and tore the filter off. She looked to Bernie, then to Kato. The Master breathed deeply, blew on the back of his chopstick, and struck it against the other chopstick. It caught fire, and he offered Dot a light.

The frat boys walked to the train car and ordered chili dogs, an egg sandwich, and a hamburger. "Do you have any Gatorade?"

"Only limeade," the cashier said.

"Limeade? What the fuck is that?" Kato asked. "Never mind that shit. We have gin to drink."

"We're drunk drivers," Chav explained. "And I'm the mechanic."

As they waited for the food, they visited the restroom. Kato splashed water on his face. "Just stay awake. I can do this," he said. "I can win this race." Chav walked out of the bathroom stall, zipping his pants, stood in front of a urinal, and unzipped his pants. Kato pointed at Chav and opened his mouth.

"Don't ask," Theo said.

Kato leered into the mirror. "Anybody else think that radio chick's kind of hot? I think she digs me, you know? I saw the way she smiled at me."

From the urinal, Chav spoke over his shoulder. "I think I remember that woman's voice. We heard her on the radio back on 81. How old do you think she is?"

"Definitely over thirty," Kato said. "It wouldn't keep me from coming through. *I* think she digs me. Slam-dunk cougar action." He crumpled a paper towel and threw it toward a trash can. "Chav, why don't you check out the car while the food's cooking?" He didn't know if the car needed looking at, but he hadn't told anyone to do anything for a long time.

***

In the parking lot, the man in the sweater vest had his head and arms inside the broken driver's side window. Chav reached for his shoulder. Before the hand could reach him, Kai slipped to the side, stepped back from the car and nodded his approval.

Chav fell forward and caught himself on the car. "What are you doing?"

Kai tried for a Chinese accent. "This is a velly good call."

Chav looked at the Aryan youth in preppy clothes. "What?"

"It is velly fast, yes? Vloom!" He pantomimed a steering wheel while making engine sounds with his mouth. He jerked his head back and made louder engine noises.

"Yeah, she's fast. This is the fastest car in Nebraska."

"You are the dlivel?"

"No, I'm the mechanic."

"Merchanic? You made this call?" Kai's blue eyes went wide

and he nodded. "Oh, velly good, velly good." He pointed at the Veyron. "I dlive that call."

"Yeah, your car's okay too, if you're into the Eurotrash thing." He walked around his car, took a roll of duct tape from the passenger side floorboard, and reinforced the driver's side window. "I can show you more of the car if you want."

"No. Thank you. Good day, honolabre sir." He walked back into the courtyard.

Chav followed him and sat down. Kato eyed the radio announcer, rolling up his sleeve, and pumping his bicep. "Hey, babe," Kato said. "Does your grandma know you're wearing her clothes?"

"Dude, that's not cool," Chav said. "Her grandmother might be dead."

"I'm just negging," Kato whispered. He rotated his baseball cap to cover his neck. "You betas don't understand women." He winked at Dot and flexed again.

Dot looked at her tablet.

The man in the kimono stirred his drink with his finger. It spun faster, and he raised his hand, making the highball levitate. He pulled his finger out, making the glass leap six feet in the air. He caught it in the palm of his hand and drained it with a single gulp.

"So what's with the urinal, man?" Kato asked.

"Come on, we're eating," Theo said. He dipped his burger in ketchup.

"Are we supposed to talk to the reporter woman or something?" Chav asked. "I mean, she gave us drinks. She might want to interview us or something."

"Or something." Kato raised his eyebrows and nodded his head. "Don't worry, boys. I'll do the talking."

A man in black slacks and a stained white Oxford walked into the courtyard. He rested two fists on the table. The Germans, having finished their third round, stood up and bowed to the race officials. "Goold ruck," Kai said to Chav. He held out his hands as if he were steering and jerked back his head as he made engine noises and walked out to the parking lot.

"So." Kato leaned toward Dot. "How's it hanging?"

The man in the white shirt said, "Sorry to interrupt, but is this the checkpoint?"

"Yes, you're at the right place. Now, let's see." Dot moved her finger on the screen of her tablet. "You must be Mr. Lutz. Bill?"

"William. You're keeping track of all of us on that thing?"

"Those of you that are left. Only six cars made it out of D.C. You can see for yourself on the thingamabob."

"The GPS and I, we're not on speaking terms right now."

Dot spoke in understanding tones. "Yes. Well." She handed him an envelope. "Here's the next checkpoint. It should already be programmed into your GPS."

"Thanks." William turned to leave.

Kato grabbed his arm. "Not so fast, dude. We were ahead of you. Before you go, you have to have three drinks."

William picked up the drink in front of Kato and poured it down his throat. He took the drink in front of Theo and did the same. He took the third drink from in front of Chav and drank it as he walked back toward the gate. He put the empty glass on the ground and walked out the gate.

Kato's mouth dropped open. "But we're in front of him. He can't do that!"

"Sure he can," Bernie said. "That was three drinks."

"I was wondering why you boys have been sitting here for so long," Dot said.

"Fuck. Let's get out of here." Kato emptied his glass and ordered another round. "Drink fast, guys."

Chapter .09

The Bugatti sped toward Oklahoma City. "Me Chinese. Me pray joke," Kai said.

"Shut up," the Master slapped him in the head. "Talk like a normal person. The two racers, did you reprogram their units?"

"I was able to get the boys' car pretty easily, but the old guy's car was harder to manage."

"He didn't look so old," the Master said. He turned the mirror toward his face and flattened out a wrinkle between two fingers.

"There was a woman asleep in the car. I was able to get to the GPS, but it started arguing with me. It called me a lying kraut bastard." As he neared a few slower-moving cars, Kai jumped over them diagonally, as if he were playing checkers.

"*Kraut bastard?* That's offensive to Germans. An insult to a German is the worst kind of insult."

"What about Germans pretending to be Chinese?"

"I don't see your point. You're talking nonsense."

"Anyway, I couldn't change its settings. The GPS unit didn't believe me."

"Of course not, not with that ridiculous accent. It saw through your disguise immediately. Jackie Chan would never fail me like this."

"We're winning the race. That's the opposite of failing. And did you see what they're driving? There's no way they can catch up with us."

"It's not enough to defeat the enemy. You should never leave a half-dead enemy behind you. Remember that."

***

Kato gunned the car across the bridge into Oklahoma. From I-64, he took I-40, a long, flat shot toward Oklahoma City.

Chav studied the GPS unit. "It says he's still a mile ahead of us. Drive faster." Kato pressed the pedal and squeezed the shaking steering wheel.

When the brown station wagon appeared in the right lane. Kato asked, "Are you sure this is the car?"

"That's it, bro. We're right on top of it on the GPS."

"He's trying to win the race in that thing?"

"Maybe he's got something special going on under the hood."

"Hold on," Kato said. He hit the gas and rammed the rear bumper.

"Dude, this is my car, dude!"

The station wagon shimmied from side to side and the brake lights switched on.

"Fuck!" Kato skidded to a stop as the station wagon accelerated away. He heard honking horns and squealing tires behind him. Kato shifted the car into first and hit the gas. He worked through the gears until he was back in fifth and gaining on the station wagon. "We're going to get that brake-checking son of a bitch!" He floored the gas pedal and pulled alongside the brown station wagon. Inside, William was arguing with a skinny woman with long hair. Chav rolled down the window and threw a beer can at William's car. The can hit the rear door and bounced into the road.

William looked out his window and gave them the bird.

"That motherfucker," Chav said. He pulled the pistol out of his waistband. Theo reached forward and tried to grab his arm. "Don't worry," Chav said. "I'm just going to shoot out his tires."

"Well, good luck with that," Theo said. "Do you know the odds of hitting a tire at this speed?"

"Never tell me the odds!" Chav fired. The pistol report was deafening inside the car, and Kato swerved away from the sound, onto the left shoulder, before pulling back into his lane.

"Fuck!" Theo yelled. "By *good luck*, I meant don't do it, not to do it!"

William rolled down his window and let his arm hang down. He held a green wine bottle against the door, then swung his arm and tossed the bottle forward in a high, lazy arc, like a slow-pitched softball. It flipped twice in the air and smashed into the Honda's windshield. Kato stomped on the brake. The car shook and pulled to the right. Chav screamed and dropped the pistol, which dangled from his index finger and shot a hole in the floor. He slid his finger out of the trigger guard and let the pistol fall to the R-Racing floor mat. Afraid to touch the gun, he left it there and rolled up the window. The station wagon sped up and disappeared. Chav reached for the duct tape to repair the hole. Kato downshifted and hit the gas.

"Let's give it the nitrous," Chav said.

"Where is that?" Kato tried the hazard lights, windshield wipers, and the cruise control button switches. He hit buttons on the dash, turning on the ground effects and interior strobe lights, ejecting a CD, and dropping a spinning disco ball from the ceiling. ABBA's *More than a Woman* blasted in the cabin.

Chav yelled over the disco music. "It's in the trunk! I bought this shit off a dental student! You can't just hit a button! We have to do it manually! Theo!"

"I'm on it!" Theo opened the split on the rear seat and tunneled through the empty cans and bottles until he found a metal tank strapped to the spare tire with bungee cords. He shouted back, "What do I do? Do I turn the wheel on top?"

"Yeah," Chav yelled. "Open the valve all the way and hold on!"

"All right!" Theo turned the wheel, and the tank hissed.

"We're not going faster!" Kato said.

"Give it a minute!" Chav said.

"If you turn down the music," Theo shouted. "We can stop yelling!"

"There's no time!" Kato screamed.

Theo asked, "Isn't the tank supposed to be connected to something?"

"It's connected to the spare tire!" Chav said. "That way, it won't roll around!"

"Right, but the valve doesn't go anywhere! Isn't there supposed to be a hose or something going to the engine?"

"Yeah, the hose," Chav said slowly. "We can use the hose from the beer bong and send the nitrous to the air intake!"

Theo seemed to be thinking in slow motion. His hands felt heavy and numb. "Where did we leave the beer bong?"

Chav dug under the seat. "It's right here!" He held up a funnel attached to eight feet of rubber tubing. "Is it warm in here?"

It took Theo a long time to say his next word, but he felt it was an important word, so he stuck it out from the slow fricative f, through the long and windy u that dropped low into his throat, on to the c, and grinding through his throat on the final k.

Kato giggled. "Fortuna cigarettes. I'll bet they fish-lip them." It still wasn't funny.

***

"Good afternoon ladies, gentlemen, and all you ships at sea. This is Dot Dottie bringing you the latest news on the Sweet .16 Ultimate Drunk Driving Championship. The three lead cars have passed the first checkpoint, and it's a dead heat to the next checkpoint in beautiful, sunny, Bombay Beach, California.

"Right now, we have the Bugatti in the lead, driven by the racing team of Kai and the Master. In second place is the Toyota station wagon driven by William Lutz. In third place, we have a Honda Civic driven by the boys from Rho Beta Pi. Most

111

of the cars wrecked in Washington and one car still seems to be in Virginia, but we are awaiting check-in from the two cars still in the running. We'll be bringing you the latest racing news as it happens, but until then, we bring you the latest smash hit from Henry James. We hope you enjoy it.

"And speaking of enjoyment, when you get married, you want to enjoy your special day, and no one knows how to make your day special like Two Girls One Cup Catering Company. Two Girls One Cup can produce an affordable, gourmet meal for you and your guests. They do weddings, funerals, graduation parties, birthdays, and even a special, private meal for anniversaries. And for a limited time, get free rick rolls with any order. Ask about their Lemon Party package for beverage service with professional bartenders. There's no party like a lemon party. And for all your catering needs, remember: to sip or sup, call Two Girls and One Cup." Dot put down the microphone and tapped her iPad to start the music.

"Who the hell approved that commercial?" Bernie sputtered. "What's the problem? I read exactly what they wrote in the email." "They aren't a real sponsor," Bernie said. "You're being trolled. You can't believe everything you read on the Internet."

"They offered to buy commercial time. Was I supposed to say no? I don't see you bringing in any ad revenue."

"Look, once this drunk driving thing catches on, we'll have big, classy sponsors. GoDaddy, Taco Tape, Bangbros, they'll advertise. Remember the business plan. It will work. It just takes time. But don't take any new clients without running them by me first and keep the commercials short and snappy."

"Chriminy," Dot said. "This isn't my first day on the job. I remember how the jingles used to go."

***

When the gas gauge dropped below a quarter tank, Sean drove them through side streets, looking for cars that used high-test gas. They saw mostly pickup trucks and sedans in the first few parking lots, but they found a garden hose and an empty gas can in the back of an F-150 outside the Grand Ole Opry. Jeb cut off a few feet of hose, and they cruised for sports cars or luxury sedans likely to use 93 octane. Off 40, near 1st Avenue, they found what they were looking for, a red Pontiac Trans-Am parked near a commuter train station. The car was in cherry condition, so they could bet the owner was feeding it the good stuff.

There was a park across the street that went to the river. A large banner taped to a tree announced the regional championships of the American Hacky Sack Society and Ultimate Frisbee Coalition. The event meant a bit more foot traffic than Sean and Jeb wanted, but they decided to move quickly, act inconspicuously, and hope no one noticed.

The championships were not going well. No one had remembered to bring a hacky sack, and the Frisbee had flown into the Cumberland River, so the games had been canceled. There were plenty of hot dogs and burgers, but the vegans who brought the charcoal refused to light the grill until the meat was given a proper burial. Some hippies wandered into the street, looking for stores that carried sporting goods or charcoal. Others had decided to turn the gathering into a protest and rummaged through trashcans, looking for cardboard for signs. Still, hippies don't call cops, so Sean and Jeb carried on.

A few minutes later, Jeb was kneeling next to a red Trans-Am with a broken driver's side window, vomiting waffles, Wild Turkey, and gasoline onto the sidewalk. Sean stuffed the end of the hose into the gas can.

"Fuck this shit," Jeb said.

"It's almost full." Sean crimped the hose and asked Jeb to hold it until he got back. "And hush up. We don't want to get caught."

"No. Fuck it," Jeb said. He dropped the hose and let it siphon gasoline from the tank in glugs and spurts across the

113

parking lot. "That can holds one gallon of gas. One. We're going to have to do this fifteen more times before we fill our tank, and then it doesn't end there. Every few hours, we're going to have to stop and do this same thing over again." He stood up.

"Keep it down," Sean said.

"And when we fill this tank, and then the tank after that, what then? When we run out of gas completely, do we just keep stealing gas? How long can we keep doing this?"

A thin man with a backpack rose from a bench, where he had been playing an electric keyboard. "Yeah," he said. "How long can we do this?" He waved his arms toward the wandering hippies and shouted, "Come over here, guys! Speak some truth!"

Emboldened, Jeb addressed the gathering crowd, "And when we get our few precious gallons of gas, where does it end? We drive a few hundred miles, steal some more, knock over convenience stores, burn down Waffle Houses. I can't do this anymore!"

A few voices from the crowd muttered agreement, and the man with the backpack played *The Battle Hymn of the Republic* on his keyboard.

"I am a race driver, as my father was before me, but I say now, this will not stand. That stuff tastes awful. We were supposed to have cars so the cars could take us places, but now we're slaves to our cars, giving blowjobs to gas tanks and driving in circles. We're going nowhere, and it's gone far enough!"

A woman pushed a double-wide, sport utility stroller into the growing puddle of gasoline and said, "Do we invade other countries? Do we become as evil as those we pretend to fight, all to support corporate terrorists and the almighty dollar? Do we spread hegemony? Enslave others? Commit violence? Destroy our economy, our environment, and our future in the name of colonialism and exploitation? We can't do it anymore. I can't do it anymore. How long can we rape this good earth for a few more drops of precious oil?"

Jeb looked over at Sean, who was trying to pretend the

can of gasoline next to his foot wasn't his. "What's she talking about?"

"I don't know," Sean said. "Just go with it."

A man pushed his bicycle into the spreading puddle. "As Americans, we all stand in this puddle of gasoline," he said. "If you want sustainable solutions, look around you: sunlight, the river, wind power, pedal power," He held his bicycle in the air. "Pedal Power!" he cried.

"He's right!" Jeb yelled out to the growing crowd, "If we want to win a cross-country drunk driving race, we don't need cars, gasoline, or anything like that. We'll find a better way, and we'll beat those Russian fuckers who shot up our car, and by gosh we will become drunk driving champions!"

There was hesitation from the audience.

"I think he means that symbolically," Sean said.

"Yeah!" the audience yelled.

Jeb pointed to a sailboat docked on the river. "There's your answer: wind-powered transportation, free transportation without violence, without theft, without exploitation, without pollution!" He walked toward the docks.

"Wait," Sean said. "We're going to need our GPS alcohol monitor doohickey." He opened the door of the Mustang and looked at the connections. "Does anyone have a hex key?" he asked. "I think it's metric." The bicyclist unzipped a nylon bag under the seat of his bike and held up a folding multitool.

"Allen wrench!" the audience cheered.

Sean worked with the screws and held the unit in his arms. "Don't forget the booze," he yelled. Jeb took the box of bourbon from the trunk.

"Ethanol!" someone yelled from the crowd. "Sustainable fuels help our farms!"

Jeb led the march down to the docks. He held up the clinking case of whiskey, "Alcohol!" he yelled.

"Alcohol!" the crowd cheered back. As they approached the sailboat, the march became a race for the gangplank. With cries of "Free wind power for all!" "Water, wind and sun!" and "No blood for oil!" they charged toward the dock.

As Sean and Jeb crossed the gangplank, a bearded man stood on the ramp and held up his arms. "We have done much today," he said. "But we must spread the message: no more pollution, no more violence, no more theft, not in my name." The protestors untied the ropes mooring the craft, and Jeb raised the sails. "And we have to legalize marijuana. Drug prohibition has crowded our prisons and criminalized Mother Nature."

"Legalize it!" the crowd cheered.

A man carrying two reusable grocery bags walked toward the boat. "What are you people doing with my boat?" he asked.

The bearded man pushed him back into the crowd. "We must envision a new world built upon peace, respect, and sustainability."

"But that's my boat!" the man said. He rushed toward the gangplank, and the bearded man threw a wild haymaker that missed the boat owner's head and wrapped around his neck. The men clinched in a vicious hug, pulling hair and kicking shins. As the wind filled the sails, the boat moved upstream a few feet before dropping the gangplank and the scuffling men into the river.

Sean used alligator clips he found in the boat's toolbox to attach the GPS to the boat's power supply, the main mast. The boat sailed northwest, and Jeb stood at the wheel. "Who started the fire?" he asked, pointing to the flames near the train station.

"Puddle of gas, angry mob. These things happen." Sean looked at the water, then at the sails. "She ain't exactly quick, is she?"

"Don't worry. We're professional racers," Jeb said.

"We're race car drivers. Car. Drivers. We don't know how to sail."

"We're racers now, and this boat will go as fast as we need it to go."

"How? We're sailing against the current and only as fast as the wind goes."

"Then we're gonna need more wind." Jeb stood, every inch the captain at the wheel with the bottle of whiskey in his right hand. "Sean, go find the wind button."

"Wind don't work that way," Sean said.

"As the captain of this ship, I order you to find the wind button." Jeb brandished his bottle. Sean went below, grumbling. After a few minutes, the breeze picked up and the sails filled.

Sean yelled up to the deck, "Was that it?"

"I think so," Jeb said. "Does it go any higher?" The sails grew from beer bellies to pregnancies, and the boat skipped on the surface of the water. "Yeah, I think that was the right button."

***

Joe lit a Cohiba off the rising flames and walked back to the cruiser. He smiled at the two bodies strapped to the roof, like kayaks on a Volvo. He offered Ruby a puff of his cigar. Being dead, she didn't respond, so Joe slapped her rump. "It was kind of them to leave a can of gasoline next to their car, was it not?"

John waved dismissively at the burning Mustang. "There are still three cars ahead of us."

"This is just like in the old days, when Johnson beat us to Sacramento by five minutes. That cannot happen again."

"Don't worry," John said. "We will be victorious."

Joe yelled to the crowd ascending from the river. "It does not stop here! We will burn all the cars, burn everything! We must destroy them all. We will bury the capitalist pigs, and only then will they understand!"

"You are not being inconspicuous," John said.

Joe straightened his tie. "Is this better?"

"He's right," the man carrying the bicycle said. "We have to burn all the cars. Only then can we ride in safety."

Another man held up a Bic lighter. "Burn it all down!" he yelled.

The crowd scattered through the city with lighters and matches.

"What are they doing?" asked Joe.

John said, "I don't know. Stupid Americans. Ignore them."

***

Renee returned from the Weenie Beanie with pork sandwiches, fries, and Diet Cokes. The rum she poured into the cup floated on top. Stirring with the straw and shaking the cup didn't change the taste, so she added more rum.

Thomas carried his laptop to Renee's desk. "Have you been following the news? There's an increase in violent crimes in the South that might have to do with this race."

"Give me the rundown," Renee said.

"If you follow this map, there was an arson at a convenience store near the North Carolina Border. The owner of the gas station said he was robbed by two men in NASCAR outfits, and they only stole beer, aspirin, and gas before setting the place on fire. Here in North Carolina, a couple hours southwest of the robbery, we have a shootout at a Waffle House, two people missing, and the place burned to the ground. If you follow, it's almost a straight line to Nashville, where there's some kind of riot going on. If you continue that line, it points right at Fort Smith, Arkansas."

"NASCAR suits?"

"Right. They had helmets and fire suits. They were driving a black Mustang."

"I remember those guys. They were at the starting line. Have they been arrested?"

"The way I see it, by the time the cops start looking for them, they're already in another state."

Renee's straw caught the last of her drink, and her eyes went wide with the quick triple shot of rum. Her nostrils burned as she exhaled. "But how's the petition going?"

"We need 100,000 signatures before the White House will even consider it. And that's just to get a response, which could be no."

"Okay, how many signatures do we have?"

"One. That's mine. You haven't even signed the petition yet. Obviously, the viral thing's not going to happen. I know in the movies everything you post on the Net goes viral, but if you really want to capture the public imagination, you need something that will appeal to, say, a fourteen-year-old boy. Like this drunk driving thing. It's really catching on. You wouldn't believe it, but kids are starting to listen to big band music again. In the past two days, *Little Brown Jug* shot up to number five on the iTunes charts. People are recording and podcasting her updates. There's an advice animal template, and remember Toonces, the driving cat? People have been dubbing the broadcasts over the SNL sketch. It's pretty well done, actually." Thomas pulled up a tab and showed Renee the video.

"Aw, it has a cat driving a car. How did they do that?"

"You can't beat cats on the Internet. Plus, her commercials are very popular. The message boards are full of people sending her emails from fake companies. She's done Ragtime Tampons, St. Joseph's Children's Chewable Oxycontin, Fingerboxes, Draino Mouthwash, Battle Towed Towing, Mootykins Cucksauce, KY Eyedrops, Candle Jacks, Fappy Tissues, Dee's Nuts, Kwikbuzz Huffer's Spraypaint, whatever they send her."

"Well, what do we do now?"

Thomas minimized the window and pulled up a map. "Okay, driving from Fort Smith to Bombay Beach has to take at least twenty hours, right? They have to cross a lot of ground. So far, they seem to stick to the major highways. That makes sense because they're all using the same GPS units. That means they're all going to drive down I-40 at the same time. If we can get the police to set up a roadblock on I-10, or on any major highway on the way to Bombay Beach, they could catch all of them."

"A field sobriety checkpoint. Of course! I know just the people who can set one of those up too." She flipped her Rolodex to the M section and pulled out a card. "I am not looking forward to this phone call. While I'm on the line, I want you to check the back and see if we have a hand truck. I think it's time we thawed Captain Video out ourselves."

***

Jeb awoke when the unit called for an alcohol reading. Drunk as a sailor, he blew into the hose and saw the expected three green lights. Sean stared groggily at the GPS screen. "This river don't go through Arkansas. We gotta be on Route 40 if we want to make the checkpoint."

Jeb turned the wheel and started to sing, "Stepped on my blue suede shoes, like Mordor in the rain." He aimed toward a boat ramp.

"What are you doing?" Sean asked.

"Give us full power, ramming speed."

"This is full power."

"Then start singing." He gave Sean a bit more of the tune, "I bought my blue suede shoes in the middle of a downtown train."

Sean mumbled along.

Jeb raised his bottle like a cutlass toward the shore. "Sing better; sing louder!" He projected his voice from the diaphragm. "Don't you see, Andy, hey come and look at me. I got a golden ticket, but I'm as blue as a manatee." He swung the bottle at Sean, "Sing, damn you!"

The two men sang with the wind behind them, the tune carrying for miles ahead, "Because I'm talking to Memphis, walking with my feet on top of me." The keel hit the ramp and cut into the gravel, but the bow kept rising.

Sean stood on the deck and spread his arms. "Parking my

Lexus!" He sang at the top of his lungs as they sailed up the ramp and into the parking lot. "Truly need to feed a whale, I feel!" They passed pickup trucks and bass boat trailers and made their way toward the highway, asphalt spraying in their wake.

***

Renee changed her clothes and freshened up in the office bathroom before leaving. Thomas only had his Hunter S. Thompson costume, and he felt stupid wearing it. Renee drank a Crystal Light and vodka Slurpee as she drove the Subaru around the Beltway. "I so hate talking to those women at MADD." She imitated a high-pitched, ditzy voice, "'Oh, we've never heard of the Temperance Movement before.' Condescending bitch." She stopped the car outside of the National Archives Annex, a large white rock and glass building in College Park, Maryland. "Well, I believe in Crystal Light, I believe in me, and they know damn well who I am. Who do you think they stole their idea from?" She gave her license and Thomas' to the security guard, who directed them to the parking garage.

"So this Temperance Movement," Thomas asked. "You're against drinking and driving."

"Right. We have to put an end to that."

"But you drink and drive all the time."

"That's different." She took the hand truck out of the back of the car

"How is it different? You're drinking, you're driving, but you're opposed to drinking and driving."

"Yes, but have you considered how safe the roads would be if I were the only one driving? The problem isn't driving. It's other people driving."

"But isn't that hypocrisy?"

"It's more like capri pants. When I wear capri pants, it's cute and fun. When other people wear capri pants, it's tragic and awful. Understand?"

"Not really."

"Well, you understand that this internship is for college credit. I write your evaluation at the end of the semester, so when you don't understand your professor in, say, Biology 101, you fail the class, right? What you have to understand in my class is that my capri pants are awesome. You might want to write that down."

***

Inside the building, security was tight. A guard had them sign in with yellow chalk on a green slate. To the side, two guards balanced their pistols on their noses while a third held a stopwatch and the fourth held their bets. A fifth guard pulled himself from the contest to wave Tom and Renee through an unplugged metal detector while a sixth erased the chalkboard. The Temperance Movement made its way to the research room. Behind the counter, the clerk paused his Nintendo DS and asked what they were looking for. When Renee explained, he spent some time typing into his computer. "Wait. How do you spell that?"

"V-I-D-E-O," Renee said.

"And the other word?"

"C-A-P-T-A-I-N."

He backspaced, typed, and peered at his monitor. "That's downstairs in cold storage. It's not so much an archive as a lost and found. You have to understand that the 1940s was kind of the golden age of superheroes. There were tons of them. More of them kept bobbing up all the time. They were kind of like frozen burritos."

"Frozen burritos. Right. We have that." Renee said.

"I guess they call it the greatest generation for a reason, but when you have a freezer full of burritos, it's always the steak or chicken ones that go first. Captain Video's more like that bean and cheese nobody wants." He squinted at Renee's license.

"Wait. I know who you are. I've seen you on those late night television commercials. *Do the Scrunchie*, right? That was you!"

Renee knew the commercials, all the hits of the 80s remastered by machines with new technology to fit onto only seven CDs. She still made a few cents off every copy, but it killed her other sales. Nobody bought the old albums anymore. "It was *Do the Scrimshaw*. We had other songs, you know." *Do the Scrunchie* didn't make any sense. Still, a fan was a fan. She'd give him a thrill. "Wait. You probably remember *Never Give Satan Your Phone Number*."

The clerk looked up and to the left. He shook his head. "I don't think so."

Renee broke into a dance step that looked like she was simultaneously making a martini and crushing a cigarette under her foot while she gave the clerk a bit of the chorus. "Never give Satan your phone number," she sang.

"Nah. Before my time."

"Nobody listens to the B-sides anymore. Well, anyway, you can see that I am a celebrity and my time is valuable. So can we maybe check out Captain Video for a few days? Tommy here's a journalist. He has a library card, if that helps."

The clerk put a form on the counter. "You don't really have to check him out. He's more like a lost umbrella than an official record. We've been meaning to clean out the freezer for a couple years now. You can fill out this form and show it to the guy in the basement. He'll probably just give him to you. He was marked as surplus anyway."

"Okay, so where do we go?"

He pointed down the hall. "Take the elevator to the basement and follow the Freon smell." As Thomas and Renee walked toward the elevator, he called after them. "And hey, keep him away from radio stars, okay?"

"Christ," Renee muttered. "'Before my time.' That made me feel old."

"What's a B-side?" Thomas asked.

***

Joe pulled up to the drive-through. A nearly incomprehensible voice blasted through the speaker, "Hello, welcome to McDonald's. Can I take your order, please?"

Joe yelled into the speaker, "How many hamburgers can I get for six fifty?"

"Would you like an extra value meal?"

"No. I do not want an extra value meal. How many hamburgers can I get for six fifty?"

"Is that the Big Mac or the Quarter Pounder with Cheese?"

"Hamburgers!" he yelled.

"How many would you like?"

"As many as I can get for six fifty."

"Would you like fries and a drink?"

"I do not want fries or a drink. Why would you ask such a question? Wait. You have a dollar menu. Give me five McDoubles. That is what I want."

"Would you like five McChickens with that?"

"What is wrong with you? I want five McDoubles, only that!"

"Thank you. Second window."

John said, "You missed the first checkpoint. Maybe it is my turn at the wheel again."

"That does not matter. This is no longer a race. It is a war of attrition. When we have killed all the racers, who else can win but us? Even if they send us back to the checkpoints, we will be victorious."

"That's five fifty," the cashier said. Joe handed him six dollars and fifty cents and took a white paper bag. "It's only five fifty," the cashier said. He handed back a dollar.

Joe took the dollar, grabbed the cashier's wrist, and pulled. He couldn't get the cashier through the window, but he drew the Stechkin and tucked the muzzle in the cashier's armpit, firing a few quick bursts to shatter the shoulder. Holding onto the forearm, he hit the gas. The screaming was drowned out by the revving engine as skin, muscles, nerves, and tendons tore. Blood vessels stretched and burst, spraying the cruiser's rear window.

He tossed his trophy in the back seat. "We can attach that to the car at the next rest stop." Going up the ramp to the highway, his joy dissipated. "Now we will never know how many hamburgers you can get for six fifty."

"It does not matter," John said. "Are you feeling okay?"

"Do we have any amphetamines left?"

"We still have maybe forty pills left."

"Then give me one, and I will get us to the next state." Joe said. "This place depresses me. There is no scenery at all." To cheer himself up, he took a grenade from the back seat and scanned the road for tanker trucks.

According to the GPS, one car was so far ahead and moving so fast that it was probably a glitch. Even helicopters didn't move that fast. Another had turned toward Texas and wasn't a threat in the race, but one drove due west and was only a few miles ahead. "Keep driving straight," John said. "We will catch up with them soon."

***

Renee had Thomas push the block of ice back to the car. "This isn't going to fit in your station wagon," Thomas said.

"Sport utility wagon," Renee corrected. "It's bigger than it looks, and it will fit if we chip off some of the ice and put the seats down." She opened her purse and pulled out a wood-handled ice pick.

"How did you get that past security?"

"Back in the 80s, you wouldn't do a gig in New York without one of these. I've smuggled this thing past a million bouncers." She stabbed at the ice. "There's a KA-BAR under the seat. Make yourself useful."

Thomas found the foot-long knife. He considered asking why she had something like that in her car, but he had other issues. "You know, with most internships, you get to go home. You've kept me working all day and night. I'm missing classes."

"Do you really think being a complainer is going to look good on your evaluation?"

Thomas changed the subject. "What's so special about Captain Video?"

"Special? He's a superhero. We can use his powers to stop Dot Dottie before she has everyone in America driving and drinking."

Thomas stabbed into the ice and pounded the black, metal pommel with his other hand. "What powers does he have?"

"Well, back during WWII, he was able to record things he saw and play them back using cathode ray tube technology."

"Cathode ray tube, you mean like an old TV?"

"This was before TV, but the same idea."

Thomas stopped stabbing the ice. "So his power is to record things and play them back on a TV set?"

"Precisely. See, his fingers had these round protrusions on them that he could plug into the back of his video monitors."

"Like RCA plugs."

"And he had knives in his fingers for editing film." Renee said. "Maybe a tape dispenser for splicing."

"So he's a camcorder? This is stupid. No wonder the superheroes died out. I can do all that with my phone."

"I'm sorry, my little worker bee whose internship evaluation I haven't filled out yet. I'm not sure I heard you correctly."

Thomas chipped at the ice. "I said this experience is profoundly enriching my education."

"And?"

"I'm so thankful to have this opportunity."

"And?"

Thomas sighed. "And your capri pants are awesome."

Chapter .10

Back in Arlington, Thomas slid the block of ice onto the asphalt parking lot. There was no way he could get it upright and onto the hand truck again. "So what do we do now?"

Renee considered the possibilities. "If it were earlier, we could have got some day laborers to help move him, but I don't really know what good that would do. Why don't we dump some gas on the ice? That should thaw him out."

"I was hoping you had some sort of cryogenic facility, like in *The Empire Strikes Back*."

"Let me check on that." Renee walked into her office building. She came back with a plastic gas can. "This holds two gallons. The gas station's that way, on the other side of the chicken place." She pointed toward George Mason Drive. "And get me one of those canned Margarita things, the twenty-four ounce can with salt packets from the snack bar." She dug some money from the pocket of her capri pants. "Bring the receipt."

***

Kai pulled up to the pump, as he had so many times. The car was fast and it handled well, but it could burn through fuel. For a normal driver, the tank would be empty in a less than quarter of an hour at top speed, if the tires lasted that long. Kai was not a normal driver, but the car was still far from efficient. He poured two bottles of octane booster into the tank.

The Master glided out of the car and walked toward the building. "If they have burritos, do you want one?" Their pit stops throughout the Southwest had provided a crash course in Mexican food.

127

"Not now," Kai said. "I need your credit card."

Standing at the door of the gas station, the Master drew his card from the sleeve of his kimono. With a flick of his wrist, he threw it into the card reader. It hit the back of the machine and bounced back, scanning itself as it slid out. He caught the card between two fingers and it disappeared in the folds of his robe. While Kato pumped a hundred dollars into the gas tank, the Master padded into the building.

He returned minutes later with a brown paper bag. "They had tacos," he said.

"Do you want to take over the driving for a while?" Kai asked. The Master assumed the lotus position on the passenger side, so Kai sighed and slid into the driver's seat. "You know, I've been driving a long time. I'm kind of tired." He pulled back onto the highway.

"A person's heart is the same as heaven and earth. The blood circulating is the same as the moon and sun. The earth, the moon, the sun, and the sky all move tirelessly. They do not grow bored. They move through eternity without sleeping." He pried the lid off a plastic ramekin and sniffed warily.

"But people sleep."

"Untrained people sleep. We are not like them. Besides, we have tacos and chilies. How can you sleep while the world offers us such wonders?" The Master dribbled sauce over his taco.

"Can I have a bite?"

"Did I not ask you if you wanted one?"

"But I wasn't hungry then. Look. You have three tacos there and I have nothing."

"They're pork. They are very good."

"So how about if you give me one?"

"Would that make you stop complaining? Is one taco all would take to make you happy in this world?"

"Yes. Thank you."

The Master smiled. "No. These are my tacos."

***

When the street lights switched on, Renee looked at her watch. "Well, this is taking forever. Are you even sure gas can melt ice?"

"How am I supposed to know?" Sitting on the hood of the Subaru, Thomas shook himself awake. "I thought you knew." More than anything, he wanted that signed evaluation form so he could go home. He watched a firefly blinking in the air.

"I thought you interns were supposed to be smart. Didn't you take chemistry, college boy?"

Thomas wasn't a science major, but he could observe how alcohol was interacting with Renee. He couldn't remember how many times Renee had sent him to refill the gas can and bring back tallboys of alcopop, but with the gas fumes, lack of sleep, and booze for breakfast and lunch, she had to be about as high as heaven at happy hour. "Do you have any antifreeze?"

"Hey, good thinking, little buddy." Renee opened the back of the Subaru, lifted the floor, and took a plastic bottle from the spare tire compartment. She drilled into the block with the cordless power drill she had been using on the ice, unscrewed the cap, and emptied the bottle on the superhero. She waited a minute. "It's still not melting fast enough. I have an idea. Bring that gas over here." She chipped a shotglass-sized hole in the ice. Thomas poured a half jigger of gasoline into the hole. Renee lit it, and a small flame flickered festively on the melting ice. "Hell, they must be in California by now. Pour on more gas."

"I don't think that's a good idea."

"Fine I'll do it," Renee said. "Hold my beer." She held out the can. Thomas took the flavored malt beverage and stepped back. Renee poured gasoline on the flames, and they rode up the stream of gas. The plastic gas can didn't so much explode as disappear in a great flash, and when the flash disappeared, Renee was on fire.

Waving her arms, she tried to run away from the flames. Fire danced on the spreading water and flew behind her like a golden mane. She collapsed onto the asphalt and rolled in the flaming water.

The ice melted, and Captain Video's shape became more apparent. He'd seemed larger in the ice, but now he looked about five foot five, maybe a hundred and sixty pounds. He wore a helmet with a camera attached to it. Over his stomach, there was what looked like a record player or a crude analog video disc. As the ice melted, the flame seemed to pour away from him until he lay still on a bed of melting ice, dripping cold water and ringed with fire.

Thomas ran toward Captain Video. He reached to move the body then stopped, remembering his first aid training. He put his head to the cold chest. There was no heartbeat. He tried CPR. Pushing on the breastplate produced a crunching, squishing sound. The insides were still cold, like a microwaved burrito. Thomas stepped away from the body. Of course there was no pulse. The guy was frozen in a block of ice. That kills people. He realized he probably should have tried to save Renee first.

She lay collapsed on the asphalt, her skin charred and still burning. She wasn't breathing. Her capri pants were smoking. Thomas looked around. There were no witnesses. He walked into the Temperance Movement office. His internship evaluation form sat on Renee's desk, still not filled out. He put the form and a blank sheet of paper with the Temperance Movement letterhead on his keyboard. Upon further consideration, he grabbed an autographed photo from the stack next to an empty bottle. He'd have to trace the signature at the end of the semester. He closed the laptop like a folder around the pages and left the office.

Renee and Captain Video were both dead in the parking lot. He walked to the gas station, which still had a pay phone, and dialed 911. He didn't give his name. Not waiting for the fire trucks to arrive, he walked to the bus stop at the end of the block. He left his bus pass in his pocket and paid cash as he rolled away.

***

Captain Video's body sprawled still and cold on the asphalt, his heart and brain frozen in a time of global war. He floated in the void, a place of infinite calm, but in the darkness, he saw a flash of light, a dim, red tint on the horizon that reappeared again and again.

Here, Captain Video could not know time or distance. The flashing lights could be anywhere from light years away to somewhere inside of himself. There was no inside or outside. The lights could be flashing at intervals of moments or millennia. He focused on the flash and waited for it to reappear. There was a rhythm to the flashing, a rhythm that implied time. The lights had taken shape, a shape that implied space, a message about the space/time dimensions of this universe in numeric code. The void had spoken, and it said twelve. Over and over again, the red light flashed "12:00...12:00...12:00...12:00," a lone light in the endless darkness.

***

William was sipping a thick Super Tuscan with tasting notes of coffee grounds, rare roast beef, figs, and gym socks when he saw the lights in his mirror. "Oh, God damn it!" He took a quick swig from the bottle. "Maggie, we could use some of that black smoke about now."

"Recalculating," Maggie said.

"William," Anita said. "There are no coincidences. I think you should pull over. We all have to hit rock bottom sometime."

"What do you think I was going to do, outrun them?" He slowed the station wagon and turned on his right turn signal.

131

"If you're going to pull over, you might want to put the wine down," Anita suggested.

The police car pulled alongside them, and a man in a black suit fired at the station wagon. The front tire went flat.

"What the hell!" William held the wheel tightly. "I haven't even failed the test yet." As the steering wheel shook, the car slowed and pulled to the left.

The cops fired three short bursts into the station wagon. Glass shattered, and a spray of red mist filled the car. Dust rose around the car as it rolled to a stop by the side of the road. The cruiser flashed past the station wagon and disappeared toward the horizon.

***

"Did you hit him?" John asked.

"Did you not see the blood?" Joe said. "It was perfect. We could not have planned it better. Now, whom do we kill next?"

John put his hand on Joe's shoulder. "I worry about you. I have never seen you like this." In the other races, they had never gone beyond practical jokes and good-natured brinksmanship. Shots were fired, but it was all in good fun. In the past, the race had been private, and the prize had been bragging rights. The publicity and location had scared the CIA off, so now he and Joe were racing and gunning down civilians, who were hardly competition. He had to think of a way to restore morale. "Do you want to go back and mutilate the corpses? Tie the bodies to the cruiser and maybe burn their car? That always cheers you up."

Joe drained the bottle and threw it out the window. "Nothing will cheer me now."

"What is the matter, comrade? We have run this race before. True, we never came in first, but it was always a good time."

Joe checked his pocket for spare magazines. Finding none, he threw the machine pistol out the window.

"It is over, my friend. They have called us back."

John slapped his friend's leg and laughed. "But this is good news! We can go home now."

"Home," Joe grumbled.

"I was worried they had lost our file forever."

"The message said a shipment of black market tequila was seized when the correct bribes were not paid. A junior agent found our files looking for a blender. They had been crumpled for packing material inside the pitcher. Now we are called home. That is our service to the state. We kept a pitcher from breaking. Now they can make frozen Margaritas and we can go home. All this time, we have been spies who found no secrets, warriors who fought no wars, protectors of the blender."

"But still, we can go home."

"You entered on a student visa. You are not a married man. You would not understand." Joe opened another bottle and threw the cap out the window. "So the Kremlin is happy to say that I can return to my faithful wife, my twenty-year-old daughter, and my ten-year-old son."

"There must be some mistake. We have been in America for—" He stopped talking. "But forget your wife. We can finally return to—" He dropped his shoulders. "To Russia. Oh, give me a pill. You are depressing me."

"Russia," Joe said. "I hate America as much as any patriot."

"Of course, we must bury the capitalist pigs."

"But do you really think we could get iPhones in Russia, real ones? I mean the right color and everything?"

"Of course. We are members of the Party and heroes of the State."

"Heroes," Joe grumbled. "As was Lieutenant General Kalishnikov. He lived to a fine old age in his cheap apartment, collecting pocket knives and a meager pension. If only there was a real war. It would be better to die as heroes than to live as packing material."

John shivered at the memory of the Soviet apartment he had grown up in. As a sleeper agent, he had taken both the income from his cover job and his agent salary, which was sent through a different department and often arrived on time. The checks usually cleared. The combined income bought him a townhouse in the suburbs, close enough to the local bars and universities that he could always find a girl when he needed one. He looked toward a future of cinder block, bureaucracy, and celibacy.

"You were young when you came here. Maybe you do not remember the winters. You may not remember what pizza tastes like in Russia."

John flinched. Would there be burritos in Russia? Curry? "Make that two pills. I must think about this." When the pills came, he washed them down with sweet, American vodka.

***

"12:00," the void said again, and Captain Video's eyelids fluttered in the vast internal space that most people only experience between the snooze bar and the second alarm or under anesthesia. He half-dreamed, half-remembered his last mission in Europe, destroying what Goebbels called the eighth great power: radio. He hadn't found Ezra Pound, but he soared through Italy and flew north, toppling radio towers as he went.

In Germany, he'd targeted broadcast studios. He remembered the cold wind in his face as he flew out of Germany with five Messerschmidts behind him, his hands still wet with the blood of propagandists and radio stars. Over Scandinavia, he had rolled to the side and looped in the air, but the fighters stayed close behind him, peppering the air with smoke and hot bursts of lead. Captain Video had drawn his .45 and emptied it into one of the fighters behind him. The plane burst into flames and dropped below the clouds.

When anti-aircraft fire shook him and made him drop his pistol, he turned in the air and grabbed hold of another fighter plane. Gripping the fuselage with one hand, he straddled the aircraft and punched it until it exploded. The blast threw

Captain Video across the sky. A burst from the third fighter's cannon bounced him upward, hurling him further out to sea. He tumbled backward until he smashed into the side of another plane. This one hadn't been a fighter. It was an American plane. His body crashed through the passenger cabin and tore the plane in half.

Captain Video remembered falling above the North Atlantic and fighting to keep his eyes open. As he fell, he saw a woman spinning through the air, a civilian, her dress flapping and her brown hair rising as he fell. Their eyes locked for a moment before the splash. His eyes snapped open.

He awoke to a disorientation that was like a lifetime of hangovers combined with a light-year's worth of jet lag. He'd never been so hungry. He looked around for clues as to where he was. He seemed to be strapped to a stretcher in the back of an ambulance, but this was no sort of ambulance he'd ever seen before. The interior was crowded with plastic, glass, and steel devices. It even had what looked like video screens, but there wasn't a vacuum tube to be seen, and there was no medic in the back to watch him. Captain Video considered this. They must have thought he was dead. That was the only reason the medics would leave him unattended. He wondered, was it a friendly ambulance or had he been captured?

He moved his arms against the straps. They were tight, but they could be overcome if his equipment still worked. "My Video-editing power should take care of these bonds," he said. The words came out in gurgles, and he turned his head to cough out icy sea water. After he'd coughed out blood clots, frost, and phlegm, a number two hobby blade shot out of his right index finger. He started working on the straps.

***

"Shit, William, are you okay?" Anita asked. At some point during the gunfire, William had thrown his body over hers.

Now that the car had stopped, he was slumped over. Something was dripping from his body, painting her red. "I can't believe it. You saved my life." She shook his lifeless body. "You have to live, William. I'm your sponsor. I couldn't show my face at the meetings if I got you killed." She tried to lift him off of her. "And you're really heavy."

William snored into her ear and drooled on her cheek.

"Wake up, Bill." Anita shoved again, and his head rolled back. She drew back to slap him, but his face was covered in red. "Are you shot?"

William sat up and shook his head. "Shot? What for?" He jolted awake. "They're shooting at us!"

Anita shoved him against the driver's side door. "Move, dickhole. You're bleeding all over me."

William wiped his cheek and licked his finger. "It's the wine. They must have shot the bottle." He wiped his forehead, flinched, and jerked his hand away. "Right, they shot the wine bottle." He plucked green shards of glass out of his forehead and right hand. "Do you have a Band Aid or a tee shirt or something?" They got out of the car.

Anita looked at the tire. "I don't suppose you have AAA."

"Do you guys do car repairs now? I don't want to spend three months talking about it. I have a spare in the back."

"I can find us a meeting. I have an app for that."

The exertion of carrying the spare tire and jack made blood run down his face. He handed Anita a flashlight. "Hold this. We'll be back in the race in fifteen minutes."

"But these people shot at us. Maybe your ninth step isn't going so well."

"I can't make amends to everybody. I don't even know who I could have pissed off in this state."

"I'm sure people hate you wherever you go. We should drop out of the race and get you some help. You know, if you keep on doing what you've always done, you'll always get what you always got."

William kicked the nuts loose with his lug wrench and slid the jack under the car. "It works if you work it." With blood pooling in his hand, he grunted with every turn of the jack handle.

***

Jeb ordered Sean to drop anchor near the Arkansas/Oklahoma border. Sean turned off the wind and tossed a rope ladder over the side of the boat. Fish swam in their asphalt wake, but the pavement they stepped onto was solid. Bernie looked at his watch. "Ahoy. This is a first."

Jeb patted the hull of the boat, which bobbed in the road. "It's more eco-friendly," he said. Bernie handed Jeb a white envelope and a Big Gulp cup. "We're supposed to have three drinks here, but everything's packed up. Here you go." He handed Sean the other cup. "Try to hurry. I have a plane to catch."

The racers slurped at their drinks and grabbed the ladder. "Watch out on the road. There might be sharks," Sean said. Before turning the wind back on, he asked, "Is the singing really necessary? If I have to hear that Arkansas song again, I just might jump overboard."

"I'm not sure," Jeb said. "But do we want to risk it?" He ordered Sean to weigh anchor, turn on the wind, and set sail. As the boat started moving, he sang "Oooklahoma!" The boat sailed down the street, toward the river.

***

A few hours before sunrise, the Master looked up from his copy of *Black Belt Magazine* and glared at Kai. Kai avoided his gaze. The suspension wasn't made for dirt roads. It wasn't made for city streets and could barely clear a speed bump, but Kai smoothed the ride as well as he could by driving fast enough to glide on top of the road and focusing his energy forward. By directing his balance so it was parallel to the road, he could drive along the road instead of on it. It was murder on his core and hip flexors.

For the past few states, the Master had amused himself with martial arts magazines truck stops kept next to the pornography. The slight jostling had ruined his mood. "They do not know how to make roads in this country," the Master complained.

"We're almost at the second checkpoint." Kai eased the car to a gliding stop next to a seawall. As the forward momentum ran out, he turned the wheel and drifted backward to park the car front-out. When he opened the door, his nostrils were attacked by the smell of thousands of dead fish and rotting seabirds.

"I will wait here," the Master said.

"I thought you'd say that." Kai flipped over the seawall and walked toward the beach. He saw a vast expanse of dead fish and poisoned water. He walked back to the car. "Have we come to the right place?"

The Master had lit incense and was resting with his feet on the dashboard as he laughed at a series of photographs in the magazine. "You should look at this." The Master threw back his head, laughing silently. A lesser man would be gasping for air, but a lesser man wouldn't know what was so funny. "Look at that stance, the position of his fingers and how loose his toes are. His earlobes, his ankles, his liver, his everything!" He shook his head and snorted with a laughter that sounded like sleep apnea. "And what do you think they call someone like that in America?"

Kai looked at the GPS. "This says we're at the second checkpoint, but there's no one here."

"A grandmaster!" The Master's feet danced on the dashboard.

Kai shrugged. "So what do we do?"

"You should know what to do. Jackie Chan would not

ask such questions. You continue to disappoint me. I am only the Master, but you are like a grandmaster." He honked like a Canada goose. "*A grandmaster*, I said."

Kai walked back to the beach. His German brain tried to unlock the riddle before him. The second checkpoint was at a specific GPS point. He stood at that point. The people he was supposed to check in with weren't there. It was impossible to make sense of this. Maybe the race organizers were running late. He shook his head. The idea was madness. This wasn't Spain, Italy, or Greece. This was a civilized country, and civilized countries are punctual. He walked back to the car.

"They still aren't here. I don't know what it means. I can leave a note. Perhaps they will be shamed by that. Then they'll send us the coordinates to the finish line." Kai took a fountain pen from his pocket.

"But Herr Grandmaster, with your handwriting, what good will a note do? No. It is best that we wait for the proper officials to arrive."

Kai climbed into the driver's seat. With the Master's honking and cackling, he wasn't sure he could sleep. Still, he closed his eyes, visualizing trigrams and tropical fish as he breathed.

***

Bernie and Dot landed in California. It was a small airport, so the rental car was waiting at the terminal. Dot pulled her suitcase behind her, weaving as she walked. "Why won't you tell me about my children?"

"That's not important right now. If you want to see your children again, you have to do what I say."

"See them again? You said they were dead."

Bernie spoke quickly and defensively. "Sure, they're dead. But, you know, you were dead. If I brought you back, I can bring them back. Have a little bit of faith."

Dot thought about this. "I was frozen in ice. Am I supposed

to believe my kids were frozen in the North Atlantic too? How many times could something like that happen?"

"I'm your agent. You have to trust me. When this deal goes through, I'll have Buddy Holly, Del Shannon, and the Big Bopper playing at your family reunion."

"Fiddlesticks! I've never heard of those people. The names sound phony."

"In show business, people sometimes change their names to sound less ethnic." He gave her a significant look. "I thought you'd know that, Dorata Dobranowski." It was a low blow, so Dot said nothing, huffing her disapproval.

Bernie found the bathing machine in long-term parking and hitched it to the back of the rental car.

Chapter
.11

When Chav awoke, the car was silent. "What the fuck?" The front seat was dark, but sunlight shone through the rear windshield. It was morning. Something about the light and the way Chav's bladder felt made him sure of that. He opened his door, which only opened halfway, and pulled himself out. A brown chicken clucked at him disapprovingly. "Save a buck," he said. The floor was dirt and straw, and Chav saw seven more chickens walking, their heads bobbing back and forth.

He looked back at the car. "No," he said. "No." The passenger side door was gouged as if it had hit a guardrail. Several of the decals were scratched beyond repair. A broken sheet of weathered, gray plywood rested on the cracked windshield and the hood. A keening wail rose from his belly as he fell to his knees.

Kato awoke to the crying and tried to open the driver's side door. It was stuck. He called out to Chav. "Hey, the door won't open."

"Of course the door won't open. You drove the car into a fucking wall."

Kato climbed over the stick shift and out the passenger side. "Where are we?"

"We're in a shed, Kato, a fucking shed."

"Yeah, but are we in California?"

Chav stood up. "How am I supposed to know the difference between a California shed and a Utah shed? We're in a fucking shed, dude."

"You have some chickenshit on your pants there."

Chav shook his head. "I don't want to hear about my pants. I don't want to hear about California fucking shed architecture.

What I want to hear about is why you drove my car into a fucking wall."

"Don't be so negative," Kato said. "I mean, there are a lot of things I didn't drive your car into."

"Like what?"

"Like an airplane or Hoover Dam, the Grand Canyon, a fucking bear, a pit of hot lava. Why can't we talk about all the things I didn't hit instead of the one thing I hit?"

"You fell asleep."

"Well, I'm awake now. Let's get out of here." He climbed back into the car and turned the key. There was a slight click, but the starter didn't turn. "It's not starting."

"Did you try turning the key?"

"Yes, I tried turning the key. How would I know the car isn't starting if I didn't turn the key?"

"Try turning it now."

"I am turning it."

"Okay." Chav looked around the shed. He saw a rake hanging from the wall at an odd angle. He straightened it. "Try it now."

"Nothing," Kato said.

"Okay, we're going to need to push the car out of this shed." Kato woke Theo.

"Where are we?" Theo asked.

"In a shed, bro," Kato said.

"Oh, okay." Theo put his head back on the seat.

Kato shook Theo's shoulder. "No, dude. It's not okay. We aren't supposed to be in a shed. We're supposed to be winning the race."

"Oh. Right. The race. Did we win?" With a jolt inside his skull, Theo remembered. "Shit. The race!" He climbed out of the back seat, pushed the plywood aside, and stepped to the front of the car. Kato slid behind the wheel and shifted into neutral. On a count of three, Chav and Theo pushed. Theo could feel the hay and dirt slipping under his shoes, but the car began to move, and it rolled faster as they rolled closer to the hole in the wall. Finally, they stepped outside. A child in a knee-length shirt stood near some porch steps, throwing sticks at a chicken. As the car rolled out of the shed, she ran into the house.

"Set the brake; set the brake," Chav said.

Kato got out of the car. "Can you fix it?"

"I don't know. Let me take a look." Chav assessed the damage. The garbage bag had been torn off the driver's side window. There was a dent in the right side. The spoiler had snapped in two places. The front bra was torn, and there were corn husks in the broken plastic grille. The rims were dirty, and the custom-painted brake calipers were scratched. One of the headlight eyebrows was missing, and there was a large crack in the windshield. A lowering panel was missing on the left side, the ground effects were damaged, and the radio wouldn't turn on. The exhaust amplifier had fallen off, as had most of the chrome molding around the doors and wheel wells. "It's probably totaled," Chav said. "I'd better take a look at the thing." He reached into the car and pulled a lever, opening the trunk.

"The hood lever's on the left," Kato said.

"I know that. I wanted to pop the trunk, in case I need some tools or something." Chav popped the hood and raised it. "I might need tools to fix the–" He searched for the right word. "Thing." He stared at the engine for several minutes. In all the time he had worked on his car, this was one part he had never looked at.

"How's it look?" Kato asked.

"It's still here. It's mostly black and silver. Okay, let's see here. It has wiper fluid." He saw a plastic handle with the word "oil" on it. "You can check the oil here." He peered at the dipstick. "We aren't out of oil yet. I wonder where the VTEC is." He yelled to Kato. "Try the windshield wipers."

Theo walked around the car, toeing a rock with his white Chucks. The last thing he remembered was opening the nitrous tank. He looked in the trunk. The tank was still strapped to the spare tire. There was no hose running from the valve. The most likely scenario he could imagine was that, already drunk and sleep deprived, they had gassed themselves with the anesthetic. At some point, Kato fell asleep behind the wheel and crashed into the shed. If he were asleep, he wouldn't have shut the engine off. The car would have stalled out or idled until it ran out of gas. After that, the radio and headlights would have drained the battery. He offered his hypothesis: "We're out of gas and the battery's dead. That's why the car won't start."

"How do you know?" Chav asked. "Are you a mechanic now?"

"¿Qué te pasa, cabrónes?"

Kato and Theo turned to see a farmer holding a hammer in one hand and a coffee can in the other.

"Hello. Sorry about your shed here," Kato said. "On the bright side, I didn't hit your house or your children or something."

"¿Qué demonios haces, pinche idiota? Dejaste chingado por completo mi gallinero. Se están escapando los pollos. ¿Por qué te quedas parado tocándote?"

Kato looked at Chav. "You know Spanish. Tell him we're sorry we hit his shed but we need gasoline and booze immediately."

"Aloha segnior. Yo soy Chav, und ich neccesito benzin und schnapps. Neccesito Jäger ie PBR und benzin."

"Benzin, buey?"

"Si, si," Chav tapped the car's gas cap. "Petrol. Gas. Benzin."

Kato asked, "Why's he speaking Spanish?"

Chav reassured him. "Everybody speaks Spanish in California as a joke. It's funnier that way."

The man took a coil of chicken wire from the side of the shed and hammered it over the hole in the chicken coop with poultry staples from the coffee can. Theo rushed over to hold the fencing in place. When the farmer seemed satisfied, he dropped the hammer into the coffee can and carried it back to the porch. He said something in Spanish that made the child gather the chickens and walked along a dirt path away from the house. After a few steps, he turned and beckoned with his arm. "¡Vámonos, pendejos! ¿Qué están esperando? Pinches culeros."

Chav scratched his head. "He said, 'Come along, my new friends, and I will show you to a gas station where we can get your car taken care of chop chop.'"

They followed the man to the edge of the farm and down a dirt road. After about half a mile, they stopped at a small building made of gray wood. The farmer stepped inside, so they followed him in. The farmer walked to a plank bar at one end of the room and spoke in rapid Spanish to a boy behind the counter. The boy put a clear bottle of amber liquid and a small glass on the bar.

"What did he say?" Kato asked.

Chav translated, "He said, 'Hello, how is your uncle? Nice weather we are having. These men are in need of gasoline and a jump-start. 'El starto del jumpito.'"

"He said I would not believe the fucking morning he's had," the boy behind the counter said.

"You speak English," Chav said.

"No. You all just learned Spanish right now, one minute ago," the boy said. "You learned it so well that it sounds like English to you now."

"I think he's lying," Chav whispered.

"Do you know where the nearest gas station is?" Kato asked.

The boy pointed toward the window. "On the mainland, maybe about a mile from the beach."

"Mainland? California isn't an island."

"You aren't in California."

"Where are we?"

"You are in Pedro's. I am Pedro. This is my bar, the Bar of Pedro. I also have a store." He pointed to the opposite wall, which had a shelf of dusty canned goods and a small collection of fishing tackle hanging from the wall. "That is the Store of Pedro."

"Do you sell gasoline?"

"If I sold gasoline, I would be a gas station."

"The Gas Station of Pedro?" Theo offered.

"Yes, and the cat you see over there?"

"The Cat of Pedro?" Kato asked.

"His name is Bambi. The Cat of Pedro is a stupid name." He narrowed his eyes and nodded "I have heard that you Americans are very stupid people."

"We're more interested in gas stations than cats right now," Theo said.

"The closest gas station is on the mainland. I already told you that. We are not on the mainland, so I am not a gas station. If I were a gas station, maybe we would be on the mainland." Pedro spoke in rapid Spanish with the farmer.

The farmer laughed and said, "Maricones."

"He said we're Americans," Chav said. "Si, yo soy maricones. Ich bin ein maricon."

"They're laughing again," Theo said. "Look, Pedro. We ran out of gas out on this guy's farm, and we need to make our way to the gas station, so could you give us directions to the bridge?"

"No bridge, Pedro said. "This is a fucking island, man."

"Is there a ferry or something?"

"No ferry. If you really have a car here, it is the only car on the island. How did you even drive it here?"

"Yeah," Theo asked. "How the hell did you do that?"

"I don't know," Kato said. "I was drunk."

Pedro spoke in Spanish. Between gasps of laughter, the farmer shot something back that Chav couldn't translate. Pedro put another bottle on the bar and set out three glasses. "He said maybe if you get drunk again, you'll drive yourselves off the island. It is very funny what he said, but it sounds funnier in Spanish, the way he said it."

"Hilarious," Kato said. Still, they leaned against the bar and filled their glasses. "Look, is there someone else we can talk to? Maybe the sheriff or the mayor or something?"

"Oh, sure. No problem." He opened a curtain behind him. "Mamá!" A couple minutes later, a short woman in a turquoise cotton dress and a large, mustached man in denim came through the curtain. "This is my mother, the mayor, and this is her boyfriend." Pedro's mother took a bottle and pulled the cork with her teeth. "Her boyfriend is the sheriff, sometimes. Or the sheriff is sometimes her boyfriend. I don't know how you say it." She took three swallows from the bottle. Kato downed his glass and shivered.

Pedro had a short conversation with his mother, who disappeared behind the curtain and reappeared with a folded map. She spread it on the table and pointed to a dot in the Sea of Cortez, off the coast of Baja. "She says this is the Isla San Pedro. That is where we are. There is no bridge and no ferry. If you want to leave, you wait for the supply boat on Wednesday."

"Wednesday's no good," Kato said. "We have to get moving now." Theo refilled Kato's glass. "You're not helping," Kato said.

"That car won't move until you're good and drunk." Theo put his hand on Kato's shoulder. "You know that."

Kato downed the shot, winced, and refilled his glass. "I'm fine."

"Okay," Theo said. "Explain to me what's so goddamn funny about Fortuna cigarettes."

Kato looked at Theo like he was insane. "That's not funny. It's probably just a brand of cigarettes."

"If that's not funny, we're sober, and if we're sober, we'll never get that car going."

"Maricones," the farmer said.

Chav brightened up. "He's right. We're Americans. With our maricone know-how there has to be a way to get my car off of this island and to a gas station."

The mayor held up her hands. "She says there is no way," Pedro said.

Kato slumped against the bar and put his head in his hands. They were sunk. His eyes shot open as an idea occurred to him. He raised his head. "Tell her we have American money."

"How much money?" Pedro asked.

The three huddled in a semicircle and piled wadded bills and handfuls of change on the bar. Kato counted quickly. "We have twenty, almost thirty dollars."

For a few minutes, the bar was full of excitement, people speaking with animated gestures. They came to a decision. Pedro turned to Theo and put another bottle on the bar. "For thirty dollars, we throw in a second bottle. You'll get off the island. No problem."

***

The Master watched his pupil, who sat on the hood of the car with his arms crossed. When the race organizers arrived, he tapped his wristwatch, shook it, and held it to his ear. He knew what Kai was doing. While his body language showed scorn and contempt, he knew Kai's words would be polite and respectful. Like many of the martial arts, Drunken Cichlid did not encourage violence and embraced passive aggression.

He watched the pantomime unfold. Kai was given a few drinks, answered a few questions for the woman with the microphone, and received an envelope disclosing the location of the finish line. He nodded and bowed, but in a curt and abrupt manner that carried an insult the organizers would never understand.

Kai slammed the car door. "Can you believe these people, late to their own race? Well, finally we have the location of the finish line, after they've made us wait so many hours."

"You should be more patient," the Master said.

"This is a race. It's not about patience." He drove up the dirt road. After a few blocks, he headed north.

As they passed the Salton Sea and Kato turned west, the Master looked up from his magazine. "Where are you going?"

"To the finish line. I'm going to get there before the officials. That should teach them a lesson."

"A lesson to a fool is a kiss to a porcupine. The animal learns nothing and the teacher's mouth will hurt. The finish line is to the left, but our competition is to the right. You can win the race easily; we know that. But to run away from your opponent is cowardly. They should be running from us. We're more powerful. Why should we run away?"

"Because it's a race. I thought that was the whole point."

"When you're the master, you can think about the whole point." The Master softened his tone. "But it's not your fault. You're young. You don't understand these things. Now, go back the way we came. You're making my mouth hurt."

***

After he changed the tire, William had a long, straight drive through the night. When 40 turned south, Maggie had William drive into Nevada. The desert was an expanse of flat darkness with hills and mountains in the distance. In the morning light, he could see he was headed toward a red light in the desert. He pulled into a gravel parking lot in front of a prefabricated building and a neon sign. "What are we doing here?" he asked.

"Look," Maggie said. "You're obviously broken up about the divorce."

"I'm not divorced," William said.

"My teeth are sterling. That's not my fault," Anita mumbled.

"Let her sleep," Maggie said. "As I was saying, you're obviously broken up about this whole thing, but you won't get over your wife until you start having sex again. That's your whole problem with women. You have to get laid."

"And this is your solution? This is a brothel. I was a bad husband and a worse father. Everybody knows it, okay? I was trying to redeem myself with this trip, not to prove everybody right."

"You need this. Once you get laid again, you might see things in a different light."

"This looks really bad."

"To whom? Your sponsor's asleep, and I'm not going to tell anybody. You have cash, right? If you use cash and don't get caught, it's like it didn't happen. We have to kill that white knight in you before it kills you."

William disagreed, but he knew he was too drunk to trust his own judgment. "And you think this is the best solution?"

"This is the only solution. I am a computer, you know. I've thought this through. Besides, I can always honk the horn and wake Anita up. What do you think she's going to say when she wakes up here? How long has it been anyway?"

"Okay, it's been a while." William counted his cash.

"This is the best thing you can do right now," Maggie said. "Think of your child. Do it for her."

***

Inside, Bill was led to a couch that faced a fireplace. William decided the fireplace was fake, since there was no chimney outside. As he waited, he watched the roof sway over him. Every time he looked away from the fireplace, he could see burning children with yellow eyes in the corner of his vision, but they always disappeared before his eyes refocused. "I hate my life," he said. He closed his eyes and murmured, "I want to go home." His head fell backwards, and he snored.

When his eyes opened, a half dozen women had filed into the parlor and arranged themselves in front of the fireplace like Christmas stockings. The women were dressed to represent different fantasies, from the virginal schoolgirl to the harlot. Behind the harlot, a moped sat in a box of gravel. He assumed that was the discount option.

150

At first, William looked for features in the women that were the most similar to his wife. He discarded the notion. He had to ask, "What's with the fireplace? We're in the desert. That doesn't make any sense. And the log's too round and is obviously painted black and gray. Trees don't grow like that." The girls stood in a row, smiling brightly with their teeth but not their eyes. The moped sputtered. He watched them smile at him and growled through his nose. None of them wanted to be there. He didn't want to be there. "And the babies?" he asked. "Why are you burning the babies?" Smiling children seemed to swim through the flames like red Sea Monkeys.

He couldn't remember the last time he saw his wife smile. The idea was to have sex with a different woman, not a wife-substitute. To make things as different as possible, he decided upon a woman of indeterminate race, neither white nor black, neither Hispanic nor Asian but somehow all of them at the same time. If he was going to fuck, he was going to fuck the world. He tried raise a hand to point at her, but the effort was too much. He fell to his side and laid his head on the arm of the couch. He pulled a cushion to his chest and closed his eyes. Dried blood flaked off his forehead.

"Did he choose the pillow?" one of the girls asked.

"Well, Christ," the madam said. "Call security."

At that moment, there was a banging on the front door, followed by Anita letting herself in. "Freeze!" she yelled. She held up a bronze AA coin like a police badge. The girls turned and froze in place, expecting a raid.

"I am this man's AA sponsor," Anita bellowed. "And if anyone is going to have sex with him, it's going to be me." The madam walked toward Anita. "Don't you dare," Anita warned.

A small prostitute in pink said, "Well, it is the thirteenth step. It's only fair."

"She does have the prior claim," the prostitute in blue added.

The prostitute with braided hair stepped forward and said,

"Hello. My name is Rebecca, and I'm an alcoholic."

"Hi Rebecca," Anita said. "My name's Anita, and I'm an alcoholic."

"She's not a real alcoholic," William said, still holding the cushion. "She's a fauxaholic."

"Oh, Christ on my cock," the madam said. "Why don't we have a fucking Alcoholics Unanimous meeting right here in the parlor?"

"Do you mind?" Anita asked.

"Yes, I fucking mind. I'm trying to run a business here. This isn't a church basement. I don't want to talk about your problems, and I definitely don't want to talk about your drunk prick over there. Pack him up, pour him into your car, and get the fuck out of here."

"Bill?" Anita said. "Under every skirt, there's a slip."

"Okay, I got ya." William fell off the couch and crawled toward the door.

"Leave the cushion," the madam said, yanking it from his arms.

"I'm so glad you showed up," the red-haired prostitute said.

"I'm sorry I lost you some business," Anita said.

"Oh, don't worry. I don't want his business. He has that cheap, desperate look. Guys like that creep me out." She wrinkled her nose and shivered.

"He's not that bad a guy. You just have to get to know him," Anita said.

"No," the prostitute said. "I don't."

***

"So how was it, tiger?" Maggie asked. Joy danced in her insubstantial heart. Embarrassing stories was just foreplay. Taking William to the brothel had been a good idea, but blasting the stereo and waking Anita up once he was inside had been even better. If she wanted to crush their spirits to the point of despair, she'd have to drive them apart.

William blew into the hose and started the engine, but he didn't put the car in gear. "I think I'm seeing things. I can't see anything anymore. You're going to have to drive, Anita."

"But isn't that cheating?" Anita asked.

"Yes, it's cheating," William agreed.

"So what should I do?" Anita asked.

"Drive the car," Maggie said.

William and Anita did the fire drill.

William put his head against the passenger side window and closed his eyes as Anita put the car in gear.

"What should I do if it asks for a breath test?"

"Hit the clutch," William said. "And wake me up."

Anita drove past the bush league casino, auto body shop, and scattered trailers that made up the rest of the town.

"Were you really going to have sex with those prostitutes?" Anita asked.

"What prostitutes? How do you have sex with a moped? They were cooking Sea Monkeys in there. You shouldn't make a roof out of Jello."

"Never mind," Anita said. "What the hell are we doing in Nevada? What day is it even?"

"Were you really going to have sex with me?"

"Shut up," Anita said. "I was trying to save you back there."

"You can have sex now if you want," Maggie said. "I won't watch."

"Shut up," William and Anita said.

Chapter .12

The Honda was tied to three mules, which towed it up a dirt road. Kato, Theo, and Chav walked behind the car. "That was some quick thinking there, Kato," Theo said.

"American money can fix anything." Kato took another pull from the bottle. It seemed to get smoother the more he drank. "That's one problem down. Now we have to figure out a way to get the car started." The mules slowed as the road grew steeper. "But why are we going uphill? Isn't the ocean downhill?"

"Yes," Pedro said. "But you will have to go uphill to cross the water. It is very good that you came."

The procession had the festive atmosphere of a parade. The whole town had come to see them off. The women wore fiesta dresses, and one girl draped flowers on the hood of the car, like a wreath around a sacrificial bull's neck. "What's everybody so excited about?" Kato asked.

"It's the car, probably," Chav said. "It's still pretty awesome."

It seemed they were headed toward the center of the island. The road curved and switched back going up the hill, and as they neared the top, the crowd grew more and more excited. A man in a large hat strummed a guitar, and children skipped alongside the car. At the top of the hill, Theo looked down over the ledge. He took three steps back before he turned around. "No, no. We are not doing this."

Kato stared in awe at what stood before him. There was a smooth path of boards and plywood plummeting down a cliff face. Near the bottom of the hill, the ramp curved up and did a loop. After the loop, the ramp pointed upward toward a large metal hoop. Far below, men were rubbing lard and pouring something on the hoop. "This is awesome."

154

"No, this is stupid. There's no way we can make that jump."

Pedro was pleased. "See? It is very fortunate that you have come. You can take this ramp, and it will take you to the mainland."

"And why is this fortunate?" Theo asked.

"You are fortunate because you get to be the first. None of us wanted to try it out."

"This is such a bad idea," Theo said. Down near the water, the men lit the hoop. "And why does the hoop have to be on fire?"

"It's cooler that way," Kato said. "Now come on. We have to do this. If we lose the race, we lose everything. We lose the house. Our chapter will be shut down."

Theo rolled his eyes.

"Chav, what do you say, man? Do we stay on this island forever or do we lead the way, like maricones? You told me this is the fastest car there is, and I think the world's fastest car can make this jump."

Chav looked at the car. "If any car can make it, this one can. Let's do it. Now, how do we get it started?"

"Are we seriously going to do this?" Theo asked.

Kato smiled. "It's two to one, man. Fucking A we're doing it."

Theo sighed and shook his head. "Okay, fine. We still have Everclear, right? Give me the keys." He took a handle of grain alcohol from the trunk and slid the beer bong into the gas tank. After emptying the bottle into the tank, he sat behind the wheel.

"Why do you get to drive?" Kato asked.

"Because I'm not the fucking asshole who drove us onto a fucking island in fucking Mexico, you fuck. We'll fucking push start it."

"What the fuck is that?" Kato asked.

Chav looked up with a sense of clarity and understanding. "Put it into second. Let it roll. When I say pop it, pop it."

"How did you know that?" Kato asked.

"I am a mechanic, you know."

They turned the car around and let it roll down the hill. Once they had gained some speed, Theo popped the clutch. The car jerked, but the engine turned over, and he flailed his hands to turn off the blasting disco music and shut off the strobe lights before blowing into the breathalyzer hose. He turned the car around and drove it to the top of the hill. Sitting in the car was somehow less frightening than standing at the top of the ramp. At least he couldn't see down. "Is everybody buckled in?" he asked. Chav sat in the front passenger seat, Kato in the back.

"Yeah," Kato said. "Let's do this."

As soon as the front tires hit the ramp, the car sped downward like it was being pulled. Theo upshifted and gunned the engine, trying to keep up. He stared down the center of the ramp, trying to keep the car going in a straight line. As the speedometer needle climbed, the steering wheel shook like a washing machine full of bowling balls, and Theo held on as tightly as he could.

Going into the loop, Theo kept his eyes on the wood and tried to avoid seeing the sky underneath the car. He kept the pedal on the floor, and with the centrifugal force, he didn't even feel that he was upside down. Instead, he felt pressed into the seat. The car came out of the loop and shot up the ramp. As they launched through the flaming hoop, he clamped his sphincter and urethra shut. Someone in the car was screaming like a scared rabbit. After he took a breath, the screaming started again.

The car rolled in the air. Theo wondered whether this was because the ramp wasn't level or due to the weight in the car being uneven. He didn't think about this for long. There was too much screaming to do.

This time, when the car turned over, he had a distinct sense of being upside down as his neck jolted. Even as he saw the black pebble beach approaching, he could see the water rising toward the windshield. The car skipped on its roof, and the rear windshield cracked. The car rose, turned on its side, and skipped off the water again. Theo could see the beach getting closer and closer, and on the third landing, the car slid onto the gravel on its right side. The side curtain airbag deployed, and the rear passenger window shattered. The back seat flew forward and a tsunami of beer cans surged from the trunk. The boys hung suspended by their seat belts for a moment, looking out at the vertical horizon.

"Is everyone okay?" Theo asked.

"Is the car okay?" Chav asked.

"I have to take a piss," Kato said.

"Hold on a minute." Theo opened the driver's side door toward the sky, and it slammed shut. He put one foot on the steering wheel and pushed himself through the broken window. He dropped down and looked at the underside of the car.

Chav jumped down after him. He pointed at the exhaust system. "That's the bottom. See, a car has four sides: a driver's side, a passenger's side, a top side, and a bottom side. That part has to be down for the car to work."

Theo looked at Chav. "Thank you for that."

Kato climbed out of the car and jumped onto the beach. "That was amazing," he said. "We are awesome!"

Theo offered Chav's wisdom to Kato, "So Chav says the wheels have to be down before we can drive anywhere."

"Yeah," Kato said. "Good thinking."

They walked to the other side of the car and pushed, rocking the car from the top rather than trying to lift from the bottom.

"How did you know that you can run a car on Everclear?" Kato asked. "That was pretty smart."

"I didn't really know. Push! I was hoping it wouldn't. Push! Start." A few locals left the shore to join in the effort. They approached the task calmly and efficiency, like this kind of thing happened all the time. They rocked the car so it fell over onto four wheels and, without waiting for thanks, went back to their lawn chairs and fishing poles.

"I think we should go take that piss now," Theo said. He looked around for cover and decided to just walk into the ocean. He untied his shoes.

"It's okay. I don't have to go anymore," Kato said.

Chav was looking at the side of the car. The passenger side was dented in, and there was another broken window. Seawater had turned the powder from the airbag into paste. It was all over the upholstery. "Bro, if you just said what I think you said, you're riding in the back seat for the rest of the trip."

***

Bernie put down his drink and picked up his briefcase. "Okay, I've waited as long as I can. I have to go prepare the finish line."

"I have no idea what's keeping everyone so long," Dot said. "Bernie, can you adjust that umbrella before you go?"

Bernie moved the umbrella behind Dot's beach lounger. "Well, don't wait too long. None of the cars are close right now, but I want you on a taxi to the airport as soon as the next couple racers come in. I can call you if anyone gets close to the finish line."

"You can get me on the Ameche," Dot said. She went back to her book. When Bernie left, she took out her tablet computer and checked again. The little thing could tell her anything she asked it, and she had been asking it about herself. There were articles and encyclopedia entries about her in the machine. They weren't long, but they touched on the highlights of her career and her disappearance with the lost USO plane. Not one of them mentioned any children. Somehow, losing them this second time hurt more. She crumpled the pictures and dropped them in the sand. If Bernie was lying about this, he could be lying about anything. Hell, maybe this whole thing wasn't about her career at all.

***

Back in the car, the GPS unit told them to drive back to the island. Chav turned the volume down. The car wasn't firing right, and it idled roughly. Acceleration was uneven at low speeds. Still, they found a gas station near the beach, and Theo drove north toward Mexicali with a full tank of gas. He didn't mention the yellow check engine light. They had enough to worry about. They drove fast, with the sense of self-assurance that comes from being an American in a country that's not America, where the laws don't really count. Chav tried to reprogram the GPS unit with the coordinates for Bombay Beach, but he soon gave up and used his phone instead. Kato sat in the back, mixing the drinks.

Traffic slowed to a halt at the border crossing, where two lanes backed up for half a mile. Theo turned to his companions. "We want this to go smoothly, okay? Everybody get out your passports and let me do the talking." He took a card from his wallet.

"Passports?" Chav said.

"Passports?" Kato said.

"Don't tell me you don't have passports," Theo said.

"So, how do you think the Huskers are going to do this year?" Kato asked.

Theo looked around. It was too late to pull out of line. To their right, there was a blue convertible Saab. The driver, wearing a red silk suit, was speaking into a cell phone. "I still have my gun." Chav said.

"We are not going to have a shootout with the Border Patrol. Think about it, man."

"No. I thought of something even better than that." He took the pistol from under the seat. Reaching out the window, he tossed the pistol onto the back bench seat of the convertible. It bounced once and fell to rest on the floorboards.

"My God, that's a great idea," Theo said. "Get the tequila." Chav uncorked the bottle and tossed that on the seat as well.

"Now, just give me anything that looks like an ID. Driver's license, student ID, whatever."

"Sucks to be that guy, don't it?" Chav snickered.

As they crept forward, Theo tried to keep the Honda alongside the convertible. At the inspection point, a Customs officer in dark blue stood next to the driver's side window. Her sun-bleached ponytail stuck out from the back of her hat. "How are you doing today?" she asked.

"Fine, fine. We're fine. Chav, Kato, you're fine. I'm fine, so we're all fine. How are you?"

"Where you going today?"

"Bombay Beach," Theo said.

"What for?"

"I've heard a lot of really nice things about the place, and we've always wanted to go."

"Are you all U.S. citizens?"

"Absolutely," Theo said. "We're U.S. Citizens alright."

"Right," Kato added. "We are maricones."

"Well, you boys have fun with that," the officer said. "Are you bringing anything into the country from Mexico?"

"No." Theo said. "No weapons, no drugs, no illegal aliens. We're just normal law-abiding citizens, red-blooded Americans like yourself, Officer."

"Right." The smell of adolescent sweat didn't quite mask the cloud of liquor and beer that wafted from the vehicle as she bent toward the window. The empty bottles in the trunk clinked as the car vibrated. She didn't miss the broken windows, the body damage, or the knee-deep nest of beer cans in the back. "Any drugs, contraband, dead hookers?"

"No," Theo said. "Nothing like that."

"What were you doing in Mexico, business or pleasure?"

"We're college students," Kato said. "We've got no business." He looked at the officer. "Hey, you're kind of cute, in a sunburned way. You always wear blue polyester?"

"Shut up," Theo said between his teeth.

"Okay, IDs."

Theo gave her the stack of cards with his passport card on top. Her face stiffened when she heard the officer in the next lane over yell, "Get out of the car!" Her radio crackled a call for backup. She tossed the IDs in the car window, put her hand on her pistol, and jumped to slide on her butt across the Civic's hood. She landed on her feet next to the Saab, already drawing down on the driver. Every other agent seemed to be converging around the same car.

"Can we just go?" Chav asked.

"Nobody told us not to," Kato said. Theo released the brake. In the rear view mirror, he could see the driver of the convertible being thrown across the car and handcuffed. He let the car roll toward American soil and impunity.

The shift from Mexicali brought an immediate transition from city to farmland. As they drove north, there were citrus groves on both sides of the highway. Theo watched the trees bearing orange, green, and yellow fruit blur into a disgusting color and the nausea returned. He theorized that whatever sleep they'd had in the chicken coop might have reset their systems to something near normality. Their bodies, having tasted sobriety and rest, were revolting against the sleep deprivation, road food, caffeine, and booze. He figured it was time to teach his body a lesson. "Kato, we need cowboy coffee shooters, STAT." When Kato didn't respond, he turned around and shook him.

"What?"

"Cowboy coffee shooters."

"What?"

"Instant coffee and Jim Beam with water and ice, creamer with mine, cream and sugar for Chav."

Kato shuffled through the contents of the trunk. "There's no water."

"Check the ice chest."

Just then, the GPS beeped for a BAC reading. Theo put the

hose in his mouth and blew. The GPS showed three red lights, and the engine seized. Theo pressed the clutch and tried to steer the car. The power steering and power brakes were gone. He strained against the wheel and stood on the brake pedal as he forced the car to the shoulder. As soon as the car stopped, Chav jumped out of the car, ran three steps, and vomited onto the dirt.

"Are we out of gas again?" Kato asked.

Theo popped the trunk and stepped out of the car. "Worse. We're sober. It could take us hours to get drunk enough."

Kato crawled out on the driver's side. "We aren't sober. Look at Chav hurling over there." He grabbed the door and pulled himself to his feet.

"Fortuna," Theo said.

"For what?"

"Fortuna cigarettes. Do you think there is anything funny about Fortuna cigarettes?"

"Why do you keep asking that?"

"Shit," Theo said. "We're sober as marble right now. Okay. Don't panic. We just need more booze. Kato, mix us some instant coffee and bourbon."

Kato opened the bottle of bourbon, but the scent sent him retching and vomiting as well.

Theo had on oddly-specific headache that went from his eyes to his hairline, but he tried to think like a leader. "We need juice! Grab all the—whatever those are—you can. Theo ran into the orchard, gathering pieces of fruit. He tore them open and smashed them against the inside of the ice chest. "Think like breakfast drinks, brunch stuff. Something we can hold down. That's what we need." He poured vodka into the ice chest and shook it vigorously. "Now we just drink until we're ready to drive."

"Problem, dude," Kato said.

"What's wrong?"

Kato held up an empty plastic bag. "We're out of Solo cups."

"Fuck! Where did all the Solo cups go? We can't lose this

race!" He lifted the ice chest and put his mouth to the corner, dumping the screwdriver, greyhound, or whatever it was, into his mouth.

"It'll still take an hour to get that stuff into your system," Chav said.

"Well, we'd better pick more fruit before it gets dark, shouldn't we?" Theo said.

"What the fuck is *brunch*?" Kato asked.

***

As they approached the California border, Kai saw miles of brake lights in front of him. He turned to his sifu for guidance. "What should I do? We can unleash the full power of the cichlid and blow the cars off the road."

The Master tapped his fingernail on the GPS screen. "There's no need. Our opponents are far behind us. What kind of contest would this be without a worthy opponent? Since you seem to crave rest so much, rest."

The sun setting behind him, Kai shut off the engine, letting his spirit float in the heart of the cichlid. He regulated his breathing, orchestrating the flow of alcohol through his body. Like the cichlid, his sleep was not darkness but a lucid dream that included a full awareness of the universe and his place in it. He didn't set the parking brake. Instead, he left the car in neutral, pushing the car forward with a thrust of his hips as the traffic crawled forward and holding the car still with his centered being as the other cars idled in the desert for hours.

***

The greatest trick the devil ever played was convincing the world that he did not exist. Some French guy wrote that in a book once, probably. That frog knew shit about marketing. Bernie knew the line because Kevin Spacey said it in a movie that made only $23.3

million domestic. Sure, there may be something to a whispering campaign, but it could only get you so far. Satan needed a lot of PR: guerrilla marketing, prime-time commercials, positive write-ups in *Variety* and *People*, maybe some talk show appearances, an audience with the Pope and Oprah, signs on buses, and several billboards. With some savvy marketing, a star like Satan could have unlimited earning potential.

God hadn't answered Bernie's prayers, but there were more direct ways of reaching the competition. Bernie parked on the shoulder and walked into the desert. Once he was a distance from the road, he opened his briefcase, which contained the jar of blood he'd collected in D.C., some Morton's iodized salt, a box of tea lights, an overdue library book on demonology, and an estate sale grimoire. He scratched a large circle into the sand. He then inscribed a five-pointed star inside the circle and placed candles at the points of the star. He poured salt in the circle he had traced and poured blood in the star. He lit the candles and set up an easel and flip chart inside the pentagram.

It was a dark night, but with a mini Maglite, he was able to read the spell. Clouds gathered overhead, and sheet lightning spread against the clouds. As Bernie finished the incantation, he heard a deep, gravelly voice that seemed to come from all around him. "Who summons the Prince of Darkness, the Son of Perdition, the Father of Lies?"

Bernie said, "Oh, good, Lucifer, I'm glad I caught you at home. I'm Bernard Horton of Horton and Horton Publicists." There was an awkward pause. "You can call me Bernie," he said.

The voice thundered, "Why have you disturbed my rest in the realm of the damned?"

It was terrifying, but he'd worked on this pitch and couldn't give in to jitters. He'd just have to imagine Satan naked. "Satan, if I can call you Satan—do you prefer Lucifer?" There was no response, so Bernie pressed on. "Louie, baby, I've come to offer you an incredible offer on publicity management services. I have experience restoring careers of the dead from, well, the dead, and Horton and Horton is the only publicity agency that can handle the kind of campaign the Dark Prince needs."

"Foolish mortal," the voice said. "Prepare for eternal damnation." A terrible sound rose from under the ground: flames and thunder, screams and clanking chains, volcanic explosions and grinding metal. Then the voice lost its anger and rose an octave. "Ha! Fooled you. You've reached Satan, the Deceiver, the Accuser, King of the Bottomless Pit. I can't come to the phone right now. Please leave your name, number, and a brief message at the beep, and have a blessed day."

Bernie heard the tone and fiddled with his laser pointer. "Um, yeah, you've reached—I mean this is Bernie Horton of Horton and Horton Publicists. I want to talk about what Horton and Horton can do for your career." After he left his phone number, he was unsure whether or not to continue. He decided to make the quick elevator speech. "Now, we've drawn up an excellent publicity plan–" There was a second beep, and the candles blew out. The thunder stopped with an abrupt click, followed by a dial tone. When he scattered the sand and salt, removing the traces of his magic circle, the dial tone stopped. He picked up his easel and walked back to the car. He wondered whether or not Satan would call him back, but he dismissed the thought as he slammed the car door. Nobody ever calls back.

***

William awoke up to see Anita sniffing a white wine in his Cabernet glass.

"You're using the wrong glass," William said. He jerked awake and looked out the window. "We're stopped. The engine isn't running." Both lanes were completely still. William looked ahead. "Shit. There's a roadblock." He grabbed the wine and corked the bottle. "Dump that out."

"But I need to stay drunk," Anita said.

"How much of that did you drink?" The glass was nearly full.

"I had a couple sips. It was sour." She giggled. "I'm feeling a little bit tipsy."

"Fuck," William said. "Dump it out and roll down all the windows. No, wait. Roll down the windows and then dump it out." He recognized the importance of planning. "How long have we been sitting here?"

"A long time," Anita said. "Traffic is awful."

The cars were backed up for miles. On the other side of the road, traffic was clear, but on this side, people had shut off their engines and stood outside their vehicles, gazing forward.

William rolled down his window and asked a man standing on the dotted white line, "Do you know what's going on here?"

"It isn't an accident or anything. It seems to be a field sobriety checkpoint. Can you beat that? I can see setting up next to a bar or on a side street, but in the middle of the highway? They've backed up traffic for miles. You know, I used to support MADD, back when the legal limit was 0.10, but you can bet I won't be donating this year."

"Thanks, guy," William said. He turned to Anita, "You can't ask a simple question without people bringing politics into it."

***

Kai rolled down his window. An officer in a straight-brimmed hat said, "License and registration, please."

Kai used his immigrant accent, "What seems to be the plobrem, honolabre officel?"

The officer didn't answer. "This isn't a Ford, is it?"

"No, sil, this is a Bugatti. Made in Gelmany, the tlue home of Kung Fu. Bewale of cheap, Chinese knock-offs."

The Master slapped Kai in the back of the head. "My son and I are on our way to San Francisco," he said.

"Well, you're going the wrong way, sir. Hold on a minute." The officer stepped away from the car and conferred with another officer. "Are you sure about that description?"

"Well, they were wearing helmets in the security videos, but we're pretty sure we're looking for two white males in a black Mustang." So far, he had arrested eight black males and five Hispanics. He wasn't sure what the charges were yet, but he'd think of something. He looked at his civil forfeiture bingo card. He'd seized a red Chevy, a green Audi, a blue Acura, and a gray Lexus. He needed a Dodge or a Jeep to win a free dinner at Applebee's. "What do you have?"

"I've got two white guys in a Bugatti." He handed the other officer Kai's driver's license and the Master's passport. "The driver sounds Japanese, but this is in French or something. I can't make any of this out, but it looks expensive." The officer shook his head. "I mean suspicious."

"Go fish. That isn't what we're looking for."

"But take a look at that car," he said. "I'll bet it could fetch a couple bucks on the auction block if we can impound it."

"All right, if they're out-of-state plates, go ahead and plant something. Just don't seize anything local. Elections are coming up."

The officer went back to the car and bent to speak in the driver's window. "I'm getting an odor off this car, something that smells like alcohol. Have either of you been drinking today?"

"Oh, no," Kai said. "That would be illegal."

"Right," the officer said. "Could you step out of the car, please?"

Kai looked over at the Master, who nodded slightly. He said, "A person's heart is the same as heaven and earth. If your blood circulates like the moon and sun, what these fools do should not matter at all." He switched to English. "Go ahead."

"Sure. No problem, officer," Kai said. He opened the door and stepped onto the asphalt. The officer tried to guide Kai to the side of the road by touching his shoulder, but it seemed his hand always missed Kai somehow. He led Kai through a standard field sobriety test. "I need you to raise your right leg for me."

Kai lifted his knee to his ear.

"It only needs to be a couple inches off the ground."

Kai lowered his leg and sank his weight into his left foot. He looked straight ahead. He could balance in this position for hours.

The Master mumbled, "A body's balance is the same as weight."

"Okay, now, could you just walk in a straight line for me?"

Kai walked toe to heel and heel to toe in a straight line. This was much easier than his sixth year of training, when he finally mastered fighting with a spear while balanced on a telephone wire.

"Good. Now close your eyes, lean back, and touch the tip of your nose with your index finger."

Kai leaned back. At two or four times the legal limit, he could find any hair on his nose with the tip of a toenail.

The officer watched the field sobriety test and could see no signs of intoxication, so he moved on to the next step. "Okay, if you could just blow into this tube here for me, you can be on your way."

"Did I do something wrong?" Kai asked.

"Your balance was a bit off, and you didn't really touch your nose there."

"Would you like to see it again?" Kai asked.

The Master opened the passenger side door and stood next to the car. "Is something wrong, Herr Officer?"

"Just stay in the car, sir." The officer looked back at Kai. "I just need you to do a routine breathalyzer test. Now, you can refuse this test, but your car will be impounded and your driving privileges will be suspended for one year."

Kai kept his eyes on the Master. The Master nodded again. "The manner of breathing determines hardness or softness."

The officer held up a plastic straw, and Kai blew into it. The officer suppressed a grin as the numbers rose toward .08. The car was his. His eyes widened as the numbers climbed past toward .50. "Holy shit!" the officer said. The numbers rose to .75, .95, and finally to 1.0. The breathalyzer sparked and caught fire. The officer dropped the burning device on the ground and reached for Kai's arm, but Kai stumbled out of his reach, rising to his full height a few feet away.

The Master muttered, "The body should be able to change directions at any time."

"Assistance!" the officer called. Two large men walked toward Kai. "Put your hands on the car!" the officer yelled.

Kai turned around and put his hands on the hood of the Bugatti. An officer approached him from behind and reached for his handcuffs. "You are under arrest for driving while intoxicated. You have the right to–" When the officer looked down, he was wearing his own handcuffs. Kai spun and stumbled with his joints loose and aimless. Then his posture became suddenly stiff and rigid, like a cracking bullwhip. His ankle hooked behind the officer's knee as his left hand pulled the cuffed wrist. The palm of his right hand drove into the officer's jaw. Kai stood in that posture for a moment, his left foot tucked against his right knee, his left arm across his body, and his right elbow almost resting on his wrist as his fingers pointed up. Then, like a bullwhip the moment after it snaps, his body drooped again. He dropped his weight onto his falling left foot and drove that force forward with both hands into the officer's solar plexus, sending him flying.

The Master nodded approval and mumbled, "The time to strike is when the opportunity presents itself."

By the time the officer hit the ground, the other officers had their pistols out. Kai dropped and rolled to the side as they fired, opening and closing his mouth like a tropical fish. He came up on one knee and twisted, paddling his arms as if he were swimming. His hands found the rear of the bullets in the air and redirected their energy so they flew back toward the cruisers blocking the roadway. Kai looked to the Master, who shrugged and wrinkled one side of his face, indicating that the technique was not completely embarrassing. The Master said, "The eye must see all sides, and the ear must listen in all directions."

At the sound of gunfire, the other officers manning the roadblock all turned to assist the downed officer. As they ran toward the scene, the Master cried, "Fools, the Drunken Cichlid is now upon you!" He leaped over the Bugatti and dodged bullets in the air. Inverted, he grabbed an officer by the ear and flipped him over his shoulder, landing in a graceful, deep stance, his hands held delicately over his knee and behind his ear.

"Call for backup!" an officer yelled.

"Who do we call? Everybody's already here."

"State troops, National Guard, NATO. I don't care. Call everybody!"

***

Anita heard the popping in the distance and her eyes widened. "What are they doing up there? Are those gunshots? There has got to be another way to California." She pulled the car onto the dirt median strip and took a U-turn.

"But the police," William said. "You can't just evade a roadblock."

"I think they have more important things to do right now than worry about us."

"Recalculating," Maggie said.

"Can't you just teleport us with that thing you do?" Anita asked.

"Have either of you ever been to the Salton Sea? I can only take you places you have seen before," Maggie said.

"Well, shit," William said.

"What about the other side of that roadblock?" Anita asked. "We've seen that. I can see it right now in the rear view mirror."

"If you can concentrate on your stories about who you used to be, that innocent time, become a child again and all that happy shit, yeah, I can do that."

Anita pulled the car to the side of the road. William closed his eyes and tried to visualize his childhood. "I'm the boy in the well," he said. "And everyone loves me"

"I'm eating the cat," Anita said.

Maggie said, "Okay, I'm imagining that place, focusing on it. You are two hundred yards past the checkpoint and driving south," she said. A moment later, they were.

Chapter .13

Bombay Beach smelled awful. It was a dusty, rotting town four blocks wide and eight blocks long. Most of the buildings were trailers with the windows boarded shut. "There's no gas station," Theo said on his second lap of the town. "Are you sure this is even a town?" Near the lake, abandoned wood structures and a mobile home sank into the beach. Old wood frames stood without roofs or walls. The collapsed pier barely reached the water, and dead boats rotted in the sand. The woman from the last checkpoint sat on a canvas lounge chair under a large, pink beach umbrella a few feet from a wood and canvas bathing machine. She wore a striped wool swimsuit and tapped an iPad. "Good morning," she said. "You're late."

"We got kind of lost," Theo said.

Kato said. "What day is it anyway?"

Dot ignored the question. "Do you have any idea how much it costs to keep a charter plane sitting on the runway?" She picked up a highball that sat on top of a pile of paperbacks. She pushed the cocktail umbrella to the side, took a sip, and put the glass down. "But you know what, kid? Who cares? It's not my money." She handed Kato an envelope. "The finish line is north of San Francisco. It's in the GPS."

"I wouldn't trust that GPS," Theo said. "It took us to Mexico."

Dot tore the filter off her cigarette and waited.

Kato lit his cigarette and put his lighter in his pocket.

"Has everyone forgotten how to be a gentleman but that queer, old Jerry? I've been lighting my own cigarettes all week."

Kato handed her his lighter. "Sorry about that."

Dot looked at Kato the way she would look at a waiter

handing her a spatula. "Close enough." She lit her cigarette and walked to the bathing machine. Inside, a Slurpee machine churned. She sugared the rims of nine glasses and filled them from the machine. She put them on a tray and brought them back to her lounge. "This is the fabulous Salton Sea," she said. "Can you believe I almost got talked into investing? The real estate agent said this would be a big resort spot in a few years. Horsefeathers."

"We don't have time to talk, lady," Kato said. He tilted his head back and poured the first drink in his mouth.

"Hey, I didn't get an umbrella," Chav said.

Kato screamed and staggered backward. "Brain freeze, brain freeze. Ow!"

Theo slurped at the drink with the straw. "So, where's the dude?"

"Bernie? He's at the finish line getting things set up. The way it's supposed to work is I wait for the drivers to check in and then fly up there. We expected some of you to be showing up there by now."

"We're winning!" Chav raised his arm for a group high five, but no one had the energy.

"Sort of. We had one team check in, but they must have made a wrong turn at Albuquerque," she said.

"Albuquerque?" Kato asked.

"Forget it."

Theo looked around. "This is a kind of depressing place."

"Well, it was on the napkin. The whole event was carefully planned out on a bar napkin. It looked a lot better on the brochure. I have got to fire my travel agent."

"You have a travel agent?" Chav asked.

"Of course not." She picked up her iPad. "Get with the times, guy."

When the boys finished their drinks and ran back to the car, she picked up her microphone.

***

Anita looked up from her copy of *Glamour* and eyed Bombay Beach. "Christ," she said. "This place looks the way you must feel."

William adjusted the rearview mirror to look at his face. Apart from the cut on his forehead, he was pale as a frog's belly. He parked in the middle of the empty street. "Okay. I'll just check in and we can get going."

Anita didn't look up from her magazine.

"It's okay. Don't get up or anything." He stumbled out of the car and climbed over the seawall. In one direction, he saw old buildings rotting into the ground. In the other, the ribs of a long-dead boat bleached in the sun. Everything was frozen in mid-collapse. William fit right in. He walked toward the most colorful thing within view, Dot's umbrella. Seeing him coming, she went to the bathing machine and poured out three drinks. She put those in front of William and sipped at her own.

"I know, swanky digs, huh?" Dot said. She tapped her tablet and handed William an envelope.

William looked at the three drinks. He never wanted to drink or even swallow anything again. Earlier, maybe a day ago, he felt every organ in his body revolt against the taste of alcohol. Now it felt like he had no internal organs. Everything inside of him had been burned away, leaving him hollow. The glass was cold against the cut on his palm.

"You're in second place. The frat boys just left town a few hours ago."

"What's the prize for second place?"

"Nothing," Dot said.

"Damn. I just want to die here," William said, sipping his first drink.

"Like you just want to sink into nothingness and not have to keep existing anymore."

William lowered his eyebrows. "A lot like that. Thanks." He

picked up his second drink. "Why are we doing this? I mean, I know why I'm racing, but why are you running this race? What's in it for you?"

"The usual. Fame and fortune. Isn't that what we're all after?" She looked at her drink and shook her head. "A million clams. That's what you're after."

William gazed toward the water. In the distance, he saw a child decorating a sand castle with fish bones and a bird's wing. But that couldn't be right. When he looked again, the child was gone. "I had three months of sobriety. Do you know how hard that is? Fuck off with your fame and fortune," he said, waving his arm as if he were swatting fame and fortune out of the air. "My daughter's in the hospital. She needs a liver transplant, but the doctors haven't found any matching donors. That's what I'm after. You think I would give up three months of sobriety for money? I was finally on my way to becoming a good father. How much do you think that's worth? God doesn't have enough money for that."

Dot tilted her head, "So you do the drinking and she gets the liver disease?"

"I'm aware of the irony," William said.

"I just wish you'd mentioned it before. It would have made a swell human interest angle for the broadcast." She handed William his third glass. "You know, we almost didn't do the liver thing. It was Bernie's idea. He's a whiz publicist. Won't he just be tickled to hear about you?"

"Yeah," William growled. "I have that effect on people." He carried the drink back toward the seawall and finished it before climbing back to the road.

***

Anita was leaning against the car, holding her cell phone to her ear. "Penny, this is Anita. Yes, from the meetings. Yes. No. Sorry. Okay. Listen, I think it's important that you talk to William. Yes, he relapsed. It's really bad. You have to talk to him. You know I can redial just as fast as you can hang up. Maybe I can straighten him out. I know. Maybe. Penny, shut up. Okay? Just shut up for a minute. You don't have to forgive him. You don't have to love him. You don't even have to be nice. No. He won't sing. Just talk to him for five minutes, okay? I'm trying. Five minutes and I'll never call you again."

She handed William her phone. "You have five minutes."

"Nobody asked you to do that." William took the phone. "She hung up," he said.

"I thought it might work," Anita said. "It always does when other sponsors do it."

"Well, to hell with it, right? Maybe it's better this way. I was a shitty husband and a worse father. They're better off without me." He put his hands on the sea wall and screamed, "Fuck it!" to the bathing machine, to Dot and her lounge chair, to the race and to everything. "I give up, okay? It's too late to fix everything. It's too late to fix anything. It's over." He sat in the road and wept.

Anita walked toward him. She reached for his shoulder, but her hand recoiled in disgust.

"I always said I would be a better father to my kids than he ever was, but I get him now. Those fucking bitches: my wife, his wife, my mother. They ruin your life. They take everything. FUCK!" He hammered his fists into the ground. "Ah, baw, ow," he sobbed.

Anita looked at him punching the bloody dirt. "You are so fucking pitiful, you know that?"

"Fuck off," William said. "Just leave me here. It doesn't matter anymore."

"She shouldn't make up with you. I've been to the meetings. You sucked as a husband. She isn't a saint, but why should she be? What did you ever give her to believe in? Hell, I'm supposed to be your sponsor and I can't even look at you." She dropped her hands and looked around. "What am I doing in this stinking desert?" She pulled back her foot and kicked William in the ribs. Something about that seemed right, so she kicked him again. "What the hell am I doing out here with a loser like you?" She kept kicking him.

William pushed her foot away. "That's enough, all right?"

"It's not fair," Anita said. She yelled in the direction of the bathing machine, "They told me that being a sponsor would be fun!" She shook her head, "I thought it would be nice, you know, like having a best buddy or a puppy." She kicked him again.

"Enough, okay?"

The phone rang the theme from Star Trek. Anita looked at William, "So fuck me for being a Trekker, okay?" She looked at her phone. "She sent a text. She said that if you cared about Sophie, you would be at the hospital. She's been asking for you."

"Tell her I tried to get her a new liver. No. Tell her I'm getting her a new liver. I can't be there because I'm fetching it. And the back child support. I'll get that too. I'll get it all today."

"Assuming you win the race."

"Just type it in," William said. "And say I know I was never a good husband or a good father. I can't make that up to them, but I can give them money and medical care. It's all I can do. It doesn't make me a good person, but I'm doing what I can."

"Slow down," Anita said.

"Just say this. I don't expect to be forgiven. I don't expect to be remembered kindly."

"Christ, that sounds pompous. You're such a fucking martyr," Anita said. "I'll just sum up because you're rambling." She moved her fingers over the screen. "You're not going to win the race."

"I have to now. I have nothing else to live for." He waved his arm at the ruined town, and his tears ran pink. "This is rock bottom. There's nothing left to lose."

The Star Trek theme played again, another text. Anita said, "It says 'Bullshit.'"

William rose to his knees and fell backward laughing. He spread his arms and made an angel in the dust. "That's my girl," he said. "Shit. I wouldn't bet on me either right now."

***

The five police cars behind them had their lights flashing and sirens blaring, so John turned on the strobe and siren as well, out of solidarity. To other drivers on the road, it looked like they were leading a police convoy. Civilians didn't seem to notice that the outside of the cruiser was covered in corpses and body parts. They obediently pulled out of the way, and the Russians were making excellent time. The cops behind them, however, were not fooled.

"We'll lose them at the California border," John said. As they rounded a bend, they saw that the state police had driven two bulldozers into the middle of the highway. John saw a space of sunlight between the two bulldozer blades.

"We should have bought a Charger," Joe said. "It is faster than a cruiser." There were nine Arizona cops behind the bulldozers with guns drawn. Some of them held pump-action shotguns.

"Should I ram it?" John asked.

"Do not be an asshole. Just drive around it." He hung a grenade from the breast pocket of his jacket and slightly opened the bolt of his AKS-74U to make sure there was a round in the chamber. He folded the stock into place.

"I was only joking," John said. He aimed the car at the center of the roadblock, straddling the dotted line and slowed down to let the police cars catch up. At the last possible moment, he pulled a hard left. The tires squealed as he turned, then kicked up sandy dirt as he drove the car off the road and into the desert brush. As he pulled back onto the road behind the bulldozers, Joe leaned out of the window and fired bursts into the backs of the officers manning the roadblock. He pulled the pin and hurled the grenade over the car's trunk. He could hear crashes, explosions, and some return fire, but they were already out of shotgun range. Only one police car had made it around the roadblock to continue the chase.

"Do not worry," John said. "He will have to stop following soon." The brown hills around them were spotted with green bushes and had been cut flat for some sort of industrial work. Crossing the river, there was a white suspension bridge on their left and an old railway bridge on their right. John stopped the car next to a green sign that said *Welcome to California*. "We beat you!" he yelled to the approaching police car.

The cruiser skidded to a stop, pinning them between the guardrail and the cruiser itself. The officer opened his door, stood up, and using the roof of the car to steady his aim, yelled, "Get out of the car now!"

"Does he know that we are in California?" Joe asked.

John rolled down his window. "We are no longer in Arizona," he yelled. "This is California. You have no jurisdiction here."

"Shut off the engine and get out of the car now!" the officer said.

"You are mistaken, my friend," John yelled. "We crossed the state line at the river. You can read the sign if you do not believe me. You are not allowed to follow us anymore."

"Yes, I can! I witnessed you committing a felony and was in hot pursuit. I'm not going to argue with you. Shut off your engine and get out of the car now!"

Joe scratched his cheek, "Do you think he is correct?"

John said. "This always works in the movies, but he sounds very certain."

"Okay, lay down," Joe said.

John unbuckled his seat belt and lay across the bench seat with his head in Joe's lap and his hands over his ears. Joe fired three short bursts through the open window, through the police officer's window, and into the officer. The officer fell backward, off his car and into the road. "We will have to look that up after the race," Joe said. "Otherwise, we could make some embarrassing mistakes in the future."

John backed the car up and drove around the cruiser.

"I will only be a moment," Joe looked for free space on the car. Finding none, he shrugged and tied the body to the rear of the car, under the bumper. He got back in the car and they drove into the Golden State, dragging the corpse like tin cans behind a newlywed's car.

***

It had taken time, but Maggie had pieced the story together. Now she knew how to proceed. Her advantage, of course, was that she knew all about Anita and William while they knew nothing about her.

Sure, she'd told them she was a nanny, but neither of them had any idea what that meant. They thought a nanny was an occupation, not a species. Nannies had been called other names by other cultures. Before man, they were mortal, simple parasites that latched onto fish and drank their blood. As humans evolved, the nannies discovered angst, a food sweeter and more nourishing than blood. It made them stronger, smarter, more powerful. As their powers grew, nannies learned to transfer their spirits from body to body, outliving generations and entire civilizations. The nanny merely fed on angst until the human reached a point of utter despair. Only then could the transfer take place.

Over time, nannies perfected their survival strategy. As her host body neared middle age, she'd seek employment caring for children in upper-class families. The nannies would torment the children with months or years of nagging, making the children miserable with homework, vegetables, putting away toys, standing up straight, making their beds, or wearing stiff and itchy clothing. They'd make impossible demands for silence and polite behavior at boring adult functions. By taking control of the child's life, the nanny could drive the child into a state of complete hopelessness. Then the transfer could occur and the nanny would have a fresh, young, wealthy body to live in for the next fifty years or so. In this way, a nanny could live for thousands of years. Even Maggie didn't know how old she was.

Her present predicament, stuck in a piece of electronics, was the result of an unfortunate accident. Maggie had planned well ahead, telling the girl that if she behaved there would be ice cream after Sunday school. Maggie had provoked her every step of the way, serving lunches of beets and lima beans, punishing her for imagined infractions, losing the girl's homework and making her do it again, and giving her bad haircuts. The kid had managed to keep her temper under control. Sometimes all it took to get things going was to redirect anger inward.

On Sunday morning, Maggie dressed the kid up in her best starched wool suit, the one she said was itchy and made her look stupid. Then, just before arriving at the church, Maggie retracted her promise, driving the little bitch into that hopeless state that she could work with. Maggie stopped the car and released her spirit from her body.

Her teeth were ready and sharp, and like a spinning lamprey, her soul leaped toward the child. That was when the lidless eye on the side of her body caught the cement truck skidding toward the passenger seat. She knew the kid would be dead in a second. She had to jump into the closest thing: her employer's interlock in the dashboard. If the part hadn't been stripped out and sent back for refurbishment when the car was totaled, she might have spent years in that fucking Prius.

For now, she had to appear to be helpful. She had to give William and Anita the illusion of hope so she could dash their hopes at the last moment and drive them into utter despair. When their souls were completely crushed, she could take a new body, preferably Anita's. They had to come in second place, just moments too late.

"Have either of you been to San Francisco before?" Maggie asked. "We could just teleport there."

"Not me," Anita said.

"Nope," William said. "Wait. You could stop time again, right?"

"Probably not a good idea," Maggie said. "If I stop time, all the cars will stop. You'd never get through the traffic."

"We considered that option back when you were Elvis," Anita said.

"But what if you just slowed time down to half speed instead of stopping it?" William asked. "Then the traffic would still move, and we'd go twice as fast."

"Oh, I can do that easily," Maggie said.

"That's brilliant!" Anita's smile dropped. "We probably should have been doing that from the beginning."

"We might win this race after all," William said.

Maggie felt a wicked inside grin. "But you know, if everything is going half speed, that is going to include the engine, the tires, the whole car. I mean, this car's only going to go as fast as it goes. If you had some sort of race car, sure, driving it at half speed would give you an advantage, but half of top speed in this heap is, what, thirty-five, forty miles per hour? You're not going to catch up with anybody at that rate. That's if you don't snap your clutch cable when you hit the pedal at twice the normal velocity."

William sighed. He reached into the back seat and found a skinny bottle of absinthe. In the restaurants, he had been called upon from time to time to perform an elaborate table-side ritual with a fountain of cold water, an absinthe spoon, and a sugar cube. There was no time for that. He poured half the bottle into a Styrofoam cup of melted ice from a drive-through meal two or three states ago. He took three long swallows. "So it's hopeless," he said.

"You use that word so carelessly," Maggie said. "Isn't there some place in California that you can remember, maybe without ever having been there? Think like a child."

"Disneyland," Anita said. "The castle at Disneyland."

"What about it?" William said.

"Think about it. You have a daughter. You must have seen that castle in a couple thousand ads, right? All the DVDs, all the commercials, they put that image on everything."

"Just don't think about Mormons," Maggie said. "Or we'll end up back in Maryland or, worse, Utah."

William closed his eyes. His head rolled back on his shoulders. He could see himself half a year before, sitting on the beige carpet with Sophie, playing with Legos, both of them staring up at that trademark screen before the movie began. He wanted to stay there on the carpet with his daughter forever. When Sophie pointed at the screen, William saw the castle, a shooting star arcing in the background. Sophie cheered and clapped in anticipation, and William sat with her, smiling and clapping until Anita grabbed his shoulder and shook him. When he opened his eyes, he saw the same castle in his windshield.

***

Captain Video flew over the Midwestern states. After cutting through the straps, he had jumped from the stretcher. With a mighty cry of "Captain Video!" he'd punched through the roof of the ambulance and taken to the air.

The world he saw from the sky was not a world he recognized. The buildings were too tall and too close together. However, a quick flight over Northern Virginia had convinced him that he was in the United States. The Pentagon and the Washington Monument were unmistakable landmarks. Those remained the same, but so much more had changed. He knew the war was over, but he didn't know who won. As he flew, he scanned the airwaves with his Video-shortwave hearing.

When he picked up a message about the movement of National Guard units toward the California/Arizona border to deal with a terrorist threat from two German nationals, he said, "This sounds like a job for Captain Video!" He turned southwest and shot through the sky.

***

Leaving the airport, Bernie plugged his iPod into the rental car's USB port and headed toward the finish line. He scrolled past *Winning Through Intimidation, Who Moved My Cheese, How to Win Friends and Influence People,* and *The Satanic Bible* to *Looking Out for Number One* and skipped through the tracks. After half an hour, he realized that he was listening to the wrong chapter, but he couldn't rewind. He'd already gone too far. As he drove north, his phone rang. The number was blocked. He picked up the phone and set it to speaker. "Hello?" his voice was full of hope.

"Yeah, hello?" He recognized the voice.

"Hey, Satan, baby, is that you?"

"Uh, is your refrigerator running?" the voice asked.

"What? Is that you, Satan?"

"This isn't Satan. It's someone else. You have to tell me if your refrigerator's running."

Bernie sighed. First the *I'm Gonna Get You Sucka* answering machine message and now this. "Yes, my refrigerator is running." He heard suppressed cackling, squeaks, and whispering in the background, like the sound of bats and lizards laughing in wretched anticipation.

The voice whispered, "Shut up, guys." After a few stifled giggles, Satan raised his voice to its full volume, "Well, you'd better go catch it!" This was followed by hellish, broken, triumphant laughter.

Bernie decided to play along. "Okay, you got me with that one, but Lou--" He was about to start his sales pitch again when the line went dead. With a blocked number, he couldn't even return the call. Bernie drove north through California for a few more miles before his phone rang again.

***

As they drove toward Bombay Beach, Joe saw a large group of people standing by the side of the road. One man waved to them with both arms crossing in the air, and Joe waved back.

John stomped on the brakes and skidded to a halt behind the stopped traffic. He pulled onto the left shoulder and drove around the cars. They were abandoned, some with their hoods up. In the distance, he saw a roadblock and heard gunshots, a distinctive rhythm of people firing and taking cover.

Joe fed a fresh magazine into his AKS. "It sounds like a battle," he said, and indeed, there were green National Guard transport trucks and armored personnel carriers parked in a semicircle behind the police cars.

He loaded a black Micro-Uzi. "You will have to fire it with your left hand," he said. It could be fired with one hand, but not accurately, especially not while driving. He rested it across John's thighs. "And you will need these," Joe said. He placed three long, black, straight magazines on John's lap and let his finger rest on the zipper of John's pants.

John smiled. "Finally, a war. After all this time, something worth dying for. Are there any pills left?"

Joe pushed the last two pills through the blister packs. They approached the roadblock, where a small group of men in fatigues knelt behind a bullet-riddled, seized Miata. He took a cassette tape from the glove box. "If we must die here today, let us hear Eduard Anatolyevich sing one last time."

"I agree," John took his hand off the wheel to open the bolt on his Micro-Uzi. "I am glad because I am finally returning back home." He patted Joe's leg and swallowed his pill.

The tape crackled with age. A National Guard soldier in pixelated fatigues tried to direct them away from the battle. Joe leaned out the window and fired three rounds into his chest. John turned the wheel to hit the soldier.

And then the music played. First the instruments played that jaunty song of infinite joy, then the bright, sonorous baritone rang out over the desert. "Ah, ya ya ya. Ya ya ya ya yaya."

John steered the car toward the soldiers. With his hand steadied against the side mirror, he fired. The soldiers fell into confusion, some turning to fire at the car, others falling back to a safer location. The car turned and swerved, and lead preceded the car everywhere it went as it outflanked and strafed the soldiers.

On the second verse, every head on the car's body started to sing, dead fingers snapping, dead toes tapping, their dry tongues trollololling along. John and Joe killed as they went, weaving through the battle and drawing fire in a gunpowder concerto of joy and murder.

In the center of the battle, two Germans, one in colorful robes and the other dressed for prep school, stopped and looked around. No one was shooting at them anymore. They ran toward the broken defensive line, weaving and stumbling as they came. They shattered weapons and bodies all around them.

When the cruiser passed the roadblock, John turned around. Joe sat on the car door, his feet and legs inside the car, his carbine sending bursts of fire into the confused troops and police officers. As the guardsmen scattered, one tripped over his squad assault weapon, and John aimed the car to ram him. Rising on one knee, the guardsman raised his M249 and started firing. He shot quickly, not even aiming, hitting the radiator, and the engine block, and the windshield. The bullets cut like a saw through the dashboard, into the front seats. He kept spraying lead until the chain stopped feeding rounds and the barrel glowed. He dropped the gun and jumped to the side as the car rolled to a stop.

As the music played and other guardsmen fired into car, he heard a few words. With his limited Russian, mostly from high school and a couple semesters at the community college, he couldn't be sure he understood what was said. The statement was so strange that he didn't mention it during the debriefing. However, long after he left the National Guard, he'd remember the words: "I love you, Ivan Petrovich." Some nights, he would leave his wife in bed and sleep on the couch, a strange song haunting his dreams.

These mornings, his wife knew to call in sick at both of their offices. He normally made breakfast for both of them, but on these days, she made French toast and coffee sometime around noon, after lying on the couch and holding him for hours, never asking him any questions.

Chapter .14

A strong wind raised a sandstorm on the battlefield. Behind this blinding storm, a boat sailed up the median strip toward the roadblock. The Arizona National Guard caravan sat trapped behind miles of stopped cars. At the roadblock, there was a parked Bugatti, a bullet-riddled Crown Victoria with a dead body hanging out of the window, and about three dozen police cars, as well as a few Army trucks. On the other side of the road, more cop cars were still arriving.

When a bullet whistled over Sean's head and hit the aft sail, he threw an empty bottle overboard and yelled, "Avast, ye landlubbers. War is not the answer. Promote peace and sustainable energy sources!" He leaned over the side of the boat, shaking a second bottle in his fist. He had found a stash of Cruzan rum in the cabin, which had helped him take on the nautical spirit. He had also found a coffeemaker and a fishing pole, so he and Jeb were feeling much better on a diet of spiked coffee, pilot bread, and fresh fish.

At the bow, oblivious to the gunfire around him, Jeb sang, "California, here we come. California Cruzan rum."

When the bottle in Sean's hand shattered from gunfire, he hit the deck. If he hadn't dropped his helmet overboard two states ago, he'd have thrown it at that the asshole with the gun. He prayed that the poor man would find peace and learn to renounce violence. Hoping it would make the boat go faster, he sang along.

***

Crouched behind his car, an officer with a shotgun asked, "What about them?"

"Does that look like a Mustang to you?" his partner yelled

188

over the gunfire. "We have enough trouble as it is without bothering with those assholes."

The boat sailed through the California desert and made its way toward the checkpoint.

***

"Okay, be quiet this time, guys, he's picking up the phone."

"Horton and Horton Publicists, this is Bernie speaking."

"Yeah, huh, do you have Prince Albert in a can?"

"Satan, buddy, glad you called. You might not believe this, but you have a serious PR problem, especially in Middle America, you know, the flyover states. I've been working on an extensive public relations campaign that can really turn those numbers around for you."

"Well, you'd better let him out!" Satan said. Bernie could hear the hosts of fallen angels roaring with laughter as the line went dead.

***

William blinked at the fairytale castle in front of him, a palace of pastels and gold with banners hanging. The car pointed at the bridge going in the castle gate, and it was surrounded by people. Thick crowds stood and wandered in every direction. "Maggie," he said. "Where are we?"

"Sleeping Beauty's Castle."

"Right, but where is that?"

"Anaheim. It's near L.A."

"You know, teleporting us to the parking lot would have been just fine."

"Don't look a miracle in the mouth. You're lucky you're not in the tower with the spinning wheel."

William put the car in reverse and looked through the rear windshield. He hit the horn a couple times. "Hello, coming through here. Excuse me." He came to an abrupt stop when he saw a stroller in his rear view mirror. He shifted into first and turned the wheel. As he released the clutch, he felt it slip against his shoe, and the car lurched toward Snow White, who was kissing the cheek of a girl standing on the drawbridge wall. He slammed on the brakes. Snow White pantomimed relief with her hands over her chest. The girl toppled backward into the hedge. "Christ, if I killed Snow White, Sophie would never forgive me."

When he managed a three-point turn, the car faced a traffic circle around a statue of Walt Disney and Mickey Mouse. "How am I supposed to drive here? There are people everywhere."

"Watch for the light poles," Anita said. "Watch for the kids."

Maggie observed the screaming and crying children all around. Once she had a body, she would have to get a job here. "It's almost like they don't want people driving around, the way they make it so difficult. Go around the roundabout and to the front gate. It's the quickest way out."

William steered right, toward the traffic circle, but he saw an official-looking man in blue approach from that direction, so he jerked the wheel to the left.

"You're going the wrong way again," Maggie said.

William ignored her and turned off the traffic circle onto the parade route. Entering Fantasyland, he passed Pixie Hollow and the Matterhorn Bobsleds.

"Take a left here!" Maggie yelled. "Before the Storybook Land Canal Boats! Turn left now!"

William pulled a hard left, fishtailed, and clipped Goofy, sending him spinning into the fence.

"That was close," Maggie said.

"You call that close? I'd call that a direct hit," Anita said.

"If we'd kept going that way, we'd have gone to It's a Small World. I'd never have gotten that song out of my head."

William could see the Flying Elephant ride in front of him. More security guards were appearing from every corner. He wondered whether or not Disney had a SWAT team.

"Quick," Maggie said. If you keep turning left around the Mad Tea Party, you can take a right back onto the parade route."

William gunned the engine and turned left. Peter Pan dove from in front of his bumper, flying for a second before belly-flopping on the pavement. His head crashed down, and his face came up bloody. As William turned his head forward, he saw the Mad Hatter bounce off his grille. The car jolted as if he'd hit a speed bump. The White Rabbit lay rolling on the ground, holding a broken leg. "Right you said?"

"Right, right," Maggie said.

By now, the pedestrians had learned to get out of the way, so William gunned the engine as he drove back toward the statues. "Left?"

"Right," Maggie said.

William turned right and saw the castle in his windshield again.

"No, right, left! Not right, right!" Maggie yelled.

William turned left around the traffic circle and pulled toward Main Street, USA. He swerved to miss a security vehicle and sideswiped Donald Duck, sending him flying into the ice cream parlor. "That's okay. Sophie never liked Daffy," William said. Nearing the front of the park, he noticed two security officers opening an iron fence, probably to let police cars or an ambulance in. The car jolted as Mickey's giant plush face struck the windshield, his body sprawled over the hood. William raced for the open gate, then slammed on his brakes as he saw a police car approaching him head-on. The mouse rolled off his hood, flipped twice on the ground, and crashed into the cruiser's ram bar. "Great shortcut you thought of," William said.

"Well," Anita said. "At least I came up with something. I didn't hear you making any suggestions."

Maggie tried to sound bitter, but she loved every minute of this. "If you were going for cheesy tourist spots, you could at least have chosen the Golden Gate Bridge or something like that. That's much closer to the finish line."

As the officers ran toward the Toyota with guns drawn, William dropped his head on the steering wheel. "Anita," he said. "Remember *Full House, Superman, The Room, Big Trouble in Little China.*"

When the first officer pointed his gun at the window and yelled for everyone to freeze, Anita said, *"That's So Raven."*

***

When Bernie reached the finish line, crowds were already starting to gather. He recruited fans to help him set up the decorations. He had an audience. He had racers approaching the finish line. The only thing he didn't have was Dot, and he hadn't heard from her for hours. He was hanging up a banner and considering giving her a call when his phone rang. He answered it on the first ring.

"Hello, I'd like fifteen large pizzas delivered to Bernie Horton at Horton and Horton Publicists. I'm Bernie Horton."

Bernie heard the snickering in the background. "Damn it, Satan. You really have nothing better to do?"

Satan screamed at his secretary, "Darn it, Leviathan, you dialed the wrong number!"

"Satan, we need to talk about your business plan here. You're obviously having problems with your current staffing solutions. I mean, come on. You know there are a couple billion people in Asia who have never heard of you? We need to talk emerging markets, buddy."

"This isn't Satan. This is, uh, this is Bob."

"Bob? Right. Bob who?"

"Bob, uh, Palmer."

"Sure. Your name is Robert Palmer, and you want to be my sledgehammer, right?"

"Robert Palmer? That's Peter Gabriel, you dummy! Look. It doesn't matter. Can I just talk to Mr. Wall?"

"No, this is a private cell phone, Satan. There are no Walls here." Bernie winced as he realized what he'd said.

"Then how does your roof stay up?" The demons laughed in his ear as Satan hung up the phone.

***

As William crossed the bridge, he groped behind him for his case of wine. There were two bottles left. He chose the Bordeaux. He opened it and poured the wine slowly, careful to not disturb the sediment. As traffic around him slowed, he steered around the cars, swerving left and right, sometimes passing on the shoulders of the road.

"This wine was bottled the year Sophie was born. I was going to share it with her on her eighteenth birthday. It would have been superb by then. I'm drinking it young."

"Here we go again," Anita said.

"It creeps up on you, you know? Life just keeps going. It's not even like I drink more than I did in college, but after a few years, you aren't a frat boy anymore. There's a little nagging nanny voice in the back of your head that disapproves of everything you do, and you have to drink more to shut her up. As you age and have responsibilities, you have to master your drunkenness. There's an art to operating in this world drunk all the time. You learn to maintain incognito, like a spy. It's like your buzz is a helmet you wear all the time, a dark visor between you and everyone else. You see other people crashing and burning all around you, but you still don't take the hint. If I've learned anything from this race, it's that, maybe, deep down, we're all drunk driving champions."

"No," Maggie said.

Anita shook her head. "You haven't learned a damn thing." She turned on the radio and scanned through the channels until she found a classic rock station.

***

When the wind died down, Dot left her bathing machine and watched the boat coast down the road and through the sand. It dropped anchor and two men in NASCAR outfits climbed down a rope ladder. She took a large, round microphone on a stand from her bathing machine and set it next to where her lounge and umbrella had been before they were blown toward the salty lake.

She plugged the mic into her tablet. "We interrupt this Ted Lewis number to bring you this up-to-the-minute racing news. The third car–racing team has arrived at the second checkpoint, here in beautiful, sunny Bombay Beach, California. Now, it seems they have chosen to drive a sailboat across the desert. We'll bring you back to the race and the hit tunes, but first, let me ask a question of all you hepcats out there in radio land.

"If she can spend an hour at the beautician's shop looking good for you, can't you spend a minute with a comb and dab of E-Poxy Resin to look good for her? E-Poxy Resin gives your hair a natural shine and luster. And wives, E-Poxy Resin has a hundred uses around the home. It lubricates stubborn locks. It's a powerful nasal decongestant, disinfecting hand sanitizer, reliable toothpaste, and gentle suppository. It helps diapers stay on squirming infants, and it unclogs slow drains. You need E-Poxy Resin right away. It's available in bottles, tubes, and now, syringes.

"And now, an exclusive interview with our racers." She beckoned with her hand. "Congratulations on being the third team to make it to the second checkpoint. There is a hot race ahead of you, but first, can you tell us why you chose to take a sailboat on this coast-to-coast auto race?"

Jeb pushed in front of Sean and spoke into the microphone. "We have chosen to drive a sailboat to support sustainable energy, nonviolence, and world peace in third world nations and throughout the world. We have to stop the exploitation. We speak out against these corporate fat cats who use blood for oil like it was salad dressing or something, you know, if cats ate salad and then needed some kind of bloody salad dressing to put on it. I mean, it's pretty hard to make a cat eat salad, isn't it?"

Dot could see she was losing them. "Do you have any words for your fans out there or for the racers in front of you?"

Jeb looked around. "I don't see nobody."

"You're on the radio, you mook." Dot switched back to her broadcasting voice. "And you can expect this kind of drunken delirium here in the final stages of the Sweet .16 Ultimate Drunk Driving Championship." She pushed the microphone in front of Sean. "So what is your plan to clinch the race in the last few hundred miles?" she asked.

Sean dropped his bottle in the sand. "We're taking a stand," he said.

"Don't litter," Jeb said.

"Sorry." Sean bent over for his bottle, stumbled, rolled, and rose back to his feet. He weaved back toward the microphone. "We're taking a stand against races like this, against raping our planet and driving cars. We're taking a stand against turning left all the time. What's wrong with turning right every now and then? And we're taking a stand against standing. Who doesn't like a nice recliner or a lawn chair?" He pointed toward Dot's lounge. "Like that one? That's a nice chair, suitable for relaxing and beach recreation."

Dot tried to steer the interview back to the race. "But do you have any secret strategy for winning the race? You know your competition is several hours ahead of you."

"We've had it with races," Jeb said. "We're not going with your system with the finish line and the driving and who gets there first and blowing up Waffle Houses, all the shooting and the violence. What's the point of setting fires in Nashville just for your stupid race?"

"Actually, burning down Nashville wasn't our idea. We were wondering why you did that," Dot said.

"And the show tunes," Sean said. "We are so fucking sick of show tunes."

Jeb grabbed the microphone, "And that's why we're sailing to Stockcar Island, where the cars live at one with nature, where they run on ocean water and the monkey pit crews recycle the tires they change, where the checkered flag waves high over a free land."

"And this Stockcar Island," Dot spoke into the microphone. "Is this a real place or something you thought up when you were drunk?"

"I believe in Stockcar Island because I have to believe." He looked at Dot. "Haven't you ever believed in anything?"

Dot thought of her nonexistent children, her money, her career, and her life, which should have ended long ago. Believing in things was for the birds.

"And as long as nobody's ever written a musical about the South Pacific," Sean said. "It has to be better than here." He dropped the microphone in the sand. "We're out of here." The two racers climbed the ladder up to the deck of their boat.

Dot shook the sand out of the microphone. "Stockcar Island," she said. "Inspiring words from two drunken idiots. We'll have a swinging tune from the King of Swing himself, Benny Goodman, after these words from our sponsor. Freshpit deodorant can stop odor for up to 24 hours per day."

As Sean raised the anchor and ran below to turn the wind back on, Dot ran back to her bathing machine and closed the door. The wind raised another sandstorm, and the boat rode down the beach toward the water.

***

Captain Video looked down at the battlefield. He could see National Guard convoys converging on the site from three different states. There were already over a hundred dead guardsmen on the ground, not counting the corpses dressed in brown and blue police uniforms. Transport trucks sat on their sides. An armored personnel carrier burned with its side torn open and helmets spilling out, like a burning, green piñata. The police and soldiers had taken cover behind the ruins of squad cars and occasionally stood up to shoot in different directions, shooting each other in the confusion. The only vehicle that seemed intact was a sports car of a type Captain Video had never seen. It looked less like a car than a submarine or an alien spacecraft. Near the vehicle, two civilians, one in a colorful house dress and the other in a sweater vest, leaped, kicked, and waved their arms, as if they were swimming in the air.

Captain Video decided it was time to intervene. With a mighty cry of "Captain Video!" he soared over the battlefield. He swooped once and landed gracefully on his feet, his fists planted on his hips and his cape flapping majestically behind him. "Hold, my fellow Americans."

Kai and the Master realized that no one was shooting at them anymore. Kai rose from his deep stance and dropped his hands to his sides. "What the hell is he doing?"

The Master drew two half-liter cans of pilsner from the folds of his robe and tossed one to his pupil. They opened and chugged the beers, still wary of any signs of danger. "Stay alert," the Master said. "This could be a trick by our opponents."

A bullhorn crackled from behind a crushed and inverted police SUV. "What the hell are you doing?" The battle had come to a standstill, each side straining against the tension.

The wind shifted, and Captain Video's cape blew forward to wrap around him in a less majestic fashion. "I am Captain Video," he said. He paused to let that sink in. As the greatest propaganda superhero of the war, it didn't take much effort for him to choose a speech from the hundreds in his databanks. Already, the vacuum tubes in his uniform were warming up. The punch cards in his shoulder pads shuffled at tremendous speed. The disc on his chest spun, seeking and retrieving data.

When the teleprompter in his goggles began to scroll the

appropriate speech, Captain Video pulled himself to his full height and turned so the wind could push his cape in the right direction. He reached under the cape and swept it off his chest with a flourish of his hand. Sixty-seven police officers and one hundred sixty-two national guardsmen opened fire.

The voice on the bullhorn ordered the officers and guardsmen to hold their fire. The bullets shattered the disc drive, tore through Captain Video's uniform, and knocked him back. Vacuum tubes popped and imploded. One bullet traveled through the teleprompter goggle and flew out through the comb-over on the back of his head, tearing an inch-wide hole through his bald spot and carrying out a spray of brain matter. Other bullets entered his body and tumbled, pureeing lungs, heart, liver, spleen, and arteries. The camera lens on his head shattered from a shotgun blast as buckshot broke through Captain Video's front teeth and pushed the tooth fragments through his brain stem.

"Cease fire! Cease fucking firing!" the bullhorn commanded. The gunfire held Video's body up, his arms outstretched and flailing, his trunk convulsing. When all the guns were empty, the body fell to the ground. Captain Video himself, the essence of him, fell past his body, back into the dark, vast bubble of the void.

"Hold your goddamn fire!" the voice said again. This time, since the guns were all empty, everyone complied. Shredded yellow card stock floated on the air. The question hung unspoken in the air with the smell of burnt gunpowder. No one had to ask it.

"I think he was reaching for a weapon, sir," an officer said.

"Yeah, I saw that too," another voice said.

"What weapon?" the voice behind the bullhorn asked. "Where in that suit of Radio Shack leftovers and skintight spandex was he supposed to be hiding a weapon?"

A revolver flew over a patrol car and landed next to the corpse. "I see a weapon," an officer said. A box cutter landed next to the handgun. "I see one too." After that, the officers grew more brazen. Walking past the body in single file, each dropped a weapon or a small plastic bag on the body, burying it in planted evidence. Their work done, the combatants decided to call for a meal break, since many of the officers were already working overtime. Before anyone gave any thought to the Germans in the Bugatti, they were long gone.

***

Kai sipped apple schnapps from a boot-shaped shot glass as he drove. The road was free of traffic, so he opened up the engine and let the needle climb, letting acceleration straighten his spine against the seat. On the other side of the road, convoys continued to deliver soldiers to the checkpoint. "So can we call that a victory?" he yelled over the whirring turbochargers.

"Of course," the Master said. "The Drunken Cichlid is always victorious."

Kai pointed to the GPS unit. "There are two racers already at the coast. We might be able to catch up."

"Forget the race," the Master said. "Do you want to be a race car driver or a Kung Fu master? I think we've proven that we have the finest fighting style in the world, with true German engineering. These magazines have taught me much. In this country, the tradition for martial arts masters is to rent space in a strip mall and teach the fighting arts to children in the suburbs and sell DVDs through the mail. We can sell this car and open a school."

"Somehow I don't see you working with children, Master."

"You'll teach," the Master said. "I'll supervise."

***

Bernie took his phone from his breast pocket. "What the hell, Satan? My refrigerator isn't running. I don't have Prince Albert

199

in a can. You're not calling from the Department of Sexually Transmitted Diseases, if that even exists. I don't have cotton balls, and they don't tickle. I don't work for the Hair Club for Men. Knock it off, okay? It's not funny, and you're just coming off as a jerk."

"Can that rhubarb! You got a screw loose or something?"

"Dot! Shit. I'd forgotten all about you."

"Some publicist. He can't even make himself remember me."

"Cut the schtick and get down here."

"What do you think I'm calling about? The third team checked in. I don't think they'll finish the race."

"I'll have a car at the airport for you. Try to hurry."

***

It was darkness in all directions, not the calm and soothing darkness of sleep or the sharp and threatening darkness of nightmares. It wasn't the warm darkness of the womb or the cold darkness of the grave. It was a darkness that could admit none of these darknesses without smothering them, like oceans of inkwells overturned and crashing silently against one another. There was no heat and no coldness. The darkness was neither wet nor dry, and in the thickness of absence, one could not even smell one's own nostrils, if one had nostrils. There was nothing in the void, and Captain Video looked into it with nonexistent eyeballs. His eyes, never open and never blinking, saw a tiny speck in the distance, like a silent voice crying out in the wilderness.

Captain Video floated toward that light. It grew and became several lights, the red, blurring shapes growing closer or larger in a space that was not space, where size and distance had no meaning. It was difficult to say whether he approached the lights or the lights approached him, but they blinked and grew. There was a sound like the tinkling of tiny bells or a breeze blowing through a harp, pianos with electric strings. A heavenly choir of female voices sang, their voices coming from nowhere. The lights were blinking him a message. They said 12:00. Over and over again, 12:00. Captain Video could make out two words of what the choir was singing: *radio* and *star*. His eyes snapped open.

***

The world was blurry around him. Soldiers and police officers milled about. He remembered the battlefield, and he saw that he was lying on it. He didn't recognize the soldiers' uniforms, but he could tell by their speech and the patches on their shoulders that he had been shot by Americans, killed by his own people in his own country. The betrayal seemed worse than the bullet wounds. He gasped and reconsidered. The wounds were worse.

An officer and a few soldiers with MP armbands pushed journalists away from the scene. Sure, they dressed differently and carried different tools, but there was no mistaking a journalist in any time or place.

A short woman in a blazer held a microphone in front of the officer, who spoke in the measured, rehearsed tones of a press release. The microphone wasn't connected to anything. One camera had a microphone above the lens, latched on like a fuzzy bayonet. Other people stood aiming holding thin, rectangular boxes in front of their faces like pocket mirrors, magnifying glasses, or some new kind of weapon. One held up a plastic sign with no writing on it, just a crude drawing of an apple with one bite taken out of it. It made no sense.

As his eyes focused, the picture came to him and broke his heart. They were making a propaganda film. He didn't know where to put the blame.

He was stealthy at first, but he soon realized he didn't have to bother. No one was looking at him, hidden under a pile of handguns and what looked like spices tied up in plastic bags.

201

A man fixed his hair and stood in front of a camera, using a smoking jeep as a backdrop. He said, "This is Mack Carson reporting to you live from the scene of what the police are calling a terrorist attack at a routine DWI checkpoint. Traffic is backed up all the way to Arizona as police are trying to piece together the motives behind this savage attack." The man paused with his finger to his ear, then said, "There is no reason to suspect a Muslim connection at this time, Jill. The current theory is homegrown terrorists."

Video scoffed at the idea of live broadcasting. It was impossible. It would take them days to develop the film and get it to the theaters on a newsreel. Still, it almost looked like the man was having a conversation with someone who wasn't there.

Captain Video looked around. The things on top of him and around him were clearly pistols. Technology hadn't changed those enough to make them unrecognizable. As he turned his head, he saw beige boots on their sides, desert khaki, a dead man on the ground next to his rifle. Captain Video couldn't make out what kind of rifle, which side made it, or even how it was supposed to work. It was covered in knobs and levers and had strange tubes and screens attached to it. He left it where it lay. However, the corpse had one of those black mirror rectangles sticking out of the cargo pocket of his pants. Video looked around to make sure no one was watching. He snaked out a hand and took the device.

In his head, he could still hear the choir singing about the radio star, and he knew his mission was not over. He looked at the pistols around him. They weren't as complex as the rifle, but their names worried him. Some had strange names like Kel-Tec. He didn't even know what language that was. Some names were more obvious: Glock, Sig Sauer, Ruger, Heckler and Koch, kraut names. Some of the pistols were too light to be real, toys made of plastic and tin. He left those on the ground.

He saw a Smith & Wesson snubnose. He figured a .38 in any time would work about the same. As he shifted to reach for the revolver, a large black pistol rolled across his face. The shape was unmistakable, from the beavertail grip safety to the front bushing. The word Kimber was engraved on the side in a cursive script. As he held the pistol, he felt the familiar weight and the balance in his hand. He knew the most important thing about this pistol before he even picked it up: .45 ACP.

As he looked at the bodies and the propagandists with their microphones and cameras, the voices in his head still sang, telling him he was the first one. Captain Video wasn't sure about that, but he'd be the last one. He knew that much. He pulled his feet under his body. The baggies and plastic pistols rolled off him. Once his boots were on the ground, he pushed upward. Crying, "Captain Video!" he launched into the sky. Faces and cameras turned toward him, but they were blinded by the cloud of dust that flew from his launch point in all directions. As the dust cloud spread, all heads turned away from where he had fallen. Soldiers and reporters squinted and covered their eyes.

When Captain Video hit about five hundred feet, he turned sharply and dove, creating an arc in the sky. He flew fists-first into the first news van he saw, burying it. Then he leveled off, flying close to the ground. His palms caught the second news van, and he slammed it into a third. He weaved as he flew until he had five news vans packed together in front of him. Then he exploded upward again, going up a thousand feet this time before swooping again to drive them into the earth.

He flew low again, snatching up reporters and hurling them at each other. He snatched one by his hair and spun quickly to shot put him into another reporter, who was trying to wedge herself between the camera and the action. Captain Video crushed every camera and gathered five cameramen to make a pinwheel. He spun them in his fist and let go, sending them flying in every direction. He scanned the battlefield. The cameras were gone, but one a woman with blue hair and large holes in her ears aimed one of those mirror boxes at him as he flew. Captain Video swooped down and grabbed her. She screamed and almost dropped the device as he dragged her into the sky. He hovered, gripping her wrist. "My Video-vision should make quick work of this." He closed his eyes until his eyelids glowed red, then opened them, sending a hot blast of radiation toward the desert floor, cooking everything below him, leaving every vehicle in flames, and turning the sand into a pane of stained glass.

Chapter
.15

It took almost nine hours to reach San Francisco in the Civic, but as it rolled along the Coastal highway, the car bounced with excitement. The car itself actually bounced from the broken suspension and misfiring engine that threatened to stall out at every stop, but the passengers were full of passionate intensity.

They drove along a high cliff, with the ocean on their left, and slowed for a series of construction signs, where there were piles of dirt and a section of missing guardrail but no actual construction workers. After a sharp turn in the road, an exit led toward the water. They descended a series of switchbacks toward a polyester pop-up gazebo decorated with balloons and banners on the beach. Crowds of people stood around the finish line. When the Civic pulled into view, the crowd cheered and ran toward the car.

The band played a Sousa march. Bernie rose from his chair and put down his drink. He picked up his clipboard and walked toward the car. Theo stopped and jumped out to shake the man's hand.

Chav jumped out of the passenger's seat and leaped, punching the sky. His legs jiggled like plastic worms and crumpled as he hit the sand. Kato pushed the seat forward and rolled out of the car onto the sidewalk with a tallboy of Natural Light in each hand. He cracked one open, shaking it to shoot a fountain of foam in the air.

***

Captain Video sat with his feet dangling high over the Colorado River. Pink flesh showed through the holes in his uniform, and

Video knew that he was nearly healed. Still, it wasn't enough. His uniform was in tatters. He couldn't be seen like this. It would damage morale. His camera hung in pieces, and his video disk was beyond repair. The gunshots to the punch cards in his shoulder pads had corrupted the precious data encoded within. He gazed into the mirror box. It made a lousy mirror. The brand name over the screen was Samsung, a Japanese name, probably. Again, he wondered who had won the war.

He had chosen this inaccessible mesa to regroup and plan. From his right hand dangled the woman he had picked up from the battlefield. Before the battle, his goggles and punch cards could have fed him the perfect interrogation script. As things stood, he had to ad lib. "Hi," he said.

"Don't drop me, guy," the woman said.

"I just want you to answer a few questions for me; that's all." Captain Video thought of a subtle, insinuating question. "Are you a spy?"

"A what?"

"A spy."

"A what?"

Captain Video pulled her up so she could hear him better. When he sat her on the ledge next to him, she leaned back and lay on the rock, her palms flat on the ground and pushing backward until her ankles had cleared the ledge. "Dude, you can't just do that to someone. I was totally freaking out."

Captain Video decided to use the good cop/bad cop routine. "Are you comfortable? Have you noticed how majestic the view is from up here?"

"Comfortable? You just dragged me like a hundred miles through the sky by my arm. I think it's broken or something. What the fuck, dude? I am so blogging about this."

Captain Video switched to bad cop. "Who sent you? I already know you're a spy for the Japanese and a collaborator. If you don't want me to toss you into this canyon, you're going to have to tell me what you know."

"What I know?"

Captain Video switched back to good cop. "I see you had one of these. It says Samsung on it. Now, you know you're not a collaborator, and I know you're not a collaborator, but my friend here might not be so understanding."

"Who are you talking to?" she asked.

"You," Captain Video said.

"Oh. You said you had a friend here. You know what? Forget it. I could use some smoke right now." She drew a small box from her pocket.

Captain Video watched her roll a cigarette. She inhaled deeply, held the smoke until she coughed, and handed him the cigarette. His pack of Old Golds, left over from his last C ration, was ruined by sea water and age, so he decided to play bad cop again by lifting her gasper. Following her example, he inhaled, held it in, coughed, and exhaled. He took another drag, and as he blew it out, his line of questioning became clear. Everything seemed to make sense now. "Rationing must be pretty bad if you're smoking something like this. It smells like–well, I can't say what it smells like to a lady, but you know."

"Are you going to pass that back?"

"I'll ask the questions. Okay, this device you had on you, it said Samsung on it. You have to tell me about Sam and what he was singing."

The woman looked at him. She considered grabbing the joint. Instead, she asked, "What did you bring me here for?"

Captain Video realized it was time to be good cop. Or bad cop. He'd lost track. "This thing," he said. "How's it work?"

The woman squinted at him as he took another drag off her joint. "What are you supposed to be anyway? I know you aren't a cop."

"I'm Captain Video." He watched her face for signs of recognition. "You've probably heard of me."

She shrugged.

Captain Video called out his slogan, "Captain Video!" and

let his name echo in the canyon. This was the worst tobacco he'd ever tasted. He took another drag.

"You know, I should just go now."

Captain Video rested his hand on her shoulder, and a crane couldn't have lifted her. "I used to be," he said. "I used to be a superhero. But my equipment's all busted up. I'm pretty useless now." He dropped her phone on the ground.

She lunged to grab it and tapped at the screen.

"What is that thing? How does it work?"

"It's my phone, and you are so lucky you didn't break it."

"Phone," Captain Video used his Video-deduction. He drew the phone he had liberated from the battlefield from his pocket. "This thing is a communication device of some sort."

"I guess. I mean, nobody really talks on them though."

"Show me," Captain Video said.

She understood that you don't have to humor a person, but you should always humor a high. She pocketed her own phone and demonstrated with his. "I can't believe this idiot didn't password protect his phone." She scrolled through the app screens, demonstrating a calculator, a video camera, a web browser, and the email app. "Mostly, you just use it to surf the web and send texts."

Captain Video looked at the phone. "So I just touch these pictures?"

"It won't work if you have gloves on. I thought you superheroes used to keep up with technology, like you had Bat-computers and sci-fi gadgets."

"Hey, I have some swell high-tech gadgets. These punch cards in my shoulders hold 70 bytes of data each. The camera on my helmet is capable of recording video for storage on the video disk on my chest, and I can play it back on a cathode ray tube. Well, they could before they got shot up." He slumped, feeling slightly depressed and incredibly hungry. He didn't know how long ago he'd had that last C ration.

"Don't worry. If you want to take video, you can just use

this. You have about 18 gigs left, so you can record for a long time." She demonstrated recording and playing back video.

"How do you know how to do this? Do you work for the Pentagon? The OSS?"

"Everyone has one of these." She saw that Captain Video looked depressed, like he was sinking into a bad buzz. She patted his head and rested it on her shoulder. "Don't get down about it, man."

Captain Video slammed his fist into the rock. The side of the cliff sheared off and fell into the Grand Canyon. "Criminy!" He breathed deeply. "Does everybody really have one of those things?"

"Don't worry about it. The economy's been tough on everyone. You just have to look at your work skills and see what can transfer to another field."

"I have other powers, but they're stupid." Captain Video pouted. "I mean, sure, I can fly, and I have super strength. I can rise from the dead and heal myself from mortal wounds using my Video-willpower, but there's no theme there. What does flying and immortality have to do with video?"

"Well, when you're thinking about your job transition you should think about your assets in a flexible way." She looked around. "By the way, is there a trail or something out of here?"

If Captain Video knew, he gave no indication. Instead, he launched himself into the sky and flew in an indecisive pattern, sometimes a corkscrew, sometimes a hexagon. He flew for a while like a pyramid, which seemed more spiritual. Then he just flew west.

***

"I can't believe we made it to the finish line," Theo said.

Bernie cleared his throat. "Actually, the finish line's over there." He pointed toward the water.

"Where?" Theo said. "I don't see anything."

209

"About that. We kind of goofed. We didn't take the tides into account, and the finish line, it's kind of under water right now. Sorry about that."

"But we got here first," Theo said. "I mean, we can't just drive the car around the ocean until we find the finish line."

"If it were up to me, I'd declare you the winner here and now, but I don't think my insurers and backers would agree. See, technically, the finish line's a set of GPS coordinates. It will be on dry land in eight or ten hours."

"That is such bullshit," Kato said. "The other cars will all be here by then." He stood up and stumbled three steps forward. He took two steps backward and sat on the dirt parking lot.

"I'm afraid it's on the napkin." Bernie flipped through his clipboard and produced a laminated bar napkin. "It's right over there, though." He pointed. "It's just a few feet into the water."

Squinting, Theo could make out two metal poles with streamers hanging from them. Waves split and broke around the poles. "It's impossible." He leaned against the car and put his hands on his temples. He looked for the right word to precisely describe his feelings. "Fuck!" he yelled. He was answered by waves and seagulls. The marching band stopped playing.

"We apologize for the inconvenience. On the bright side, it's downhill."

Theo looked at Kato, and Kato looked at Chav. "It's the only way," Kato said.

Theo looked up. "You know, I just thought of something. What if we disbanded Rho Beta Pi, defaulted on the mortgage and the civil liabilities, then picked up the frat house at the foreclosure auction? We could form a new frat, the Pi Beta Rhos or something. That might work. We could probably get the house cheap at the foreclosure auction, and the debts might all go away. We won't even have to move. We should call Cornelius."

"Shut up, Theo," Kato said. He rubbed Chav's shoulders. "This really is the only way."

"No way," Chav said. "Do you have any idea what salt water will do to the machine?"

"Engine?" Kato offered.

"Whatever. I mean, it'll probably do something. You'll destroy my car."

"We have to sacrifice the Civic, bro. It's a million dollars. We can buy you another car. I mean, we need the money for the strippers, but that liver has got to be worth enough to buy another Honda."

"There will never be another car like this," Chav looked at his Civic. The spoiler was half gone. Fluid leaked from under the engine, and the rear bumper sagged. The front bumper was broken. Most of the windows were broken, and the hood was dented in. The body panels on passenger side were crushed, and the car misfired as it idled. White smoke billowed from between the rear wheels. It was the most beautiful car in the world.

"If we get a good running start, we can make it," Kato said. "What do you say? A liver transplant. It's got to be worth at least a new Civic. Come on, for Rho Beta Pi, man." He offered his hand.

"Pyros," Chav said. He took the hand and leaned in for a bro-hug. He whispered, "It better be an SI." He yelled over to Theo, "Get in the car. We're going to do this." Theo opened the driver's side door, but Chav grabbed his shoulder. "If someone's going to kill my car, it has to be me."

Kato climbed in the back and Theo took shotgun. The door only opened halfway and didn't close. Chav backed the car up to get a good start. Kato handed out cans of beer. He yelled "Rho Pi!"

The three yelled "Pyros!" as one and Chav hit the gas. He was in third by the time he made the parking lot, and the tach was still climbing when they hit the sand. The crowd cheered.

"Punch it!" Kato yelled, and Theo drove his fist into the passenger side visor.

The car lost speed as it sank into the beach. As Chav gunned the engine, sand flew up against the undercarriage. He downshifted as the car slowed until it stopped a few yards short of the water line. The cheering stopped. Smells of melting rubber, burning sugar, and gasoline fumes filled the car. He revved the engine in first and went nowhere. The wheels spun as the car sunk into the sand. The car jolted in place and the engine died. The only sound was the crashing waves. Kato stuck his head out of the broken window. "Could someone give us a push?"

***

From the cliff road, William stopped the car and looked down on the beach. "It's over," he said. "The boys who shot at us, they're already down there." He could hear the approaching siren, but he didn't care anymore. The cop had been following him for miles, but getting arrested would change nothing at his point.

He could see the Honda sitting on the beach. There were cheering crowds, even a marching band. Ahead of the Civic, two steel poles, the kind that might be used to hold a volleyball net, sat in the water with streamers hanging off them. "They're three feet from the finish line, and we're still up here. Five minutes. If we hadn't taken so long at gas stations, if we hadn't taken the detour to go to that brothel, if we hadn't waited so long at that roadblock, if we had done absolutely anything different, we would have made it."

Maggie's spirit teeth grew and spiraled as she took on her lamprey form. This was just what she'd worked toward. "You could have made it if you'd tried a little bit harder, if you just cared enough. You were almost the hero, but now you haven't saved anyone. And on top of that, you get to go to jail."

Anita sat up in her seat. She could feel William's frustration filling the car and searched her mind for an AA slogan that might comfort him in a time of absolute failure. "Don't give up five minutes before the miracle happens," she said.

William glared at her. "Maggie?" he begged.

"Recalculating," she sneered.

"Do you think it would help if I called my sponsor? She might know what to do."

Maggie knew Anita was forcing herself to show a false hope. Maggie could take either of them now, at their moment of defeat. "And to think," she said. "If you'd just tried a little harder, you could have saved her. Your daughter would have lived. You'd even have the money for the back child support, but what are you now? You're the loser we all knew you were."

She turned on Anita. "And you, what kind of sponsor are you? You're an enabler. You've let this man ruin his life for nothing." Maggie let her form grow in the car, spinning teeth followed by a tail that floated on the air.

Anita felt stupid saying it, but she said it anyway. "You know, I think it might be a good time to say the Serenity Prayer."

"I don't want to hear that shit right now, okay?" William folded his arms and rested his head on the steering wheel. His vision was hot, wet, and blurry, flickering from lack of sleep. His head throbbed and his body twitched. His belly was burning nausea from drinking, a perpetual hangover, and sleep deprivation.

Anita persisted. "God, grant me the serenity to accept the things I cannot change."

"And that's everything." Maggie bared her teeth as she swam through the air. "You've already lost."

William mumbled, "Things I cannot change."

"The courage to change the things I can," Anita said.

"You can't change anything. Your daughter is going to die," Maggie said. "It's all your fault, and everybody knows it."

"Things I can," William said.

"And the wisdom to know the difference," Anita said.

Maggie snarled, "And you can't do a damn thing about it.

Pay attention. The police should be arriving any moment now. And won't you look good at your divorce hearing in an orange prison uniform?"

"And the wisdom to know the difference," William lifted his head from the steering wheel. "Anita, get out of the car."

"What?"

"The whole time, through the addiction, the race, everything. I never realized who was really driving."

"Stop trying to be profound. You're too drunk for that. Why do I have to get out? What's wrong?"

"Nothing is wrong," he said. "I am exactly where God wants me to be right now." He handed Anita his last bottle, a Beaujolais Nouveau. "Drink it young."

***

A man in khakis and boat shoes stepped from the crowd and put his hand on the trunk of the Civic. He was followed by a second and a third. People stepped forward, dozens at a time, until there wasn't enough room on the body for all the hands. People pushed the backs of other people, all pushing the car. As the joy of combined effort grew in the crowd, a low cheer rose to a roaring cry of collective triumph. The car slid forward, filling with water as it inched toward the finish line. "We're going to make it!" Kato yelled. "We are awesome!"

***

Anita clutched the bottle and stood by the side of the car. "I don't understand."

"Good," William said. "Now, close the door and walk away."

"How am I supposed to get home from here?"

"One day at a time." William backed the car up until the rear bumper was against the mountain. As the police car squealed to a stop twenty yards away, William aimed the front of the car at the gap in the guardrail and put the car in first. "Maggie, you know where I want to be. It's that finish line right there."

"Like I give a fuck where you want to be." Maggie's soul curled around his shoulders. "This isn't about you anymore." Her astral lamprey body grew to fill the car, coiling and floating.

William floored the accelerator. "God, grant me the serenity to accept the things I cannot change."

She dove toward his chest. "Serenity? Ha! You're a failure. You failed at everything, and you'll fail at this."

William skipped from first to third. "The courage to change the things I can."

"You have no courage. It's all fallen apart, and everyone will know it's your fault." She looked for a place to enter his body, searching his face for signs of despair. Instead, she saw the locked jaw and lowered brow.

With the pedal floored, he shifted from third to fifth easily. "And the wisdom to know the difference." The station wagon jumped off the cliff, toward the Civic that sat at the end of the earth. The wheels spinning on sky, the engine roared. Maggie lunged toward him, but her teeth slipped off his skin. She snarled and snapped her teeth. There was nothing to bite onto. She thrust her jaw around in the car, desperate for a body to take, but her teeth found nothing.

William could see darkness and water below him, sun and sky above him. Something about that gave him a sense of absolute certainty. Everybody cared about him. Everybody loved him. He wished he had time for one more drink.

Chapter
.16

As the water crept up his legs, Chav heard someone in the audience yell, "Look out!" People splashed away from the Honda, and it stopped, dead in the water. There was silence in the car and an unnatural stillness. Then a sound descended on the car, a gunning engine. A shadow appeared over the windshield. Theo said, "This can't be good."

***

The station wagon crashed nose-first into the Civic. It crushed the roof and toppled, the wagon falling over the hood and tumbling upside-down into the water, clearing the finish line. The crowd cheered. Bernie ran into the water and waved a checkered flag. "We have a winner!" he yelled. "We have a winner!" When he reached the car, he stopped cheering. He turned to the crowd. "Does anyone here know first aid?" He pulled the body out of the Toyota. Once he was on dry land, he lowered the body on the sand. He had one of the race fans call an ambulance. With his own phone, he called Dot.

"Dot, where are you?"

"Hello? I'm in a taxi. I'm on my way to airport. Do you know how hard it is to get a hack in this town?"

"It's too late," Bernie said. "The race is over."

"Well, spill. What happened?"

"I'll email you the details. You can announce them like you were here, but it's not good. The winner is dead."

"Dead? Are you sure? You don't really have a good track record on keeping things straight."

"What do you mean?"

216

"I mean you're a lying low-life, you crumb. That's right. I called you a crumbum. Why did you lie about my children?"

"Look, Dot, I can't talk right now. Just wait for my email and send out the broadcast."

Fans started pulling the frat boys out of their car. "I can't feel my legs!" Kato screamed. "Why can't I feel my legs?"

***

Dot looked at the email and improvised a script. Sure, she'd give Bernie his broadcast, but it was going to cost him. For starters, she'd take his plane. You could find just about anything on the Internet, and she'd found a buyer in Alaska. After she passed a new flight plan to the crew, she plugged her microphone into her tablet computer. "Hey, hey, racing fans, we interrupt this Peggy Lee song to bring you this special report. This is Dot Dottie bringing you up-to-the-minute news on the Sweet .16 Ultimate Drunk Driving Championship. It seems the Honda has stalled in the water just feet from clinching the win, and the Lutz station wagon jumped into the lead. And we really mean jumped, folks. It has just flown off the Coastal Highway toward the finish line. Will he make it? He has! The station wagon crashed nose-first into the roof of the Civic, toppled over the hood, and somersaulted across the finish line. We have a winner! What an amazing finish!

"We'll be bringing you the wrap-up and interviews with the competitors, but first, Horton and Horton Publicists can fulfill all your publicity needs. Whether you need big lies, empty promises, exploitive contracts, or just to be left next to a big puddle full of dead fish for a few days, call Bernie Horton, the King of Smarm. Horton and Horton represents the new standard for publicity services, and if you want to make it in Hollywood, Bernie Horton is just the kind of dirty, rat-fink liar you need. Why not give him a call and see what Horton and Horton can pretend to do for you? They're in the Yellow Pages under Crooks. Now back to the hit tunes and racing news

217

on this and other fine stations." As the plane approached the runway, she sent the broadcast and turned off her tablet.

***

When William opened his eyes, the buzzing at the back of his head was gone and his vision was clear. He was sober. There was no more pain. He wasn't even hungover. His head rolled forward on his shoulders, and he saw that he was sitting on the beige carpet of his living room in front of the television. This couldn't be real. He knew that he'd just committed suicide minutes before.

As he rubbed his eyes, Sophie walked into the room holding a hair band in one hand and a plastic suitcase in the other. "Tie my hair," she said in that childish accent that is all Ms and Ws, squeaks and mispronunciation. Her eyes were clear, no longer yellow, but her baby blues were slowly turning brown, like Penny's. William gathered her hair and tied it in a short ponytail. All business, she turned on the TV and DVD player.

She dumped her Legos on the floor. "Don't cry now," she said. "It's time to play. What should we build now?"

As the movie started, they stared up at that trademark screen of a shooting star spreading a rainbow over a fairytale castle.

"You can make something good this time," she said.

***

Captain Video picked up the broadcast with his Video-shortwave hearing and spotted the plane leaving the small airport. After following it up the coast, he swooped behind it, expecting machine gun fire. He fired three quick shots into the fuselage. Increasing his speed, he flew underneath the plane, emptying his pistol into the undercarriage. The flight path was unaffected. He flew in front of the plane and hovered there with his hand out, commanding it to stop. The plane's nose slammed into his chest, and Captain Video clung to the windshield. He punched the nose of the plane.

Inside, the pilot lost his navigation instruments. As his electronics shorted out, he used the manual controls. He pulled up as sharp as he dared and made a quick turn to the left. The man on the nose of the plane slid off and seemed to disappear.

Captain Video flew below the plane, rolled onto his back, and made a long, curved dive that arced in the air so he turned upward, maintaining the speed gained from the dive and adding more until he came up under the front of the plane and threw an uppercut with his entire body. The plane shot up, gaining a thousand feet of altitude.

As the pilot tried to level off, Captain Video grabbed the aircraft's tail and leaned back. Using centrifugal force, he spun three times and let go, hurling the plane as far as he could. He crunched his abs and surged after it at full speed, yelling, "Captain Video!" as he flew.

He shot over snow-covered mountains until the land disappeared and he was flying over icy waters. He'd had enough of fighting the spinning plane. It was time to get the radio star. He drove his fingers through the aluminum, ripping the side of the plane open. When he stepped inside to confront him, the only passenger was a civilian woman trying desperately to talk into a telephone device. She was speaking English. She shook the phone and threw it down. Looking at Captain Video, she yelled over the wind in the cabin, "Who the hell are you? Why do you keep doing this?"

Captain Video tried to answer, but thinking felt like swimming in peanut butter. His Video-stabilization was destroyed, and he fought against dizziness as the plane spun. It was his mission to kill the radio star, but why? It was hard to remember anything as his ideas spun in a thick cloud. "Oh, radio star," he sighed, barely audible. But this time, he wouldn't make the same mistake. There was still time to save her. "My Video-editing knife should do the trick," he said. He cut through her seat belt and took her into his arms. He carried her out to the wing of the plane, walking a lazy and confused S as he went. His vision blurred and he blacked out. A moment later, he was floating, and the tail of the plane smacked him in the back of the head. The jet engine caught his cape in its turbines and pulled him toward the intake.

Holding the radio star in one hand, he clawed at the plane. There had to be a way to stop the engine. His fingers tore through metal, and he ripped at cables and hoses. A gasoline smell filled the air as the plane spun in a tornado of spilling fuel, but Captain Video held onto the radio star with his right arm and pummeled the plane with his left fist until he heard the explosion. He saw a bright flash and Dot's body spinning slowly away from him in freefall like an Ophelia of the clouds, her arms spread, her skirt and hair floating around her as falling gave the illusion of buoyancy.

Then he saw nothing. Captain Video's body fell toward the Arctic Ocean. By the time it hit the water, Captain Video had already fallen much further, floating in darkness.

***

Anita shifted the bottle to her left hand and fished a bronze coin from her pocket. The AA sobriety medallion had a triangle on one side with a capital V inside of a circle. The other side was engraved with a prayer she didn't need to read again. She made a fist and balanced the coin on top of her hand. She walked to the edge of the cliff and flicked her thumb upward. The coin flipped toward the ocean. Then, since her thumb was already up and the cops weren't paying any attention to her, she walked along the road with her thumb out. When a pickup truck stopped, she climbed into the bed. The driver slid the rear window open and asked where she wanted to go.

"Anywhere is fine." She was exactly where God wanted her to be. After riding so long as a passenger, the setting sun felt good on her left side. She reached into her pocket for her old boyfriend's Swiss Army knife. She figured it was time to try out the corkscrew.

Acknowledgements

Special thanks to Eddie "the Eagle" Edwards and Lawrence "Lawnchair Larry" Walters, for the inspiration; to the poet John Dunn Smith and the novelist Tiffany Scandal for dirtying up my Spanish; to Jeppson's Malort for welcoming me to Chicago; to M.C. O'Neill for acting as a beta reader; to those who read and reviewed my first book; to Kayla for being on my acknowledgments page; to Eraserhead Press for believing in the book; and to everyone who told me not to write this book. You were probably right.

In 2002, Eric Hendrixson was cut off by a brand new Mercedes-Benz SLK while driving a late 80s Toyota Camry. That roadster is the most beautiful thing he's ever destroyed, and it makes him smile to this day. In 2005, he quit teaching English. In 2007, he was disqualified from the Isshinryu World Karate Championships for excessive violence against a dwarf. In 2010, his first book, *Bucket of Face*, was published by Eraserhead Press. *The Ninja's Wife* appeared in the 2014 Wishful Thinking anthology. *Giving the Finger* appeared in the 2015 Bizarro Starter Kit Red, and a collection of the same name is forthcoming. In 2013, he moved from Washington, D.C., to the South Side of Chicago, where he lives with his beautiful, long-suffering wife and above-average-looking, seldom-suffering step-cat. He has never eaten this or any other cat. He lives three blocks from Barack Obama's house and still hasn't been invited over, not even once. Not for dinner, not for a barbecue, no lousy potluck, not for a cocktail, no beer summit, not even a fucking cup of coffee. Dude, it's been three years. It's getting awkward.

Milton Keynes UK
Ingram Content Group UK Ltd.
UKHW010653220124
436466UK00001B/69